Aure the Topaz

Book 1 in the Aglaril Cycle

Rich Feitelberg

ManaSoft Books

PRINTING HISTORY
Early Lulu Edition November, 2010
Aziza Publishing Edition October, 2013
First CreateSpace Editon November, 2014
2nd printing, January, 2016

Visit http://feitelberg.net/aglaril/

Facebook: http://www.facebook.com/pages/aglarilcycle

ISBN 13: 978-1-4563-3777-3

PRINTED IN THE UNITED STATES OF AMERICA

Back Cover Photo: Liz Feitelberg Photography, taken at Panospin Studios

Contents

In memory of Jay DeLuca and Charlie Shaffer,
without whom the kingdom of Thalacia,
and this story, would not exist.

Acknowledgements

I wish to thank all the people who gave me guidance and feedback through the many drafts and revisions of this book:

Anna Pratt
Brenda Mirabile
Stuart Schiffman
Dale Phillips
Zachary Zelano
Ian Seekell
Sarah Smith
Joe Ross
The South Shore Writer's Group
Chantal Boudreau
Alison Fields

From *A History of the Elves* by the Prince of the Realm, Everron of the clan Mealidil

… and so it was that in the First Age, when the world was new, the elves found the *Aglaril*, seven gems of unparalleled beauty. To each they gave a name:

First came Vorn the Onyx, wielder of darkness.
Then came Luin the Sapphire, source of water.
Third was Calen the Emerald, bestower of life.
Next came Carne the Ruby, firebrand and destroyer.
Telep the Diamond was fifth, herald of ice.
Next to last was Aure the Topaz, giver of light.
Last, came Orod the Amethyst, king of all …

From the prophecies of Amelidel, elven mage and seer:

… Behold! The invaders of Andropolis will be vanquished and the kingdom of Thalacia will be restored to its former glory, but only when these signs have come to pass:

First, one shall come among you who will find and collect the *Aglaril*.
Second, the heir to the House of Richmond will be proclaimed.
Third, *Balodol* will be remade.

Map of Thalacia

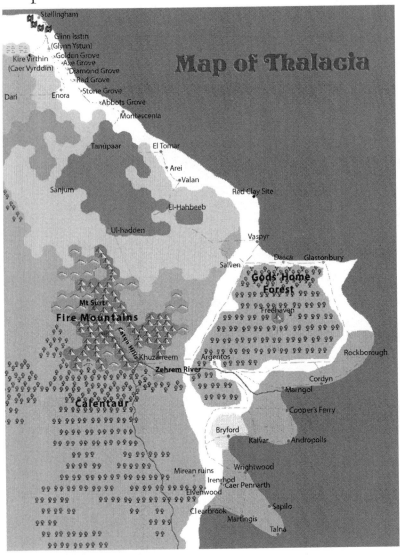

Duchy of Wrightwood and Surrounding Lands

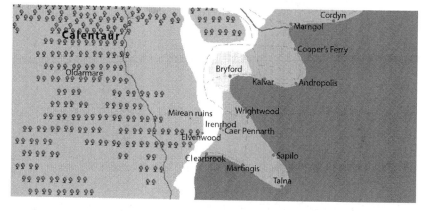

CHAPTER 1
AUDIENCE WITH HIS GRACE

The audience hall in Wrightwood Manor was large and stately. White marble with red veins covered the floor and a narrow red carpet ran down the middle of the chamber from the large double doors at the back, to the dais at the front.

The doors opened and Father Evan Pierce, a priest of the Order of St. Michael and a demon hunter, strode into the room followed by one hundred Michaeline knights. Each knight wore a breastplate of polished metal emblazoned with a silver sword. The group clanked and clanged across the hall until they reached the end of the carpet.

At the foot of the dais, Evan knelt on one knee and bowed his head. The knights behind him did the same.

"Your Grace," said Evan.

Seated atop the dais in an elegantly carved chair of bone and ivory, His Grace, Duke Wrightwood looked at the others in the hall dispassionately. He gestured with one hand. "Arise and report. How fared you in the Mirean ruins?"

Evan stood and smiled. "Very well, Your Grace. We captured two necromancers and killed two others. The pentagram they were preparing was cleansed and destroyed, thereby thwarting any plans they had for using it."

His Grace pursed his lips. "And what of their leader, Jormundan? Captured or killed?"

Evan sighed and frowned. "Neither, I'm afraid. He escaped, vanishing like a ghost at the end of a difficult battle that almost killed Sir Ahlan and me."

Duke Wrightwood's jaw tensed a little at this news and his blue eyes flashed with a fire Evan knew well. "Then we have no clues as to his plans for stealing magic jewelry of great power."

"Not exactly, Your Grace. Because we forced him to flee, he left behind his horse. Inside one of the saddlebags, we found a message to him." Evan drew out a scroll from behind his belt and handed the parchment to a nearby page, who presented it to Duke Wrightwood. His Grace snatched up the document. He unrolled the scroll and read the message.

> Jormundan,
>
> I believe I have found what we have been seeking these many months. If the stories I've heard are true, the prize is in the port town of C. I am sailing there now and should arrive in a few days to confirm. I will rendezvous with you at the standard location outside the town of S.

Signed,
Ebalin,
Sailor's Guild

Duke Wrightwood lowered the parchment and looked blankly at Evan. "This would seem to confirm the intelligence I've already received. Jormundan is in league with thieves."

"Yes, and they plan to steal something soon," noted Evan.

"We just don't know what," observed His Grace. "Based on earlier reports, it could be magic jewelry or a magic gem."

"We don't know where the theft will occur either," said Evan.

His Grace raised an eyebrow. "Does it matter? I can think of several towns of C and they are all too far away and not within the Duchy. So even if you could arrive in time to stop the theft, you'd have no jurisdiction."

"What about Clearbrook?" Evan asked. "I know it's unlikely, but it is worth investigating."

His Grace sighed. "All right. It is worth being certain. Take your men and head out immediately."

Evan paused and Duke Wrightwood sensed the priest had something else on his mind. "Is there something more?"

"Only a small indulgence, Your Grace."

"Go on."

"The people of Clearbrook are gentle folk. Marching into town with one hundred men will cause quite a commotion, possibly to the point of dissuading the thief from acting. Since our only hope of finding Jormundan now is to capture the thief, I suggest I go to Clearbrook myself, under the presumption that I'm there to rest."

His Grace briefly considered this idea and then shook his head. "No. You'll need the support of a few knights — Sir Ahlan, Sir Ambrose, and Sir Geoffrey at the very least."

"While they are all fine knights, I'm certain I can get the support I need from the town guard. A lieutenant in the guard there is an old friend of mine. I can also travel faster alone."

His Grace rubbed his chin, considering Evan's words. "You'll be taking a big risk. But, as you say, it is doubtful they would go to such a sleepy and quiet town. Very well. Go to Clearbrook alone and investigate any unusual activities there. If the thief does show up, apprehend him and keep him from stealing the magic item he wants."

Evan bowed. "Thank you, Your Grace. I'll leave at once."

CHAPTER 2

THE GREY HORSE INN

A wagon pulled by two horses stopped outside the open market in Clearbrook and was still for several minutes. The wagon's stocky driver, Neal Buchetto, chewed on a strip of dried beef, as he waited for the person sitting next to him to disembark. Neal's passenger was a fifteen-year-old boy. The lad was mesmerized by the bustle of the bazaar, oblivious to everything else around him. He watched as people haggled over the price of meat, bread, fish, yarn, and countless other items.

How could so many people fit into such a small space? the boy wondered. *How non-elven.*

Neal finished his snack, picked a bit of beef out of his crooked teeth with his grimy finger, and cleared his throat. "End of the line, Daniel."

The youth jumped a little at the sound of Neal's voice and then turned to face him. "Yes," he said. "Thank you." He stood and bowed.

Neal scratched his greasy black hair and sighed. Daniel was the first human the wagon driver had ever met who did not understand the custom of shaking hands. Not that it mattered to Neal. He was not one to insist on proper etiquette or protocol.

Daniel grabbed his sack, climbed down from the wagon, and slung the bag over his shoulder.

"One final piece of advice," said Neal. "Until you've learned how to haggle, stay out of the market. Otherwise, they'll take you for all you're worth."

"Thank you, again," Daniel said, bowing.

Neal waved and drove the wagon down the street and out of sight.

The lad's curiosity was piqued as he stood outside the market. He craned his head and tried to see what marvels he might find without actually going inside. Then he remembered Neal's words and his true purpose in town.

There will be time to explore the market later, he told himself. *First, there is business to be about. I wonder if any of my family lives in Clearbrook?*

He doubted it, but he was in Clearbrook now. Daniel saw no reason to waste the opportunity and decided to begin his search here.

The teen turned around and gazed down the road Neal had taken. It was lined with shops and houses. Daniel's sky-blue eyes grew larger as he tried to take it all in. *In Kaimin's name, this is beyond anything I ever imagined. Only the fabled palace of Ostrond could be grander.*

Starting down the street, Daniel began to put his plan into effect. He would wander about the town a little this morning and then see who in town might know about his family.

* * *

Daniel roamed the streets for hours taking in the sights. As he walked, he met shopkeepers and some of the other town residents.

He talked with everyone he met and asked if they knew about his family. Most people gaped at him. Between the bowing, the walking barefoot in the chill, and the way he stared at them, most folks didn't know what to make of Daniel. Some shopkeepers ignored the lad's odd behavior and questions, and attempted to sell him whatever merchandise they had. Others genuinely wanted to help but had no knowledge of anyone with the surname *Salvatori*.

Late in the afternoon, he came to the Grey Horse Inn. He was tired by then and all he wanted was to rest. Daniel went inside.

The innkeeper, Frank Jones, heard the doors to the Inn open. He looked up from the receipts he was counting, and saw Daniel enter and close the doors behind him. Frank's brown eyes examined Daniel's bare feet, white trousers, and long white coat belted at the waist. They were all dust-covered from his walk through town.

Humph, thought Frank. *Looks like a poor street urchin who wants money.*

Despite this assessment, Frank stopped his work and rested his hands on his stomach, which protruded like a large melon. He watched as the teen approached the ten-foot-wide mahogany counter that Frank stood behind.

"Is there a room here I could use for sleeping?" asked Daniel.

Frank's eyebrows rose. *Then again, most street urchins don't speak so well. Perhaps he's just a poor unfortunate down on his luck.*

"Yes," said the innkeeper. "Rooms are five silvers a night."

Daniel pulled out some coins and counted them. He had enough for several nights, but he remembered what Neal had told him on the trip to town. He would need as much money as he could earn and probably a job besides to finance the search for his family.

"Actually, I could use a job more than a room to sleep in. Are there any openings here?"

Frank stared at the boy. *Even more curious. Who is this strange lad?* He scratched his head. *If he is just someone down on his luck, who am I not to help? In a way, he reminds me of my old friend Evan Pierce, but I don't suppose this lad is a prankster or will be shipped off to the school for wayward boys by Father O'Malley. On the other hand, why take the chance? Perhaps I can help prevent this lad from suffering the same fate by giving him a job.*

"Yes, I need a dishwasher. You interested?" Frank finally replied.

"Yes," said Daniel. "I agree to wash dishes for you."

"Good," said Frank. "What's your name?"

"Daniel." He bowed; Frank ignored the gesture.

"Well, Daniel, I'm Frank Jones, the innkeeper of the Grey Horse. I'll show you where you can put your things and rest a little. We'll need to get you some shoes too; you can't go barefoot in the kitchen. You'll start in the morning."

* * *

Frank showed Daniel the small common area used by some of the Inn's staff to sleep. It was a narrow space with just enough room for six straw mats, three along the left wall and three along the right. Four of the mats had backpacks or satchels on them and appeared to be reserved for use by others. Daniel left his belongings next to one of the unused mats and followed Frank into the next room.

Tables and chairs filled the immediate area near the double doors that Frank and Daniel used. On the far wall, a doublewide hearth heated the room. Cobblestones covered an area about nine feet wide and three feet deep in front of the fireplace, forming a crude stage. A tall, attractive man stood by the fire addressing the patrons of the Inn. His blue eyes sparkled and he gestured with his hands as he spoke. His strong, confident voice filled the air too and resonated with the passion of the story he told.

As Frank and Daniel entered the room, the innkeeper said, "That's James up on the stage. He's the Inn's bard."

Daniel listened to a portion of the story James told. The lad recognized it too; it was the tale of Kaimin and Kellear:

"Kaimin and Kellear were twin brothers who lived before the making of the world. Kellear was ruler of water, oceans, rivers, and lakes. Kaimin was lord of the earth and crafter of jewels, silver, and gold. Together they shaped many lands. Yet both were sometimes quick to anger. And in that rage, Kellear would often flood the coast and Kaimin would cause lava to erupt, creating new areas of dry land and conquering the sea.

"They argued constantly, like most brothers, over the smallest points: a length of coast, the course of a river, or the size of a lake. They seemed not to care so long as they argued. Yet they agreed on one thing — the beauty of Lothanna.

"Lothanna, giver of fruits and flowers, trailed after Kellear and Kaimin and flowers grew where she tread. Now, Lothanna's beauty was second only to Elas's, Queen of the Heavens; and early after the world began, Kellear and Kaimin both swore oaths of love to Lothanna.

"Yet Lothanna could not choose whom she loved best. To help her settle the matter, she devised a contest: each brother was to demonstrate his love for her. Kellear made fine water sprays that caught the sunlight and created rainbows over Lothanna's gardens and orchards. Kaimin crafted silver inlaid with seven gems, to create a circlet for Lothanna.

"And when Lothanna saw the circlet, she loved Kaimin best. Kellear was furious and flooded the land with a great storm. He disappeared after that, preferring to be alone; and they say on cold, windy nights, you can hear Kellear's lament of loneliness and unrequited love."

While Daniel listened to the tale, Frank scanned the tables in front of James.

"Ah, there she is," Frank said at last. He touched Daniel's arm, gestured, and said, "This way."

They made their way through the clutter of tables and came to one on the right side of the room. Seated at the table watching James perform was an elven woman clad in a pink blouse, black trousers, and black boots. She was pretty and slim with long dark hair and pointed ears. She heard Frank's approach and, as he drew near, turned to see that he was not alone.

"Iriel, this is Daniel, our new dishwasher," Frank said to the woman. "Daniel, this is Iriel," he continued and gestured to the elf. "She's our serving girl."

Daniel bowed. Iriel didn't seem to notice him; she gave Daniel no more than a glance and turned her gaze back to James.

"Shouldn't you be waiting tables?" Frank asked Iriel.

She turned back again to face Frank. "I'm having a break," replied the elf.

Frank exhaled sharply through his nose and gave Iriel a sidelong glance. Why was she always on break when James performed? He shook his head and shifted his attention to the bard.

The sudden eruption of applause made Iriel peer up at the stage once more. She saw James bow with a flourish and prepare to tell another tale. Then something registered in her mind; her eyes flitted back to Daniel. Her brow knitted as she noticed the lad's clothes. She scanned his face and realized he was staring at her. She got that a lot from humans and ignored it for the moment.

"Daniel," said Iriel. "Why do you wear the uniform of a *Qua'ril* master?"

"I *am* a *Qua'ril* master," said Daniel.

Iriel raised an eyebrow and stood. Had she made a mistake just now not giving Daniel the proper respect he was due? She had never heard of a human mastering the elven martial arts. Was that even possible? "A human *Qua'ril* master?"

"Yes."

"Truly?" said the elf. "How old are you?"

"Fifteen."

Iriel's eyes grew round. "Amazing," she said quietly. "Forgive my lack of respect earlier." She bowed to him. "But if you are a master of the Art, why do you wash dishes for Mr. Jones?"

"I am searching for members of my family," said Daniel. "But I don't know where they are. I plan to work here to earn money to finance my journey."

"Are you lost?" Iriel asked.

"No," replied the lad. "My parents died when I was a baby. The elves rescued and raised me."

The corners of Iriel's green eyes drooped in sadness and her mouth opened with a frown. Her heart felt heavy and she twirled a strand of her hair to stop herself from hugging Daniel. He was alone and searching for his family. It was the saddest thing Iriel had heard in months; her heart went out to him.

Then another thought popped into her mind. "Your search is a sacred quest, isn't it?"

"A *garal*; yes, it is," Daniel said.

"Then I will help you if it is permitted," said Iriel. "And so will James."

Daniel crinkled his brow. "Honest? Both of you?"

"Yes, I will talk to him. Leave it to me."

"Thank you," Daniel said with a smile. "You are most kind, like most of the elves I know."

"It is the least I can do." She bowed again. He returned the gesture, smiled back at her, and stared like a puppy gazing at its new owner.

CHAPTER 3
THE FIRE MAGE

B rashani walked along a dirt road in the town of Irenrhod. He came to a small tavern, the Drunken Mage, paused, and glanced up at the establishment. The front of the saloon was not much to look at — peeling red paint and dirty white shutters mostly; but Brashani liked the place because the drinks were cheap. Today was different, though; he was here to meet someone and acquire some information.

He went inside. The tavern was filled with patrons, tobacco smoke, and women who provided pleasant company for men … at a price. He found an empty table and sat down. A barmaid wearing a low-cut black dress approached him.

Brashani smiled to himself, enjoying the outline and slight bulge of the barmaid's nipples. He caught himself staring and averted his eyes.

"Beer," said the wizard.

The barmaid smiled warmly at the order and gave him a flash of her round, firm ass. He noticed, but she was gone to place the order before he could sneak a pinch.

Just as well. I'm here on business.

Brashani looked around. An associate of his, a short, balding man named Derek, sat at the bar alone with his back toward the wizard. Only Derek's golden shirt and tan trousers were visible. With luck, Derek would have the information Brashani had paid for. As the barmaid spoke to the barkeep, Derek got up, came over, and sat down at Brashani's table.

"Well?" asked the mage.

"They know you know," said Derek.

Brashani growled. He did not need to ask how the necromancers in town knew. They were wizards like Brashani; all they needed to do was cast the proper spell, gaze into a crystal ball, or perform a ritual of Revealing and the whole sordid affair would become plain to them.

"The fact that it was an accident probably means nothing to them," commented Brashani.

"You're right; it doesn't. Whether you were eavesdropping on purpose or you accidentally wound up scrying their meeting because your magic went haywire, it is all the same to them. The fact is, you know their business; and that's a threat to them. So they have only one option."

"Kill me."

"Pretty much," Derek said, nodding in agreement.

"Which leaves me only one option — leave town."

"'Fraid so. Fighting them is suicide."

"I know. Five against one is lousy odds. And I certainly couldn't go to the authorities in Irenrhod. They're crooks and probably in league with the necromancers. I'll be dead by morning if I talk to town officials."

"Where will you go?" asked Derek.

Brashani's eyes shifted from side to side. "I've no idea. South, I guess, so they won't follow me."

"Got a horse?"

The wizard laughed. "I barely have money for food. How can I afford a horse?"

"Then you'd better start walking. It will take a week to reach even the closest town and the leaves on the trees have already begun to turn; winter will be here soon."

Brashani sighed and stood. Derek rose to his feet too and shook Brashani's hand. "Good luck."

"Thanks. I'm going to need it."

* * *

Brashani walked down the south road that led to Clearbrook and stopped to listen every few minutes. It had been several hours and so far, the necromancers had not tried to follow him. Maybe he would live to see tomorrow.

Maybe.

Somehow, Brashani didn't think it would be that easy.

Necromancers don't have a reputation of being very forgiving. On the other hand, if they are planning the theft of a magic gem, perhaps the fact that I have left Irenrhod makes me too difficult a target to pursue. Completing that job must require a lot of coordination and must be far more important to them than killing me. Guess it depends on whether they will tolerate loose ends.

Brashani guessed they would not and that it was only a matter of time before they tracked him down. He knew how that went. Several years as an investigator for the town guard in Marngol had taught him the general process necromancers followed. They would wait until the victim was certain he was safe and then they would strike.

Good thing I know how to ward against death magic.

Then another thought wormed its way to the front of Brashani's mind. It was his old investigator training taking hold, he realized. He tried to put the notion out of his head, but the thought kept coming back.

What did the necromancers want the gem for?

Who cares? he answered himself. *Probably to power a magic item.*

And what sort of device would a necromancer want to create?

Brashani pondered this and realized he had no idea. But whatever it was, it would not be good.

* * *

Brashani slept poorly that night, starting at every noise despite the wards he had set. The next morning, he felt awful; and by midday he needed to stop and rest again. He saw a tree by the side of the road up ahead.

Perfect. I'll rest there.

He sat down beneath the tree.

Wish I had something more than stale bread to eat. His stomach growled. He ignored it.

He rested his head against the trunk of the tree and before long, he was dozing. A vivid scene appeared before him. A giant worm, a hundred feet long and the size of three men in height, was tunneling underground, eating all the trees in the vicinity. Brashani saw the worm approach and eat his tree and him with it. He felt the razor-sharp teeth in the creature's mouth impale him.

He screamed and awoke to find himself under the tree. He heard a noise. In the distance, the worm approached again; he was still dreaming he realized. Brashani tried to stand and run before the worm came again, but it was no good. The monster was faster than he was, and even though he ran several yards down the road, it caught up to him and devoured him again and again.

Brashani jumped up and found himself awake and standing beneath the tree under which he had decided to rest. He was breathing hard, perspiring heavily and the collar of his tunic was soaked through.

Had the dream been a warning from the necromancers? No, not even they can reach into my mind. But that means they've taken no action against me. Are they going to leave me alive? Yes, alive to wonder. Bastards. They're trying to use my own fear against me.

Brashani tensed his jaw with anger and his fear melted away. *Well, if that's their plan, they're messing with the wrong wizard.* He felt his old confidence resurface. He had not felt that since the Massacre. Perhaps it was time to fight necromancers again. Perhaps. But he would need a source of income to do it. He could get a job when he reached Clearbrook, of course; but unless there were death mages in town, it would be hard to fight them long distance.

He sighed. It was probably just as well. He was not a young man any more. Better to continue south and hope for the best.

At least he was alive. And that counted for something. Not much — not with his luck.

CHAPTER 4

IN LOVE WITH AN ELF

James sat in the common room and sipped coffee. He yawned and wished he were still in bed. His performance last night had run extremely late … later than usual. He had only gotten up now because it would give him a chance to be alone with Iriel before the Grey Horse opened and the Inn's patrons kept her too busy to talk.

What time is it, anyway? he wondered, idly. He could not remember whether the clock tower had rung five or six times when he had awoken that morning.

James took another gulp of coffee and thought about the previous night's performance. *It went well. I told lots of tales. The one about the carpenter's wife was especially well received.* He chuckled to himself. *Yeah, that's always good for a laugh. The audience must have thought so, too; I made twenty-five silvers in tips. That's not bad. It's certainly better than my best night at the Silver Snake. I think on my best night there, I earned five silvers.*

He sipped more coffee. *Of course, that was because the owner of the Silver Snake, my old boss, Ralph Gustuvson, took ninety percent of the tips to pay for his overhead. Not exactly fair, if you ask me.*

It was one of the reasons James had left Ralph and the Silver Snake, and traveled south to Clearbrook without lining up another job first.

Lucky for me, Frank was hiring, James thought in passing. *I might have had to perform in the town square otherwise.*

Iriel came out of the kitchen carrying two plates. James gazed up at her as she entered. Her green eyes sparkled and she smiled at him. Her loose white blouse rustled as she moved and a matching apron covered her waist and thighs. Her dark hair was tied back with a strip of leather and a wooden dowel, leaving her temples and pointed ears exposed.

And I'm lucky to have met her too, he mused.

James still could not believe that Iriel was interested in him. Him. A bard.

And not the best, by any means. What is it she sees in me?

He had a vague notion. Iriel, for all her years, was still very inexperienced in the ways of the world. James, on the other hand, had traveled much of the kingdom and had seen many things. From this, the bard concluded that Iriel was attracted to him because of his knowledge, but that was only a guess.

Iriel set one plate on the table in front of James and the other on James's right. She sat down and began eating.

James looked at his food: two eggs, toast, and fried potatoes. He glanced at her plate; it was covered with green leafy things.

Iriel raised her head and paused after swallowing the first taste of her food. "How was the show last night?"

The show? James thought. *Iriel's Thalacian needs a little work.* He tasted his food before answering. "Good," he said after he swallowed some eggs. "The crowd was lively and enjoyed my performance. They tipped well too."

"That's nice," she said then yawned and stretched. "I want to view your show, but Mr. Jones works me so early in the morning, I go to sleep by nine."

"I know," said James. "It's all right. You have to work. We all do. So, you'll come when you can; maybe on your next day off."

She smiled at James and kissed the side of his face. "How did you become so understanding and so giving? Most humans are intolerant oafs," she said and smiled warmly at him.

James did not answer the question; it seemed rhetorical. But he did pause for a moment. *Giving? Why did she say that? And that smile … usually she looks at me that way when she wants something.* James considered what scheme she might be hatching and realized he was too tired to sort that out.

She continued without pausing. "I am most fortunate … or as you taught me to say, I am … lucky."

He smiled at her. "Yes, we both are lucky to have found one another."

Iriel ate a little more of her food. James heard it snap as she folded one leaf of greenery in quarters with her fork. "Did you meet the dishwasher Mr. Jones hired?" Iriel asked.

"No," said James. "But I saw him sleeping in the room we share. Blond hair wearing a white coat and matching pants. He looks a little young to be working here."

"His name is Daniel. He's fifteen and a *Qua'ril* master."

James sipped his coffee while Iriel spoke and nearly choked when she included that last part. His fatigue vanished, replaced with surprise.

He coughed a few times, then asked, "A *Qua'ril* master? A human fifteen-year-old? How's that possible?"

Iriel told James what she had learned about Daniel the previous afternoon: he had been taught the art of *Qua'ril* by the elves. They had raised him because elven rangers found him as an infant after his parents died. After relating all she knew, she added, "As a *Qua'ril* master, he commands great respect from all elves."

"Oh? Why is that?"

"The study of the elven martial arts requires concentration and a deep commitment to a special way of life," she explained.

James thought he detected a reverent tone in Iriel's voice, but that made no sense. "Like a human monk?" he asked.

"Similar, but not exactly the same. There are no vows to be taken. Only an inner dedication to the Art and the way of life it requires," she replied.

"I see," said James. "I'm sensing you like Daniel."

"Yes, of course. And respect him too. There isn't an elf alive who would not treat a *Qua'ril* master in this way."

Yeah, there's definitely a reverent tone. Wonder why? James ate a bit more of his food and swallowed. "If he's so important among elves, why is he in Clearbrook?"

"He's looking for his family."

"Do they live in town?"

"He doesn't know where they live. He plans to search the whole kingdom."

"He does?" James furrowed his brow. "That's a tall order."

"But he does not have to, right?"

"What do you mean?"

"Didn't you tell me there are books with names in them that trace family lineage?"

"Yes, that's true," he nodded. "Families with a coat of arms or other crests are recorded in the *Heraldic Registry of Names*. The information is maintained by heralds throughout Thalacia and the

Heralds' Guild circulates the records among the chapter houses in various towns throughout the kingdom."

"That's what I thought," said Iriel.

James chewed a bit more food and swallowed. "But that option may not apply to him if his family is too poor to have even the simplest of crests. And even if his family has a crest, he'll never be able to search the records himself."

"Why not?"

"Because the heralds who maintain these records guard them jealously. You usually have to pay a fee before they will share the information they have."

"Would they let you search the records for free?"

"Probably, if I asked. The Guild of Bardic Lore and the Heralds' Guild have an arrangement to share information." James paused as he realized where this was going. He swallowed with a gulp and wanted to groan. Iriel was beautiful and was one of the nicest people he had ever met, but sometimes she wore her heart on her sleeve. So far in the last week, she had gone out of her way to help three lost kittens, two stray dogs, and an injured sparrow. James had understood at the time; she was an elf and helping animals was part of her nature. Besides, helping animals was one thing; helping people was always more complex and more trouble.

He put down his fork. All the pieces finally fit and Iriel's scheme was now clear to him. "You want me to help him, don't you?"

"I promised we both would."

"Without asking me?" Iriel did not answer. "Well, forget it. I finally have a job I like. I'm not giving it up to help a stranger."

"You would let a young boy wander the countryside ... or even worse — your untamed cities and towns alone?"

"Yes, if it means giving up this job. Besides, you said he's a *Qua'ril* master; he can take care of himself."

"Would you do it for me?" she asked and smiled sweetly at him; her eyes widened and appeared innocent.

James felt the attraction that had drawn him to the elf in the first place. It was like a magic spell she had turned on suddenly and James felt his heart sink. As much as he hated what he was about to say, he heard the words escape his lips. "Yes, I suppose so."

"Thank you." She kissed him again, this time on the lips. "I knew you would help."

James smiled weakly at her. "What makes you certain he'll accept our help?"

"He seemed willing yesterday ... when I offered it."

James sighed and rolled his eyes to the ceiling. He was afraid of that. Daniel had already accepted the aid Iriel had offered.

"And just when is all this supposed to happen?"

"Once we save enough money."

James's mood brightened. "Oh, well, then there's plenty of time to prepare." He returned to his eggs.

Iriel shrugged. "I suppose. How much money will we need?"

"Depends on how long the search will take," said James. "But if I had to guess, I'd say a hundred gold sovereigns ... each." He knew that figure was high and would take forever to save, but with that much money in his pocket he could probably retire, in which case he would not mind giving up his job.

"All right," Iriel said as she stood. "Introduce yourself when he wakes. Try to help him locate any family in town."

"I'll do my best," replied James as Iriel took her plate away and returned to the kitchen.

CHAPTER 5
THE BARD AND THE BOY

James entered the common room and ran his eyes over each person seated at a table. After about a minute, he spied Daniel sitting alone, eating a plate of vegetables.

There he is, he thought and approached the lad. He watched the teen spear several items from his plate with a knife. *Odd,* the bard thought. *Didn't the elves teach him how to use a fork?*

He sat down at Daniel's table. "Daniel, I'm James Claymont, the Inn's bard. Iriel told me you might be here. Pleased to meet you." James extended his hand.

Daniel looked at it blankly for a minute as he chewed a hunk of potato, then a look of recognition came to his face. He swallowed. "Humans shake hands as a greeting, don't they?"

"Usually," replied James with a smirk.

Daniel nodded his head and shook James's hand.

"How do you like working here?" asked James.

Daniel shrugged. "Am I supposed to like it?" He harpooned a chunk of carrot.

James smiled. "No, I suppose not. In fact, most people don't like their jobs, but it helps if you do."

Daniel cocked his head to one side and swallowed. "If most people don't like their jobs, then why do they do them?"

"Money."

Daniel nodded his head. "I understand. That is why I work for Mr. Jones. Is that why you are a bard?" He lanced an onion.

"No, I'm a bard because I like to entertain people and learn about them."

Daniel chewed and swallowed. "Is that why you are here? To learn about me?"

James slid his jaw to one side for a moment and raised his eyebrows. *He's perceptive. I'll give him that.*

"In a manner of speaking, yes. Iriel only told me a little about you and why you are here, but I'd like some more information."

"Okay," he said flatly. "What do you want to know?"

"Well, to begin with, did you like living among the elves?"

Daniel shrugged. "I guess, but I didn't actually live among the elves." He bit into a large piece of yellow turnip.

"No?" James's forehead wrinkled in confusion. "Didn't they raise you?"

Daniel nodded his head as he chewed. After swallowing, he said, "Yes, until I was seven. Then I was selected to learn the Art and went to live in a secluded part of the forest with my master."

"The Art? You mean *Qua'ril*?"

"Yes."

James scratched his head and his eyebrows knitted. "How'd you manage to convince the elves to teach you the Art?"

Daniel swallowed the remainder of the turnip, then cocked his head to one side again. "I don't understand your question."

"The elves don't teach their form of martial arts to non-elves. You must've had to convince them to do it."

Daniel shook his head and stabbed at a stalk of celery. "No. My master picked me."

"Then you were lucky."

"My master says there is no such thing as luck. Only balance, focus, and control." He bit into the stalk.

"Those are the fundamentals of *Qua'ril?*"

Daniel nodded his head and chewed.

"I see. Well, there's more to life than balance, focus, and control."

The lad swallowed. "Like what?"

"Like fun."

"Fun?" said Daniel. "How does one have fun?"

James paused. *I don't know what the elves taught him, but any teen that doesn't know how to use a fork or how to have fun needs help.* A chill went down his spine at the thought. *Maybe that's what Iriel sensed from talking to him yesterday. No wonder she offered to help. I should have known better than to doubt her this morning.*

He wanted to bang himself on the head in the hopes of knocking some sense into his brain, but he saw Daniel staring at him, waiting for an answer.

He cleared his throat. "Well, there are lots of ways to have fun: sitting in a tavern, having a few drinks, listening to stories, or singing songs are some of the more common ways."

"But there are other ways?" Daniel asked and tossed the rest of the celery into his mouth.

"There are. Basically if you enjoy it, then it is fun."

Daniel chewed and swallowed. "So work is not fun — for most people."

"Exactly."

"Could helping others be fun?" He chomped another potato.

"It could be." James raised an eyebrow. "Why do you ask?"

Daniel swallowed. "Because I can't pay you or Iriel for the help she has offered to give me, and if people only do things that they don't enjoy for money, then the only way you and Iriel will help me is if it is fun, right?"

"Uh …" James did not even know where to begin with that one. He scratched his head and sighed. *The logic is sound, based on what I told him, but it doesn't take into account a lot of things.*

Daniel rolled up the lettuce leaf at the bottom of the plate and tore off a section.

"Not exactly," James said at last. "Iriel and I will help you because we like you. We want to help. Money and fun have nothing to do with it."

The teen swallowed. "I see. You do it out of friendship."

"That's right."

Daniel blinked. "Huh. I don't think I've had any friends before." He put the rest of the lettuce in his mouth.

James raised his eyebrows. "None?"

The lad shook his head and swallowed. "Not since I began studying the Art. It was just my master and me."

"You must have been lonely."

Daniel cocked his head. "Lonely?" He paused to consider the idea. "No, but I had no friends."

James sighed. "Well, you do now." He smiled and Daniel smiled back. It was a weak smile, as if he were unaccustomed to doing it, but it was a smile.

Daniel ate several more carrots and pushed his plate away. "So, how will you help me?"

James raised a hand with his forefinger extended and pointed it at Daniel. "Well, I've been thinking about that. Most churches keep a record of births and deaths. We can go to the church in town and see if anyone named Salvatori has ever lived here."

The lad's face brightened. "Okay, that would be great. I will finally find some answers."

"Answers?" repeated James, as grooves appeared along his forehead. "I don't think so. The chances of finding anything you're looking for are slim. So don't expect too much."

"Even a 'No' is an answer," said Daniel. "When can we go?"

"Right," James responded slowly. "How's tomorrow?"

"Okay, I will be ready."

"I'll meet you here about this time and we'll go to the church together."

Daniel stood up and bowed. "Thank you."

"You're welcome," James said. He stood. "And there's no need to bow."

The lad did not seem to hear James. He just picked up his plate and went into the kitchen.

* * *

The next day James and Daniel walked across town to the church. It was a large, long, whitewashed wooden building. A set of double doors faced the street and a high steeple towered over them as they approached. James saw stained glass windows along the left side of the church depicting the faces of saints.

The land around the church was flat and covered in short, dry brown grass. James walked across the lawn and paused by the front doors. He turned back to look for Daniel; the bard's eyes narrowed and he tapped his foot impatiently when he saw the lad had stopped walking about halfway across the lawn to gaze up at the church. James waved at Daniel to hurry up, but the teen did not move.

James sighed and threw up his hands. He walked back toward Daniel. "What's so fascinating?" snapped the bard.

"Everything," said Daniel, his eyes round and wide. "The elves don't have buildings like this."

"Well, let's not stand around here all day. You have to get back to work soon and Father O'Malley is waiting for us."

James started for the front doors again and glanced behind him. Daniel walked a few paces back. The bard pulled open one of the heavy wooden doors and went inside. Daniel followed and closed the door behind him.

The foyer was dark, lit only by a few candles. Another set of double doors led deeper into the church. Two low tables stood on either side of the doors. On the right table was an empty plate; on the left table a wooden box with a small slit cut in the top.

Daniel ran his eyes over the entire area and James saw them grow wide. They appeared nearly ready to jump out of Daniel's head. James smiled to himself. *What's it like to be so full of wonder?* The bard had no idea; he had never been that way — curious perhaps, but not full of wonder.

James opened one of the inner doors and stepped into the sanctuary. The wooden floorboards creaked as the bard walked down the center aisle and passed row after row of benches. Several chandeliers, suspended by long chains and filled with candles, hung from the high ceiling. Light streamed in through the stained glass windows and cast odd shapes against the white plastered walls.

At the far end of the sanctuary, James saw a man dressed in a black shirt and trousers and wearing a high white collar. The man's hair was white and he was reading from a book. He shifted his gaze at the sound of the floor creaking and saw James coming toward him. A smile came to the man's face; he closed the book and walked up to meet the bard.

"Father O'Malley?"

"Yes," said the man.

"You may not remember me. We met at the Grey Horse Inn a few weeks ago."

The priest scratched his head. "Oh, yes." He smiled. "That was the night Frank hosted a meeting for Mayor Bigsbee and the town leaders."

"Yes," said James. "That's right. I was the entertainment."

"I remember," said Father O'Malley. "You're … James Claymont." They shook hands.

The bard smiled. "Right again."

"Good to see you again. You performed quite well that night. You even managed to tell some stories I had never heard before."

"Oh? Which ones?"

"The elven stories. In all my travels as a young man, I never had a chance to visit Oldarmare or learn much about their culture."

"How unfortunate. They are a very interesting people. I spent a summer there just prior to training as a bard."

"In Kaimin's name …" whispered Daniel as he stared up at the stained glass windows.

Father O'Malley peered around James to see who had spoken. The bard turned and saw the lad was still standing by the entrance.

"Daniel," James hissed. "Come meet Father O'Malley." He gestured for the teen to come forward.

The lad ignored the bard and glanced around the room once more before finally walking down the aisle. As he stepped up next to James, Daniel bowed before Father O'Malley. "The windows are very beautiful."

"Thank you," the priest said. His brow furrowed and his eyes caught James's. "A friend of yours?"

The bard sighed. "Yes. This is Daniel. He's a *Qua'ril* master and was raised by elves."

Father O'Malley raised an eyebrow. "Was he?" He turned back to Daniel and, bending from the middle of his torso, he bowed. "Pleased to meet you. You are most fortunate. At so young an age to have done something I always wanted to do."

"What's that?" asked Daniel.

"Studying among the elves," he said and smiled. He turned back to James. "How can I help you?"

"Daniel is an orphan looking for members of his family. I thought we could peruse the records of births and deaths and see if anyone from his family has ever lived in Clearbrook."

"All right. We have records that go back three hundred years, when the town was first settled. Searching them may take a while."

"No problem," said James. "I can spare a few hours."

"I can't," said Daniel. "Mr. Jones is expecting me back in the kitchen in about an hour."

"You work for Frank?" Father O'Malley asked Daniel.

"Yes, as a dishwasher."

"Good honest work for a boy your age, I'm sure."

Daniel frowned. "What does my age have to do with my work?"

James rolled his eyes. *Why does he have to be so literal?*

Father O'Malley smiled weakly. "I only meant it is good that you have steady work."

"Where are the records?" asked James hastily.

"In the church's library. Come with me. I'll show you."

"Good," said James. "Daniel, why don't you go back to the Inn so you don't get into trouble? I'll search the records to see what I can find. We can talk more about it tomorrow."

Daniel shrugged. "All right."

"It was good to meet you," said Father O'Malley as Daniel turned away.

In response, Daniel turned back and bowed again. Then he walked up the aisle and out of the church.

Father O'Malley gestured with his left hand. "This way."

James inclined his head in acknowledgment and followed the priest through a side door into the library.

* * *

James was waiting for Daniel in the common room the following day when the lad came out of the kitchen with a plate of vegetables for lunch. Daniel saw the bard, walked over to his table, and sat down. He smiled at James.

"I looked for you last night after my shift was over," said Daniel. "But you were on stage performing. I was going to wait for you to take a break, but Iriel told me not to."

"I know. She told me. And it was just as well. There's not much to tell."

"You didn't find anything?" Daniel's smile faded and his eyes darkened.

"I didn't find any of your relatives, no."

"I thought ... You said ..." James felt his cheeks redden. Daniel paused, then asked, "So now what do we do?"

"Let me think about it. There may be a wizard in town who can help."

"All right," Daniel said and speared some vegetables with his knife.

James sat there with his right hand over his mouth and deep in thought. *Why do I feel so bad? It's as if I've let him down, but that's nonsense. It was unlikely at best to find any of Daniel's relatives in the church records,* the bard told himself. *And I told him that.*

He sighed. *So what now? A trip to Wrightwood? Maybe.* He wanted to think about that and make certain there were no other options to pursue in town.

He wanted a drink. *Iriel might have some ideas too.* He would be certain to ask her.

CHAPTER 6
ASKING FOR HELP

B rashani sat in the common room of the Grey Horse Inn. Sweat beaded on his forehead and dust covered his brown leather boots and beige trousers. Iriel walked up to him.

"Can I take your order?"

Brashani nodded his head, wiping his forehead with the sleeve of his white shirt. "Old Troll ale, if you have any; otherwise, a stein of beer."

"Anything to eat?"

"Hmmm ... no, not now. But if I get hungry, I'll give you a holler."

Iriel gave him a sideways glance that made Brashani think she did not approve of his drinking.

Too bad, he thought. *Who is she to pass judgment? Has she just walked from Irenrhod to Clearbrook over the last week? I doubt it.*

He was hot, tired, and thirsty. He had also escaped a brush with death from the necromancers that controlled Irenrhod. If he wanted a drink then, by the Twelve powers, he was going to have one.

Iriel left to place the order and Brashani glanced about the room. He saw an old man standing by the fireplace. He was doing sleight-of-hand tricks.

Hrumph, Brashani said to himself. *That's what magic has come to now.*

Then another thought crossed Brashani's mind and he turned back to examine the man in detail. Slender and frail, the magician had a proud bearing, as if he had a noble past. Brashani had seen that demeanor before, years ago, back when he was employed. It was the bearing many mages once had.

It should be easy to determine if he was a mage. But not here, not now.

Iriel returned with a stein of beer. She placed it on the table and left without a word.

Brashani took a swig and felt the liquid revive his parched throat. He sighed. *Perfect. That hit the spot.*

He licked his lips to savor the taste of the beer on them and drank again. All the while, Brashani watched the old man perform tricks that were beneath any mage.

I can't watch him any more; it's too degrading. He turned away and thought about what he would do now. *I need a job and a place to live, assuming that's even possible. If Clearbrook is like most of the towns I've lived in, I'll be unemployed and living on the street.*

Brashani grumbled to himself at that prospect and decided not to accept that outcome for a change. His old confidence surged for a moment and he longed for his old life back. He knew that the only way to reclaim it was not to just accept what life handed him; he needed to work for the things he wanted and that would mean looking for a job and a hovel somewhere in town. The mage squirmed in his chair because both tasks would be unpleasant, but he resigned himself to doing these chores ... eventually.

He wanted to stroll around town first to get a sense of the people and learn where things were. He would enjoy that at least. Learning about a new place was always interesting. Perhaps the townsfolk would surprise him and be more open to wizards. He doubted it, but it was possible.

And, before I look for a place to live, I'm going to need to see which parts of town are safe and which are not.

Once he was familiar with the town and its people, Brashani would have a few questions for his fellow wizard about how he could fit in. In the meantime, he would enjoy his beer and hope the elder mage did not embarrass himself too much.

* * *

Brashani spent a few hours walking through Clearbrook. The people seemed friendly and pleasant, and the town seemed like any average-sized town in the kingdom.

He noted that there were no magic shops in town. *Figures. As I expected, these people must be mana phobes.* He shook his head and sighed. *On the other hand, I won't have to pay the high prices I usually find in a magic store.*

Investigating the town further, the wizard found only a single jewelry store and no one of appreciable wealth aside from the gem merchant and the town mayor.

That's good, thought the wizard. *That means the necromancers won't be coming here. Unless the gem merchant is hiding the jewel they want.*

Brashani thought about approaching the town jeweler and asking if he knew anything about a fabulous gem because the urge to know if Clearbrook was a potential destination for the necromancers was strong. If the town was a possible target for the Irenrhod dark mages, he'd have to move on.

He rolled around the idea of talking to the town jeweler in his mind and dismissed it.

That's not standard procedure, he reminded himself.

Standard procedure, at least the one he followed back when he was an investigator for the town guard, called for a divination to learn whatever he could. But without a magic shop, that would be hard.

Guess I'll have to improvise and visit the apothecary for the ingredients I need. And maybe the wizard I saw earlier can help me. If not, I might be stopped before I start.

* * *

Brashani sat down at an empty table in the common room of the Grey Horse Inn. The old man had finished his performance and was taking his final bow. Brashani watched the man make his way through the room and stood up to meet the magician at the double doors that separated the common room from the foyer.

"Excuse me," said Brashani. "Do you have a minute? I'd like to talk to you."

The old man stopped; his forehead furrowed. "Me?" he asked. "You want to talk to me?"

"Yes."

The man eyed Brashani. "Do I know you?"

"No, we've never met, but we share some things in common."

"Such as?"

Brashani held out his hand and a small fire appeared in his palm. It burned for a few seconds and then disappeared without leaving a mark or scar on the wizard's skin.

The old man's eyes narrowed. "What do you want?" he said suspiciously. "I don't do that sort of thing any more."

"Oh? Why not?"

"I'm retired."

Brashani gestured toward the stage of the common room with his head. "Then why all the sleight of hand?"

The elder man's head moved up and down as he sized up the other wizard. If Brashani did not know any better, he'd think the old man was giving him a 'who-the-hell-are you?' look.

"Not that it's any of your business," said the old wizard, "but if you must know, I need a little money to make ends meet. But otherwise, I'm done conjuring and wielding magic."

"That's fine," Brashani said and smiled. "I don't need you to conjure, just to help me with a divination."

"I don't know," the senior mage said with hesitation. "Sounds tricky. Those things never come off the way you want them to and you end up with more questions than answers."

"Sometimes," Brashani conceded. "But I'm a natural fire mage. So pyromancy comes a little more easily for me."

"Hmmm," said the other man. "Never tried that. How does it work?"

"I burn some herbs, inhale the smoke, and stare into the fire. With luck, I'll see images which will tell me what I need to know."

"What do you need me for?"

"To keep me grounded. If I stare at the fire too long, my spirit can leave my body and I will lose myself."

"Sounds dangerous. I'll pass."

Brashani said nothing for a moment. *How obtuse is this guy? Pyromancy isn't dangerous. Didn't he learn the fundamentals of magic?* He sighed.

"It's not dangerous," he said at last. "Just shake me gently after five minutes."

The old man scratched his head. "That's it?"

"That's it."

"Well, if that's all, I will help you. When and where?"

"Now, if you are free and have somewhere private."

"I know just the place."

CHAPTER 7
A GLIMPSE OF THE FUTURE

B rashani followed the old man out of the Grey Horse.

"I'm Brashani Khumesh, by the way."

"Molin Black."

They shook hands.

"When did you retire?" asked Brashani.

"When King Leonard dismissed all the court mages without so much as a 'Thank you for your service,' about thirty years ago."

"Typical." The fire mage shook his head in disgust. *We're people, not toys.* "Had you served the crown long?"

"Most of my life. King Kenilworth, Leonard's father, hired me."

Brashani raised his eyebrows, impressed. "That was a long time ago. In those days, mages were respected."

"True."

"Were you there when Andropolis and Azahnon fell?"

Molin sighed. "No. I saw no point in staying in the city after being dismissed."

"That decision may have saved your life."

"Ironic, isn't it?" Molin said, as a half smile played on his lips. He paused for a second then asked, "Mind telling me why you want to do a divination in the first place?"

"Not at all," said Brashani. "A magic gem will be stolen by some necromancers. I'm trying to figure out whether the theft will happen here in this town."

Molin laughed and slapped his knee. "That's rich. A magic gem? Necromancers? In this out-of-the-way village? I doubt it."

Brashani narrowed his eyes and frowned. "Why?"

"Because I don't know anyone in town who owns such a thing."

His face brightened, but Brashani heard the irritation in his own voice as he spoke. "They wouldn't advertise it."

"I know that," said Molin with a touch of anger. "Which means the thief would have to know the person. And there's practically no criminal element here."

"That's not necessarily true," said Brashani. "The thief only needs to know the location and existence of the gem."

"But why go to all that trouble?" asked Molin. "If they want a magic gem, they can just pay to have one made."

"I don't know," replied Brashani. "The gem must be special in some way. Hopefully, the divination will answer a lot of questions."

That was a lie and Brashani knew it. The divination was not likely to tell him much at all, but Molin was so opinionated that the younger wizard just wanted to shut him up. *How had he been a court mage to a king? He seems to be so clueless, so ready to jump to an assumption.* Brashani did not understand how Molin could have functioned as a wizard at all.

They approached the open market. The cacophony of people hawking their wares drifted toward them. The smell of fresh bread, meat, cheese, parchment, ink, and a thousand other aromas assaulted Brashani like a wall. He closed his eyes tightly.

Brashani paused for a moment and rubbed his eyes to soothe them. When he opened them again, he saw Molin turn right into a narrow alley and disappear down an opening in the foundation of a building. The fire mage followed. As he approached, Brashani saw an old wooden cellar door that had been lifted up and swung over to the right, to reveal a doorway and some worn and warped granite stairs that were hard to stand on.

Brashani managed to make it down the three stairs without falling, although he was certain he was going to break his neck as he descended them. Dust and cobwebs clung to the corners and edges of the walls. Oil lamps hung from pegs and cast a dim, smoky light. A straw mat occupied the far corner and a used leather satchel lay next to it, stuffed with clothes.

Molin stood in the center of the basement near a circle of stones. Inside the circular arrangement of rocks were soot and ashes.

"You live here?" asked Brashani.

"Yes," said Molin, "it's all I can afford now."

The fire mage scratched his head, confused. "It is? I would have thought that you made a good living when you worked for Kenilworth."

Molin smirked. "That's what everyone thinks, but I didn't. At the time, it didn't matter because I expected to retire in the royal palace. Then Kenilworth died and Leonard changed the rules. So now I'm forced to live like this." He gestured about, indicating the basement.

"Well, if it helps any, many mages live like this. I do."

"It doesn't and I'd rather not dwell on it. Let's proceed," Molin said dismissively. Brashani guessed he had hit a nerve and decided not to press the point.

"All right. Let me prepare."

Brashani took out a pouch of herbs he had purchased at the apothecary and arranged the bundle in the pattern he needed. Then, he sat on the dirt floor and gazed at the charred center of the stone ring. A fire sprang to life among the ashes.

He tossed the herb bundle into the flame and waited for it to smoke and burn. He inhaled the smoke deeply. Brashani coughed a little and his eyes stung when suddenly an image appeared in the heart of the flame.

He saw a gem about the size of a corn kernel, resting on a velvet cloth in a display case made of glass and wood. Next to it stood the serving girl he had seen earlier from the Grey Horse. She was guarding it, while people gawked at the jewel.

Brashani tried to hone in on the gem, to determine the color and kind of stone it was, but the image shifted before he could see it clearly, and the next image showed the glass top open and the display case empty.

He watched as the scene shifted again to a swamp. Deep in the middle of the marshland was an old shack in need of repair. Odd bits of wood had been nailed to the front and sides of the hut, giving it an abandoned appearance.

The image melted away and Brashani saw a large hole in the side of the Grey Horse Inn. Frank Jones stood inside the Inn surveying the damage, wringing a dirty apron, and cursing.

Brashani shut his eyes and the smoke caused them to fill with tears. He blinked several times to regain his vision and saw Molin staring at him.

So there is a magic gem here and it will be stolen. Probably by necromancers. So what do I do? Move on or stay and fight?

He wanted to move on, but at the same time, he felt his old confidence again. The wizard tried to ignore it, but it would not be denied. This was the first time in over two decades that Brashani had a chance to make a difference again. He needed to take that chance or go run and hide as he had been doing for so long. Frankly, he was tired of running and living like a beggar. It was time to make a stand or he would regret it, and he knew it. He smiled. For the first time in years, he felt like himself again.

"Can you get me a job at the Grey Horse Inn?"

CHAPTER 8

BRASHANI GETS A JOB

"You want to work there?" asked Molin.

"It looks like I have to."

"Why?"

"Because, as it turns out, you're wrong." Molin grimaced. The fire mage ignored the other man's expression and continued. "The gem these necromancers want is in town, or will be soon, and it will be on display at the Grey Horse. I saw the serving girl from the Inn standing guard over it."

Molin narrowed his eyes. "But why would a magic gem be on display at the Inn? It makes no sense."

"I don't know, but that's what I saw and that's where it will be stolen from."

"Even if you're right, what business is it of yours?"

"It's none of my business," Brashani conceded. "But I was an investigator for the town guard in a former life. If they are coming here to steal a magic gem, it must be important. I may be able to stop them; but I'll have to work there, or perhaps even guard it, to even have a chance to do so."

"Sounds dangerous. Why bother?" asked Molin, apathetically.

"It will be dangerous, but I've tangled with death mages before. I can handle myself." Brashani did not feel as confident as he sounded. Combating necromancers was never easy and never went the way you expected. He had to remember that and not get ahead of himself or be presumptuous.

"If you say so, but this is all a little too far-fetched for me to believe."

"Then you won't help me?"

The elder wizard shrugged. "Personally, I think you are wasting your time, but if you want a job at the Grey Horse, let's go back." He gestured in the direction of the Inn. "I'll introduce you to Frank Jones, the owner."

"Thanks," Brashani replied with a smile.

* * *

Frank sat down at the table with Molin and Brashani. Concern showed in the eyes of the innkeeper and his forehead furrowed with lines of doubt.

"Molin tells me you want a job here," Frank began.

"That's right," Brashani said, a slight smile on his lips.

"I don't really have an opening, but I can make one if you can impress me. What can you do?"

"Sleight of hand, like Molin."

Frank shrugged. "So what? Molin does that. I don't need two people doing card tricks."

Brashani thought for a moment and suppressed a smile. "What about breathing fire? Does Molin do that?"

Frank slid his jaw to one side and raised his eyebrows. "Say, that would be good. Let me see you do it."

"One moment." Brashani was silent briefly and then opened his mouth. A jet of flame roared out across the table. The wizard closed his mouth and the fire was snuffed out.

"Excellent," Frank said with a broad grin. "But that's not an act."

"No," Brashani agreed. "But I can do all kinds of tricks with fire. I'll work out a routine and show it to you."

"Okay. If you can do that, you're hired."

Brashani smiled. His luck was turning — maybe.

CHAPTER 9

EVAN RETURNS HOME

It was a cold, clear Thursday when Evan reined in his horse. He leaned forward and patted him on the neck. Alsvinn neighed and tossed his head about.

"Easy, Alsvinn." Evan pulled on the reins to keep control of his horse. "I know you'd like to charge ahead, but this is my old hometown. We need to be a little calmer than normal. These are gentle people."

The steed seemed to understand his rider and grew quiet.

Evan peered down the dirt road to the village of Clearbrook. He had left Wrightwood eight days earlier and had been riding at a moderate but steady pace ever since. Now, near his destination, the autumn air smelled crisp and sweet. Evan breathed deeply, enjoying the aroma.

He exhaled and a small cloud formed in front of his mouth. In the distance, bare trees, with limbs like gnarled hands, looked as if they were trying to catch light and warmth. Dead brown leaves tumbled across Evan's path in the slight breeze and crunched under Alsvinn's hooves.

As Evan trotted along, he saw no one on the road that led into town. It was only after he passed the homes and stores that stood along the edge of town that he began to see people. They appeared to be going about their business: splitting firewood, shoeing horses, raking leaves, or walking down the street with their cloaks pulled tightly around them. Each person Evan saw greeted him warmly with a "Good morning, Father," or a smile and a nod of the head.

Evan smiled and waved back, or returned their greetings, "And good morning to you."

Further ahead, Evan began to hear the din of the open market and, as he came closer, saw it alive with activity. People dressed in long coats or short coats, and carrying bags, sacks, or purses perused clothes, leather, carpets, and food in endless varieties. Moving from one stall to another was slow, often requiring others to move first; but everyone made do. The merchants in each stall welcomed each new face, hawked their wares, and recited specials of the day. When someone made an offer or showed even the slightest bit of interest in buying, the stall owner haggled over the price or cajoled the customer into buying.

Evan began to turn away when he caught the sight of a middle-aged woman with auburn curly hair and a blue scarf wrapped around her head. She had full cheeks, which the cold air had turned red and which made her face resemble a plump tomato.

She looks like that lady I exorcised in Wrightwood, Christine Robeson ... how many years has it been? He flushed a little when he realized that nine years had passed. *But that couldn't be she, could it?* Evan watched her as she looked over the tuna, salmon, cod, and haddock that hung on hooks suspended from a wooden bar over the fishmonger's stall.

The woman looked up and caught Evan's gaze. She inclined her head politely, but showed no sign of recognition. Evan averted his eyes. *Guess I was mistaken.*

Spurring Alsvinn forward, Evan pushed on into the town square. The town's clock tower, at the north end of the quadrangle, chimed the half hour. In the middle of the square, there was a small low fountain with a two-foot tall brick wall around it. Over the fountain stood a bronze statue of King Illium, Thalacia's first king. The monarch held his fabled sword, Sadarxio, in one hand, and had his arm outstretched, with the blade pointed up to the heavens. His stance was regal, proclaiming his power and majesty as he gazed upon the legendary blade.

Evan cantered out of the west side of the square and down the road. At the end of the lane was an inn with a sign depicting a gray stallion standing on its hind legs. The Michaeline priest saw the building and smiled. He had reached his destination, the Grey Horse Inn.

Alsvinn responded to Evan's tug on the reins and stopped in front of the Inn. Evan dismounted and looked up at the Grey Horse. He marveled that it appeared the same as when he'd left town, fifteen years earlier. Three wooden stairs led up to a set of wooden double doors. The doors were worn, but stood firm against the cold autumnal air. Across the front of the building, whitewashed shingles had warped and were stained with black mildew along their edges.

Evan tied the reins of his steed to a nearby hitching post and brushed off miles of dust from his clothes. The demon hunter climbed the stairs, feeling fifteen again. He reached for the handles to both doors, recalling old memories. He had come here often to spend time with his best friend, Frank Jones.

Those had been carefree days. At least they had been until Evan began committing pranks all over town. The Michaeline priest scratched his head.

Why was I so angry and arrogant? I could have hurt someone. As the pained face of Father O'Malley flashed across his mind, he realized he had.

Evan had been placed in Father O'Malley's care after both of Evan's parents had died and, at the time, he had not understood why. *Perhaps that's why I was so angry.* Evan was not completely sure. Father O'Malley had not treated Evan poorly or given Evan any reason to be angry; but despite this fact, Evan perpetrated a variety of pranks in the six weeks immediately following the deaths of his parents. Finally, Father O'Malley decided it was time to discipline Evan severely and sent him away to St. Bertram's School for Wayward Boys.

Evan sighed and pushed open the doors to the lobby. Wonder filled him; the Inn's interior had been completely altered, even as the exterior remained untouched by time. Originally, there had only been a pine counter, a flight of stairs leading to guest rooms across from the counter, an old storeroom to the left of the entrance, and a small kitchen in back. Now, Evan saw that the storeroom had been finished off and converted into a large unfurnished hall. The pine counter had been replaced with mahogany. Across from him, on the far wall of the Inn's foyer, were twin doors leading into a common room. Clearly, the owner of the Grey Horse had been busy renovating.

Frank stood behind the counter wearing a clean apron as Evan entered. "By the saints," he said, his eyes widening. "I don't believe it. Evan. Evan Pierce." He smiled. "I was just thinking of you last week."

Evan looked at his old friend and grinned back.

Frank came out from behind the counter and shook Evan's hand. "What brings you to Clearbrook?" He slapped Evan's shoulder.

"Rest. My brother demon hunters and I just finished cleaning out some necromancers from the ruins of Mirea, and His Grace gave me a few days to rest. So here I am. Got a room?"

"You want to stay here?"

"Why not? You run a good inn and I need a place to stay."

Frank shrugged. "I figured, as a Michaeline priest, you'd want to stay in a fancier place."

Evan's eyes were round with surprise as he studied his friend's face. "Frank, it's me. Evan. I may be a priest of St. Michael, but I'm still the same person you used to go fishing with."

"Are you?"

"Of course, why would you think otherwise?"

"Look at you. The priest's collar, the red cross on your shirt, the sword at your side. You look like one of the Michaeline masters of St. Bartholomew."

"Well, I'm not, and you have nothing to fear. So relax."

"If you say so. Here, let me see which rooms are open."

Frank went to look through his records while Evan went outside to stable Alsvinn. As he returned to the lobby, Evan thought about Frank's reaction.

I expected Frank to think of me more as an old friend and less as a Michaeline priest, not the other way around. I wonder if the reputation of St. Bartholomew, our stronghold outside of Stellingham, is affecting Frank. Heaven knows there are plenty of stories circulating about priests from St. Bartholomew branding folks as evil or as heretics, burning their crops, seizing their businesses, and imprisoning and torturing the accused. Most of these stories are unfounded, yet somehow the Order's true purpose — to stop evil and protect folks from the undead — has been twisted by people who did not understand. Is Frank one of those people?

Evan did not think so, but he decided the subject was better left alone.

* * *

Frank offered Evan a choice of several rooms upstairs. After picking one, Evan went to unpack and change his clothes. He pushed the door to his room open and scanned the area for signs of evil. A large four-poster bed filled the center of the room. Pale green, cotton drapes covered the windows and a chest for storing quilts and blankets sat at the foot of the bed. A night table with a lamp on it had been placed to the right of the bed, and to the left was a wide table next to a narrow fireplace.

No signs of evil here.

Evan dropped his saddlebags just inside the door and flopped on the bed. It was soft. He thought about sleeping, but, aside from a few aches that were the result of riding for the last several hours, Evan was not overly tired. His stomach growled; he was hungry, but he needed to unpack and change his clothes first.

Rolling off the bed, Evan examined his wardrobe and wished he had packed some non-priestly clothes so he could more easily blend in.

Guess I'll have to go shopping, Evan thought, feeling torn. He had not dressed as a layperson since he had become a priest and demon hunter. It seemed that to do so now would be like a sheepdog wearing a ram's pelt and pretending to be part of the flock. Yet these were his people; he had grown up here. He did not want to make them anxious by wearing the traditional garb of his order.

Better to pose as one of them, he thought. *And who knows? Maybe wearing something less formal will help Frank forget that I'm a Michaeline priest.* He sighed and formed a plan of action. *I'll eat first and then shop for some clothes.*

Evan finished his unpacking and went downstairs into the common room. Only a few tables were occupied. As he sat down at an empty table, Frank approached.

"Frank, are you waiting tables?" asked Evan.

"For the next few days, yes."

"Why? Where's your serving girl?"

"In the great hall, along with my dishwasher, bard, and two old wizards I hired to entertain my guests. They are guarding Tindolen's gem," the innkeeper said with resignation.

Evan shook his head to clear it. Something did not make sense. Tindolen was Clearbrook's elven jeweler and had been for over two hundred years. But why was Frank's staff guarding one of the elf's gems?

"They're ..." Evan stopped in disbelief. "But they aren't guardsmen. Why are they standing watch? Can't Tindolen afford his own men?"

"It's a long story," Frank explained. "Tindolen offered to display the gem here to celebrate St. Sebastian's week."

"St. Sebastian's week?" said Evan. "But no one's done that since the dukef invasion. In fact, I don't think I've heard St. Sebastian's name since leaving the seminary. Most folks have forgotten about him and his message of tolerance and cooperation among all races."

Frank nodded his head. "I know, but you can't tell that to Bigsbee."

Evan's eyes widened and he raised his eyebrows. "Bigsbee! Is he still in office? How long has it been? Twenty years?"

"About that."

"No wonder none of this makes sense. He's never had a good idea and almost always confuses the details of any situation."

"Except this time," said the innkeeper. "Mayor Bigsbee decided it was time to celebrate St. Sebastian's week. He just goes on and on about how it is time to heal the differences that have kept humans and elves apart."

That, at least, Evan conceded to himself, was a noble goal. *But until the dukefs are willing to give back the land they have taken, return the property and monies they have stolen, and compensate the families of the people they killed during the invasion of the old capital, Andropolis, it is unlikely there can be a lasting peace or racial tolerance.*

"And so," Frank continued, "as a way to observe the occasion, His Honor asked for people to set up displays that showcase the cooperation that once existed between the two races."

"And Tindolen's gem is his display?" Evan surmised.

"Right," said Frank.

"But how does a gem highlight the cooperation between the races?"

"It's an Elf-gem."

The color in Evan's face drained away. "But that's impossible. All seven Elf-gems were lost when the Crown of Power they had been set into was destroyed."

"I know, but Tindolen insists it is real."

Evan stood. The gem, if authentic, could easily be the prize referred to in the letter he had shown His Grace a week ago. Which meant that Jormundan planned to steal it; but, even more important, if the gem was real, it was valuable to the entire kingdom.

"Lose your appetite?" asked Frank.

"No, but I want to see that jewel first. If it's genuine, Bigsbee needs to assign guards to protect it and I need to talk to Tindolen. This could be our chance to eliminate the dukefs once and for all."

Frank understood his friend's point and said nothing. He just watched Evan dash out of the common room and across the foyer.

CHAPTER 10
TOPAZ TALKING

Evan forgot about his hunger as he rushed across the lobby and stepped into the great hall. About halfway down the wall opposite the doorway, an extra wide hearth burned with a moderate fire. A display case, resting on an oak platform that sat a foot and a half off the floor, was at the far end of the room. The enclosure had a glass top and front panel; the other sides were made of pine.

Five dwarves with long white beards stood along the front of the case. Each dwarf wore a blue cloak with a hood and stared intently at the jewel inside the glass.

"Bah!" said one of the dwarves. "It's all an act. Let's go. We have better things to do with our time." The other dwarves nodded in agreement and together they strode out of the great hall in single file.

Evan watched them go and then turned to face the clean-shaven man and the elven woman who stood behind the display. The man was tall and attractive; his blue eyes sparkled and his brown hair was neatly combed. The image of a lyre was clearly visible on his left breast. Evan recognized the patch as the one worn by members of the College of Bardic Lore.

The elf was pretty and slim, with dark hair that reached her thighs and bright green eyes. She wore a loose beige blouse that revealed nothing of her figure. Olive trousers and a black leather belt completed her attire. Hanging from the belt, in a burgundy leather case, was a dagger with a pearl embedded in the hilt.

Evan inclined his head to both of them. "They're right, of course. This can't be a real Elf-gem."

"You doubt my uncle's word too?" asked the elf.

"Your uncle …" Evan paused as recognition came to him; his face brightened. "You're Tindolen's niece, Iriel."

The woman's eyes widened and she reached out with her right hand to the bard. "James," she said. "He knows my name!" Addressing Evan, she said, "How do you know who I am? We have never met before. Only a spellcaster reading my mind could know this."

James saw the red Michaeline cross on Evan's shirt and his priest's collar. "He's not a wizard; he's a priest, a Michaeline priest." He unfurled the coiled whip that hung off his belt and narrowed his eyes. "But even so, mind reading isn't appreciated by Iriel or me."

Evan raised his arms and opened his hands so that they were flat and parallel to his chest, with the palms facing James and Iriel. "Calm down. I'm not a mind reader, just a good friend of Tindolen's. I spent many hours at Tindolen's jewelry shop as a boy. I used to listen to him talk for hours about his family back in Oldarmare, and most especially, about his eldest niece."

James and Iriel both sighed and relaxed; the bard lowered his whip and said quietly, "Sorry."

Evan let his arms drop to his side. "He's quite proud of you, Iriel."

The elf shrugged. "That could be, but he has many nieces and nephews. Still, I suppose I am fortunate; out of all my cousins, he sent only for me." She smiled and her eyes brightened like emeralds. "I love living and working with humans. I'm learning so much! And Uncle has been so helpful. He got me this job working for Mr. Jones as a serving girl." Then Evan's words registered and her smile faded. She seemed to recognize the priest. "You're Evan Pierce."

Evan inclined his head. "Guilty as charged."

She gently elbowed James. "Uncle used to send letters home about Evan's pranks in town, James."

"Nothing too embarrassing, I hope," said Evan, flushing a little.

"I do not think so. But at the time, I was amazed at each new act of mischief you got yourself into. I admired your creativity, your curiosity, and your adventurous spirit."

"Yes, well ... the simple fact is I was a boy. I needed to grow up and become responsible for my actions."

"Sounds boring," replied Iriel, with a smile.

Evan glanced at the gem behind the glass as the elf spoke. Resting on a velvet cloth was a dark mustard topaz, round like a marble and the size of a shelled peanut.

The gem looks ordinary, but then what would a magic gem look like?

From the little Evan knew about gems, most topazes were not cut this small or this perfectly round. These characteristics alone made the gem rare and special, but that did not mean it was magical.

You can't tell anything by the appearance. Evan grimaced and narrowed his eyes. *How had a gem from the beginning of the world survived?* The priest couldn't say and he had a hard time believing it was even possible.

Evan began to turn away when he noticed James had coiled up his whip and attached it to a clip on his belt. Catching Evan's eye, James extended his hand. "We've not been properly introduced. I'm James Claymont."

"Pleased to meet you," Evan said as he shook hands. He studied the bard a moment and noticed that, in addition to being well-groomed, James was also well dressed. He was outfitted in a gray shirt and trousers, and wore black leather boots and a black leather belt. *Very sharp.* "What brings you to Clearbrook?"

"A change of scenery mostly," began James. "I worked in Bryford at the Silver Snake for five years and it was becoming old and stale. So, I decided it was time to start anew elsewhere. And you? What brings you here?"

"Rest, initially. But I didn't know there was an Elf-gem here. I may have to change my plans now if the jewel is authentic."

Iriel raised an eyebrow. "Of course, it's authentic. Uncle said so."

"So you are taking his word for it then?"

"I am; he wouldn't lie."

No, thought Evan, *but he might not tell the whole truth.* Tindolen had been known to go his own way on many town issues.

"But," said Evan, "the only way I know that you can tell whether you have an Elf-gem is to place it next to another one." He gestured with his hands and brought them together. "If both gems brighten, both gems are real."

The elf shrugged. "There could be other tests."

Perhaps, but Evan's doubt told him otherwise. "Do you know if Tindolen put magic wards on the display case to protect it?"

"He did, why?"

"Just wondering," said Evan. "Since professional guards are not standing watch over his gem, I was curious if he had taken any other precautions."

"He's done the best he can. The protection wards should stop anyone but the most powerful of spellcasters."

"Glad to hear it. Good to meet you both."

"Good to meet you too," Iriel said and smiled.

"A pleasure," James said with a wave.

Evan turned to leave. He needed to talk to Mayor Bigsbee and Tindolen. He did not relish the thought of confronting His Honor, but he had no choice. If the gem was genuine, it needed more protection and should not be on display at all. It was too important. He would need to take the gem to His Grace so that an expedition could be mounted and the other six Elf-gems located. Only then could the Crown of Power be remade and used against the dukefs.

* * *

Daniel yawned, stood, and straightened his white *Qua'ril* uniform. He saw light streaming into the room he shared with the other members of the Inn's staff and realized it was almost time for guard duty.

He stretched and then spread apart his feet to assume a *Qua'ril* stance. With luck, he could get some exercises in before he reported to the great hall. Daniel paused and listened for the voice he had been hearing for the last two days. It was not there.

Good. Maybe whatever it was is gone.

He grimaced, and doubt played in his clear blue eyes.

Daniel began his exercises, slowly moving, defensive posture flowing into one of attack and then changing back into a position of defense again. Back and forth he moved from a defensive stance to one of attack and back again.

A voice in his head resumed as he moved. It began as a hum and grew to a low unintelligible babble. Daniel concentrated on his exercises, ignoring the noise and hoping it would go away.

Two days earlier, the voice had been unclear and indistinct, sounding like wind howling in a bad storm. The weather had been bright and sunny that day, so Daniel had dismissed the noise and concluded it was his imagination.

Fear bubbled to the surface and the lad began to shake uncontrollably. He inhaled deeply, exhaled slowly, and turned his attention to the terror he felt, applying the *Qua'ril* disciplines of control and focus. His fright ebbed and his shaking lessened gradually. After about a minute, he was able to continue exercising.

The voice became clearer as he proceeded with his training, just as it had for the last two days. Initially, the noise had changed from a raging storm to a distant voice gasping for air. Yesterday the voice had changed again, from a distant voice to a mournful cry.

Daniel silently wished for the noise to end, but it persisted unabated. His hands became clammy and he realized his effort at controlling his fear was beginning to wane.

He sighed and wondered why *only he* heard the voice. No one else around him seemed to, and this scared him too.

Am I going mad?

The voice said, *Hlee.* Daniel froze in mid-stride.

Hlee, the voice said again.

Maybe it is not my imagination after all.

Daniel sat on the floor and slowed his breathing. He fixed his mind on the sound. The voice burst into his brain, becoming louder and more powerful. Unbearable pain stabbed at his temples.

The lad fought to stay conscious and let his concentration lapse. The pain in his head subsided slowly, and he gave himself a moment to recover before resuming his meditation and training his attention more intensely on the voice. It became clearer and more distinct, as if it were coming from a person standing next to him.

Hlee, the voice repeated over and over again.

Daniel smiled to himself. He was not going mad. There was a voice — disembodied perhaps — calling to him. But why? And from where?

Perhaps if I meditate and apply basic Qua'ril *principles,* he thought, *the voice might become clearer and easier to understand. But I can't do it now; it will have to wait until I'm on guard duty. I should be able to sit in a corner of the great hall unnoticed and meditate.*

He stood and yawned once more. Seconds later, Daniel ran out of the shared room to assume his post in the great hall.

CHAPTER 11
AMELIDEL'S PROPHECY

Tindolen locked the door to his jewelry shop with a frown. He was not happy about closing his store at this hour of the day. It meant a loss of business, but Mayor Bigsbee wanted to talk about how the celebration of St. Sebastian's week was going and Tindolen was in charge of the event. They could have used Tindolen's store for the conversation; Tindolen had even suggested it. His Honor had discounted that option, saying he preferred taking a walk instead so that potential customers would not interrupt them.

After testing that the door to his store was secure, the elf turned and strolled down the street with Mayor Bigsbee. His Honor was a large man who stood six feet tall. His four-foot girth almost made him wider than the elf was tall. His face was round and red, as if he were constantly blushing, and he had gray eyes and brown hair that had started to fade to gray. Dressed in blue, as he was now, Bigsbee bore a striking resemblance to a walking blueberry.

Compared to Bigsbee, the gem merchant was anything but comical. The elf was five feet tall and had a bronze-tinted complexion. He had dark hair that flowed down to his shoulder blades; his eyes sparkled like emeralds. He was dressed in black trousers and a matching jacket, a green paisley waistcoat, a jade bow tie, and a white shirt. Several rings adorned fingers on both hands. Tindolen liked to wear lots of rings as a way to advertise and generate business. Usually they were recently acquired merchandise, but occasionally he wore hard-to-sell items too.

"How has the attendance at the exhibits been?" Bigsbee inquired after taking a few strides down the street.

"Mixed," replied Tindolen. "Some exhibits are better attended than others."

"Any idea why?"

"Well, the exhibit with the lowest attendance is mine. The main issue, as I understand from my niece, is that some townsfolk don't believe my gem is genuine."

Bigsbee snorted. "Do they think we would display a fake? What would be the point?"

Tindolen continued, as if Bigsbee had not spoken. "As a result, I believe that some people are staying away, partly because they have heard the gem is not authentic and partly because they already believe in racial harmony between elves and humans. It is our cousins, the so-called dukefs, that most of the townsfolk hate."

Bigsbee gestured with his hands. "But that's exactly the point. Elves and dukefs look about the same; you can't tell, just by looking, who is evil and who isn't. The important thing is what's in the fellow's heart."

"True," Tindolen said and nodded.

"So tolerance for all elves must be the goal," Bigsbee concluded.

"Agreed, but it is our cousins who invaded your land and hold what remains of Andropolis. Until that land is restored to you, I doubt humans will be ready to tolerate my more aggressive kin."

Bigsbee's eyebrows knitted. "Surely, there must be something we can do to show the good people of this town that it is time to stop hating each other."

Tindolen was about to speak when he saw a Michaeline priest coming toward them. He pointed the man out to Bigsbee. "What's a priest of St. Michael doing here? There are no demons, necromancers, or witches to slay in Clearbrook."

Bigsbee glanced at the priest, but before His Honor could respond, the clergyman came within hearing range and addressed them. "I've been looking for both of you," he said.

Tindolen's eyes grew larger as he recognized the man's voice. Smiling, the elf strode forward, his hand outstretched.

* * *

"Evan Pierce!" Tindolen shook Evan's hand. "This is a surprise. Welcome home, my boy."

"Good to see you too, Tindolen," Evan said and returned his friend's grin.

Bigsbee stepped up alongside the elf. "You know him, Tindolen?"

"Yes," said the merchant as he stepped to one side so that Bigsbee could see Evan better. "And so do you. Do you remember the mischievous prankster Father O'Malley sent to St. Bertram's for discipline?"

"Ah, yes. Whatever happened to him?"

Tindolen rolled his eyes. "This is that boy all grown up." He pointed to Evan.

Bigsbee ran his eyes up and down over Evan. "Made a man of you, did they?"

Before Evan could answer, Tindolen asked, "What brings you to Clearbrook?"

"Rest originally. But all that's changed."

"Oh? Why is that?"

"Because I've seen your gem on display and it troubles me."

Bigsbee's face distorted, his eyes narrowed, and he furrowed his eyebrows. "Troubles you? Why?"

"Because if the gem is real, it is unprotected. More importantly, it should be in the hands of those who could put it to good use," said the priest.

Tindolen eyed his friend. "You doubt the gem's authenticity?" he asked Evan.

"I don't know what to believe," Evan admitted.

"Do you think I would say it was an *Aglari* when it was not?"

"No, that would not be like you," Evan replied.

"Then believe me when I say the gem is one of the lost *Aglaril* from King Argol's Crown of Power."

"How can you be certain without another Elf-gem?" Evan asked.

"There are … ways to be sure," the gem merchant replied.

Evan noted his friend's evasiveness. Still, if the gem was not an *Aglari*, Tindolen was risking a lot: his reputation, his business, and his good name in this town. But that still left Evan no way to be sure. He would either have to accept the merchant's word, as Iriel had done, or assume it was a fake.

The demon hunter sighed. "I see. Very well, I believe you. The gem is real. But that only makes me more concerned because the town guard is not protecting it."

Bigsbee looked abashed. "There aren't enough men to guard all the exhibits and patrol the streets too." Waving a finger at Evan,

His Honor continued, "The town's coffers only go so far, you know."

"But you can guard some of the exhibits?" asked Evan.

"Yes, of course."

Evan narrowed his eyes on Bigsbee. "Just not the one that could help us liberate Andropolis?"

Bigsbee's forehead furrowed. "Liberate Andropolis? What are you blathering about?"

"Using Tindolen's gem, we could liberate the city and free it from dukef occupation."

Tindolen's eyes shifted from side to side as he gazed at Evan. "Are you suggesting remaking *Balodol*?"

"Yes. If one Elf-gem survived, the others may have as well. And if we can locate them, the Crown of Power can be remade."

Bigsbee's eyes grew large. "You're talking about more killing and bloodshed."

"Unfortunately, yes, but it is the only way to free our lands."

Bigsbee sighed. "And where does it end?"

Evan shrugged. "I don't know, but I do know that this gem is the best chance we've had since the invasion to redress the wrong done to us."

"Evan," Tindolen said quietly, "you cannot use the Crown of Power to free Andropolis any more than I can. Only one person can do this."

Evan narrowed his eyes and pursed his lips. "Then you believe Amelidel's prophecy will be fulfilled?"

"Yes. Only an heir of the House of Richmond can use *Balodol* to eliminate the elves who seized Andropolis."

"Except there aren't any heirs to the royal house. They died in the invasion," said Evan.

Tindolen smirked. "That is the conventional wisdom, but regardless of whether an heir lives or not, the fact remains that remaking the Crown of Power by itself does not help your cause."

Evan paused to consider his friend's words. He noted Tindolen's phrasing, "conventional wisdom." It suggested the gem merchant knew more than he was letting on, which was always the case, Evan knew. More importantly, Tindolen never backed the wrong horse, as far as Evan could remember, and that suggested to the priest only one thing: one of the royal heirs was alive. If that were so, he would need to tell His Grace upon returning to Wrightwood; a search through the kingdom to find the royal heir would need to be conducted.

Turning his attention away from that speculation, Evan thought about the present and what he could do now. The obvious thing was to protect Tindolen's gem and do something about the dukefs. Their occupation of Andropolis, the old capital of Thalacia, and Azahnon, the royal palace, were constant reminders of the invasion twenty-five years earlier and the war that followed. Thousands had died as armies from surrounding duchies tried to rescue King Leonard and the royal court.

Evan had been a boy at the time, but he remembered hearing a wild rumor. An elven seer, Amelidel, prophesied that an heir to the House of Richmond who had survived would restore the monarchy by banishing the dukefs with *Balodol,* the Crown of Power, after the elves remade it with the seven Elf-gems.

This prophecy gave many people hope; but no heir ever proclaimed himself, and over the years, the prophecy was forgotten by most. Evan, on the other hand, had thought a great deal about the prediction while in seminary. Initially, he hoped the prophecy meant the House of Richmond would restore itself. However, he dismissed the idea completely after he read an account of the initial invasion that declared that no one in the royal palace had escaped the attack. Given the hatred dukefs had of humans, Evan concluded that the royal family had been slaughtered.

Nevertheless, Evan believed it was still possible to oust the dukefs ... but only with magic, distasteful as that was to him. So, until enough human mages could be trained, it seemed to Evan that the liberation of Andropolis was impossible.

At least it had been until now. The Crown of Power eliminated the need for an army of mages; and if an heir to the throne were alive, there would be a leader to rally the kingdom to war and take back what was theirs. Evan was ready to believe, and even to begin the search, until he realized that the heir, whoever it was, had yet to make him or herself known. Perhaps the heir did not know his or her true heritage. In that situation, the armies of Thalacia would have to move against the dukefs without the royal heir, which brought Evan full circle. Tindolen had just stated that only the royal heir could use the Elf-gems against the dukefs.

Then an idea crossed Evan's mind. "But isn't the prophecy only one possible future?" he asked.

Tindolen tapped his forefinger against the side of his face and considered the notion. "No," he replied after some thought. "Amelidel is a powerful seer. His prophecies are part prediction and part magic spell. Even now, the magic is guiding events so that the prophecy will come true. If you act against these events, you only delay it. You do not aid or prevent what has been foreseen."

"And how am I to know which actions help and which actions hinder the prophecy?"

"Do not force events. You came to town to rest. So rest."

"So, what you two are saying is you will not protect this gem. Furthermore, you insist that we must wait for the royal heir to announce himself and for fate to select a champion who can locate all the Elf-gems — the most important task in a generation," said Evan.

"Yes," replied Tindolen.

Evan squeezed his eyes shut and pressed his fingers against the top of his skull, as if to keep his head from exploding. Then he took his hands away and opened his eyes. They were wide and wild. He shook his open, outstretched hands. "That's insane! You are inviting theft of the gem by not protecting it," the priest exclaimed to Bigsbee. "And," he continued, as he turned to Tindolen, "you are asking me to believe in fairy tales regarding the prophecy. That somehow everything will work out with a happy ending. That's nonsense. We must act to find the royal heir and the Elf-gems."

Tindolen sighed. "Believe what you will. I can say no more."

Evan ran both hands through his hair and stared at the sky. He thought about using his authority as a member of Duke Wrightwood's court to order Tindolen to give him the gem. The merchant would refuse, no doubt, and force Evan to arrest him. That seemed harsh treatment for the elf who had been a good friend all those years ago. Alternatively, he could declare the gem to be property of the state, but he would then need a wizard to dispel the wards protecting it so that he could present it to His Grace. One of Frank's mages might be able to do that or he might need to go back to court to find a mage who could. That would take too long. St. Sebastian's week would be over by then and Tindolen would have undoubtedly hidden the Elf-gem away again.

Evan turned away from Tindolen and Bigsbee and started back to the Grey Horse Inn. He grumbled to himself, *Well, there's only one other option.* He sighed and began sketching out plans in his head.

* * *

Daniel meditated in the corner of the great hall and listened to the voice that spoke to him.

Hlee ... hlee.

Daniel tried to understand and reached out with his mind. The voice became clearer.

Heh lip eee ... heh lip eee.

I don't understand, thought Daniel. The voice replied, *Help me.*

Startled, Daniel was unsure what to do. The words repeated. *Help me. Help me.*

Help? How? Daniel thought.

Help me find my brothers.

Who are you?

I am Aure.

Aure, where are you?

Across the room.

What room?

The room you are sitting in.

Daniel opened his eyes and looked across the room. James and Iriel stood next to the display case and the ...

Aure, who ... what are you?

I am Aure, the topaz, Giver of Light.

Tindolen's gem! Daniel thought. He was hearing the voice of an *Aglari. But how?* Daniel thought.

You are telepathic and so am I, the gem replied.

CHAPTER 12
AURE AWAKES

Evan returned to the Grey Horse Inn in disbelief at how obtuse Bigsbee and Tindolen had been. The demon hunter might have expected it from Bigsbee — His Honor had missed the point and had failed to act on more than one occasion — but Tindolen was smarter than that. To trust in this prophecy so completely seemed ludicrous and irresponsible to Evan. That wasn't like Tindolen at all.

Worse still, Evan had wasted his time talking with them; going to town hall and looking for Bigsbee had been all for naught too. Even the good fortune of running into His Honor on the street meant nothing now. Part of Evan wondered, *Why did I even bother?*

But he knew why. There was a chance now, albeit a small one, to locate all of the Elf-gems, remake the Crown of Power, find the royal heir, and oust the dukes from Andropolis. They would be hard and possibly dangerous tasks, but worth the risks. The first step toward these goals was to safeguard Tindolen's topaz and keep it out of Jormundan's hands.

Considering how best to accomplish that objective, Evan decided there was only one option open to him: he would have to stand watch himself since Bigsbee refused to protect the Elf-gem with any of the town guard. The thought was not a pleasant one and he wondered if His Grace had not been right; at the very least, he should have brought Sir Ahlan with him. That would certainly make the chore of standing watch over the gem easier, but Ahlan's presence might also deter the thief from stealing the *Aglari*. Evan's only hope of locating Jormundan was to capture whoever tried to pilfer the Elf-gem and force the burglar to lead the way back to the dark mage's stronghold.

He sighed and climbed the stairs of the Grey Horse. Resigned to the night ahead of him, Evan entered the inn and stepped into the great hall. James and Iriel were still standing guard and with them were three other people. Straight ahead of Evan, a blond-haired, barefoot boy in a white jacket and trousers sat in the corner, eyes closed. A pair of black shoes rested next to the lad. They looked new and barely worn. Evan wasn't sure if the boy was asleep or concentrating deeply on some magic rite since he made no motion as Evan entered the hall.

Deeper in the room, two men stood directly in front of the fireplace. They seemed to be arguing. The man to the left of the hearth eyed Evan suspiciously as he approached. He had gray hair at the temples and in his beard. The top of his head was covered with only a few wisps of brown hair. The old man to the right of the fireplace glanced at the cleric. He had dull gray eyes; a hollow, gaunt face made him appear fragile and weak, as if he would topple over in a strong breeze. Lines etched his face. White hair and a long white beard added to his aged appearance.

Evan offered both men a friendly nod and went over to Iriel and James. "I found your uncle. He confirmed what you told me. The gem is real."

Iriel grimaced. "What is wrong with you humans? You trust so little."

"Well, the claim is pretty incredible," said James.

Iriel's brow furrowed. "You think so?"

James nodded his head. "Absolutely. It may not seem so to elves since you live longer, but for most humans, I think it is hard to believe this gem was made by your gods and given to the elves at the beginning of the world."

"I don't see why," said Iriel, indifferently.

As the bard spoke, the blond-haired boy came over and stared at the gem in the display case. Evan looked at the lad; he appeared disheveled and confused as he intensely stared at the gem.

A flash of light caught the corner of Evan's eye. Turning toward the light, Evan saw the topaz change color from a bright yellow to its original dark mustard.

"Did you see that?" Evan asked Iriel and James.

"You mean that flash of light from the gem?" responded Iriel.

"Yes," Evan replied.

"I did. What caused it?" asked James.

"I don't know." Iriel glanced nervously at James.

"Good question," said Evan.

The two men who had been arguing on the other side of the room stopped bickering and approached James and Evan, eyes wide with curiosity.

James rubbed his neck. "Maybe it was a fluke. It looks normal now." An instant later, the light flared again.

Iriel looked at the boy. He was staring at the gem. "Daniel, are you all right? You look tired."

Daniel looked up at her and murmured, "It's the gem. It speaks to me."

Evan, James, Iriel, and the two other men exchanged glances.

"You can hear it in your head, talking to you?" asked Iriel.

"Yes. I've been hearing a voice, but I wasn't sure what it was saying or where it was coming from ... until now," he replied.

"I thought only elves could hear an *Aglari* speak to them," commented James.

Evan narrowed his eyes on the lad. "And how do you know the voice is from the gem?"

Daniel cocked his head to one side. "It told me so."

"What does it say to you?" asked the balding man.

"It wants me to find its brothers," said Daniel.

Evan raised an eyebrow. "Brothers? You mean the other stones?"

Daniel paused. "Uh, yes."

"Does it know where they are?"

"No."

"Then how do you find them?" asked James.

"By using it as a guide," explained Daniel. "It will know when other *Aglaril* are near."

Evan noted the use of the elven term but that was the least of the strange happenings here. A human boy should not be able to talk to these magic elven gems. On the other hand, perhaps this is what Tindolen meant about the prophecy. Events were aligning themselves for the prophecy's fulfillment.

"I don't think Tindolen is going to let you walk around the kingdom with his gem in your pocket," observed Evan.

Daniel did not respond.

"Better get a healer," said the balding man. "The boy's as crazed as a rabid dog."

Iriel glowered at the man. "I don't think so. The *Aglaril* speak to some elves."

"But," James reminded everyone, as he gestured at the boy, "Daniel is not elven."

"Maybe he's part elven," suggested the gaunt old man.

"Perhaps," said Evan. "Or maybe the gem is talking to Daniel, elven or not, and he is hearing it."

James nodded. "You mean the same way the Elf-gems were said to speak to elven kings."

"Exactly."

"Sounds like telepathy to me," said the balding man.

The gaunt man nodded his head, "Yes. Some people have the gift."

"What makes him so special?" asked the balding man.

"Good question," said Evan. He turned to Daniel, who was still staring at the topaz. He put a hand on Daniel's shoulder and gently shook him. Daniel's eyes flickered and looked up at Evan. "Daniel, I'm Evan Pierce. I'm a priest and demon hunter. If you don't mind, I'd like to ask you a few questions about how you talk with this gem."

"All right, I'll try," said Daniel, his voice a little rough with fatigue. "But it's hard to think with the gem's voice in my head."

"When did you start hearing the gem?"

"A few days ago, but I couldn't understand the words."

"Why not?" asked Evan.

"They sounded too far away."

"Then how is it that you can hear the gem now?"

"I've been meditating and concentrating on the sound."

"Where did you learn to do that?"

"From my master, Alendil," said Daniel.

"Your *Qua'ril* master?" asked Iriel.

"Yes," replied the teen.

"You studied with the elven grandmaster of martial arts?" asked Evan. "Since when has he accepted human apprentices?"

Daniel shrugged. "I don't know. At the time, I was living among the elves as one of them; when I turned seven, he let me study with him."

Iriel's eyes widened. "Amazing. All young elven children study *Qua'ril* for a year or two to learn basic self-defense. Alendil personally trains only the most gifted."

"And why were you living among the elves?" asked Evan.

"Because they rescued me when I was a baby," Daniel replied.

"Rescued you from where?" Evan pressed.

"The ruins of the village my parents had settled near the Fire Mountains."

Evan had never heard of anyone settling near the Fire Mountains. "Why was the village in ruins?"

"Goblins had attacked it."

"How did you survive then?"

"Elven rangers arrived and drove them off before the goblins found me."

"Did anyone else survive?"

"Not that I know of."

"And they took you back to Oldarmare?"

"Yes, and cared for me."

"And so by using these *Qua'ril* techniques, learned from your master, you've managed to attune your mind to that of the gem?" Evan asked to ensure he understood.

Daniel was silent as he considered Evan's words, then answered, "Yes."

James whistled, long and low. "I think that's a first."

Evan placed his hand on top of his head and pressed down hard, as if to keep his brain from jumping out of his skull. "Incredible," he said, but what astounded him even more was Daniel's obvious involvement in Amelidel's prophecy.

Was he the royal heir? Evan thought about this. *No, that's not possible. He's too young, and neither Sandra nor Leonard was known to have had children. No, given this turn of events, I'm guessing Daniel is the one to locate the Elf-gems and that's all. But how does all of this fit into the larger picture?*

Evan wasn't sure. He needed to speak with Tindolen again.

"Are *Qua'ril* techniques magical?" asked the balding man.

Iriel shook her head. "I don't think so. Why?"

"Because how else could they yield a magical effect?"

"As I said," the gaunt man repeated, "some people have the gift. The boy must be naturally telepathic. The *Qua'ril* techniques and mental disciplines must have triggered his ability."

The balding man looked at him. "Hmmm. Maybe. We'd have to read his aura to be sure."

Evan put up a hand. "Stop, all of you. Before we do anything, we need to verify Daniel's claim of this Elf-gem speaking to him."

"How do we do that?" asked James.

"Let's talk to Tindolen," replied Evan. "It's his gem. He knows the most about it."

"I'll go find him," said Iriel.

"Good idea," said Evan.

"I'll go with you," said James.

CHAPTER 13
MARNGOL MASSACRE

Iriel and James left to find Tindolen. After they were gone, the gaunt old man turned to Evan and held out his hand. "I'm Molin Black." He pointed to the balding man. "That's Brashani Khumesh."

Evan shook Molin's hand. "Evan Pierce. You are the mages Frank hired as entertainers?"

"That's right," said Molin.

"Is there a law prohibiting us from entertaining folks?" Brashani grumbled.

Evan sighed. "No, of course not. Why would you think that?"

"Because there are plenty of other laws that prevent us from doing just about everything else. It's a wonder we are allowed to eat, breathe, and dress ourselves."

Evan recognized the hyperbole.

"Don't mind him," said Molin. He shot Brashani a sidelong glance before continuing. "He's just a troublemaker."

"Is it troublemaking to rebel against circumstances that have deprived you of your livelihood?" asked Brashani.

"You are free to practice your craft," Evan observed, "so long as no one is hurt."

"Horse feathers!" spat Brashani. "In most communities, mages are feared and shunned. So unless I want to live a segregated life in Ravenhurst, where most mages live now, I have to pretend I'm not what I am or live on the fringes of society, poor and alone like a beggar."

"That's not really anyone's fault," said Evan. "Magic is unpredictable even in the hands of the most skilled practitioners. You can't blame ordinary folks for being a little scared."

"No, but no aristocrat or religious leader has bothered to champion our side, thanks to that lead-headed knave, Constance III, and his encyclical on the evils of using magic. 'Manipulation of the life force and its elements is strictly forbidden.'"

Molin sighed in exasperation and stepped away from Evan and Brashani and stood next to the display case. Neither man noticed.

"That's right," Evan replied, "but the edict is about necromancy, not the use of magic as a whole. The passage you quoted addresses how necromancers use magic to manipulate the life force to give a semblance of life to dead things. Clearly, such actions are evil and unnatural, and are forbidden."

"That's what it is supposed to mean," said Brashani. "But your illustrious General Cosgrove, a Michaeline knight of the highest order, I believe, interpreted the edict differently."

Evan blushed at the mention of Cosgrove's name. "Yes, I know. He misinterpreted the phrase 'life force and its elements' to mean 'the elements of life' and used that as an excuse to invade Marngol and send hundreds of innocent people to their deaths."

"Precisely," said Brashani. "But it was more than an invasion in which people died; it was a massacre that overwhelmed and destroyed the town. Cosgrove came in superior numbers and attacked by surprise."

Evan cringed. "You were there, I presume."

The wizard nodded his head. "I was working as an investigator for the town guard in Marngol when Cosgrove's troops arrived by land and sea. They started killing mages before anyone knew what was happening, and by the time we did, the battle mages were scattered across the city or holed up in their towers. It was only a matter of time before the city fell."

"I'm sorry," said Evan. "Truly, I am. I can also tell you that the masters of the Michaeline order have apologized for Cosgrove's actions and stripped him of his rank. He died in one of the dungeons of St. Bartholomew a few years later."

Brashani snorted. "And their apology fixes everything? Marngol was thousands of years old, originally built by the elves in King Argol's day. It still lies in ruin, and the lives of hundreds were taken or were changed forever. I've wanted to go back and try to bury the dead and set things right, but I barely have enough money to live on.

"And what's worse," the wizard continued, "is that because of Cosgrove's actions, the dukefs were able to capture Andropolis. If not for the massacre, we would have been able to rescue King Leonard and reclaim the city."

"I do not doubt it," said Evan. "Why do you think the dukefs attacked Andropolis only a few weeks after Marngol fell? They knew our strength was halved. Many in my order believe Cosgrove was working with the dukefs in some way and demanded his execution. But no proof was ever found."

Brashani said nothing for a moment. When he finally did reply, his voice had lost some of its anger. "You're the first Michaeline priest to agree with me, at least in part, about the massacre."

"Well, we want to make amends."

"That will be difficult, but your attitude could certainly heal some wounds ... if it were shared by your fellow priests."

"I believe it is," said Evan.

"That remains to be seen," said Brashani.

Tindolen entered the great hall with James and Iriel following closely behind.

"I understand that our young friend is talking to my gem," said the senior elf.

Evan smiled to see the gem merchant again. "Yes, that seems to be the case. The gem seems to be the one initiating the conversation."

"Indeed!" cried Tindolen. "But, from what Iriel told me on the way, you do not have independent corroboration of his story."

"That's true. We only have Daniel's word for it since none of us can talk to the gem."

"But if Daniel and the gem have been talking, perhaps Daniel knows something about the *Aglari*, something known only to a select few."

"Like yourself," replied Evan.

"Exactly. I did considerable research on the *Aglari* once I found it and uncovered a few facts known only to those who bother to scrounge about in the Vault of Legends."

"The Vault of Legends," repeated James. "The elven repository of myths and fables?"

"The same," said the jeweler. He turned to face Daniel. The lad was staring at the topaz once again and Tindolen placed his hand on Daniel's shoulder. He shook the lad gently, and with glazed eyes, Daniel peered up at the gem merchant. "Daniel, have you been talking to the *Aglari*?"

"Yes, sir."

"Then tell me something about it. Something you couldn't know any other way."

"His name is Aure," Daniel replied.

Tindolen recoiled, as his eyes swelled with emotion.

"I take it from your reaction," said Evan, "that it's true. He talked to the gem."

Tindolen nodded his head. "As far as I know, the names of the *Aglaril* are recorded in only one scroll, which rests in the Vault of Legends."

"So the only way Daniel could know the gem's name is if he spoke with it."

"Yes," said Tindolen. "Amazing. As a human and a non-wizard, he shouldn't be able to talk to it at all."

"According to Daniel," James offered, "he was raised by elves and learned *Qua'ril* from them. Using these techniques, he has been able to talk with the Elf-gem telepathically."

"That's even more astounding," noted the merchant. "That means that most elves should be able to do the same thing. We all learn *Qua'ril* in our youth for basic self-defense."

Evan narrowed his eyes on his friend. "But that also means that any non-elf who learns these techniques should be able to achieve the same effect as Daniel."

"You're forgetting," Molin interjected, "that Daniel could be a natural telepath."

"Perhaps," replied Tindolen, as he considered both comments. "Or advanced training may be needed. I notice Daniel wears the traditional white *Qua'ril* uniform worn by masters of the Art."

"Regardless," said Brashani. "I don't think you want the gem talking to him. It will raise concern."

Tindolen sighed. "Such a suspicious race you are. But as I understand it, few people are coming to view the gem. So what harm can it do?"

"To others?" answered the priest, "very little, but what about Daniel? Having another voice in your head must be distracting."

"I suppose it might be," said Tindolen. "But I think that's easily fixed." He glanced at the lad. "Daniel, can you block Aure's voice?"

Daniel paused a moment. "I think so."

"Good, then do so," The gem merchant turned to face Evan. "Satisfied?" he asked the priest.

The demon hunter stroked his chin. "I suppose so, unless there's a way to tell the gem to stop sending to Daniel."

"Even if there is," said Tindolen, "from what I read, the *Aglaril* have a strong will of their own. Giving them orders is good only until they decide some other course of action is warranted."

CHAPTER 14
PROPHECY REVISITED

S atisfied that the current crisis had passed, Tindolen left the great hall and headed back to his shop. Likewise, Iriel, James, Molin, Brashani, and Daniel resumed their duties guarding the *Aglari*. Evan, on the other hand, lingered to watch Daniel. Almost as soon as he had been instructed to block the Elf-gem's voice, Daniel's composure seemed to be restored, from what Evan could tell. The lad went back to the corner of the room, sat down, and closed his eyes once more.

Is that the effect of blocking the gem's voice? Evan assumed it was, but he would have preferred to know for certain.

The sound of footsteps behind him intruded on Evan's thoughts and he spun around. Several of the local townsfolk had entered the great hall. Evan relaxed and realized he had been staring intensely at Daniel; he blushed a little at the notion.

Evan looked about the room. *Where's Tindolen? Looks like he left.* He stepped out of the great hall, walked over to the Inn's main entrance, and pushed the double doors open. To his surprise, the priest found Tindolen waiting for him by the hitching post.

"Such unpleasantness," said Tindolen, as he motioned back toward the Grey Horse. "This is no way for us to renew our friendship, is it?"

Evan shook his head. "No, it's not." He paused. "I'm sorry about my outburst earlier too."

"Think nothing of it, my boy. It is hard to understand the workings of a prophecy. I doubt Amelidel fully understands it himself."

"But I am amazed," said Evan.

"Oh? How so?" the elf asked and tilted his head to one side.

"Because if Daniel can talk to your gem, then I suppose he's the one who will locate the other Elf-gems. I wouldn't have guessed he'd be the one. And it happened just as you said it would. I've never seen anything like it."

Tindolen smiled. "Well, not everything is predestined: don't make that mistake. As I said before, events are being guided toward the prophecy's fulfillment, but individuals still control their own actions. Daniel still has free will; he may be the one to locate the *Aglaril,* or it may be he and others, or he may refuse to go on the adventure. It is too soon to know. The important thing is to let the events unfold naturally. Trying to force events to achieve a specific effect can have unforeseen consequences, many of them undesirable, and that only delays the fulfillment of the prophecy."

"I understand." Evan narrowed his eyes. "But answer me one more question."

"If I can."

"You said you had this gem for years."

"Yes."

"And you told no one about it in all those years?"

"Well, not exactly," said Tindolen with a smirk. "King Everron commanded all elves to report the whereabouts of any *Aglari* that might be found. I, as a loyal elf to my sovereign Lord, obeyed, of course."

"I thought so. And Everron never asked for it?"

"Actually, he did, but I was reluctant to part with it. Once I finally decided to deliver my *Aglari* to him, I received a message from His Majesty telling me to put it on display."

"So that was Everron's idea?" asked Evan.

"In part. When Bigsbee insisted on celebrating St. Sebastian's week, I decided I had the right venue to execute his command."

"I see. Does Everron support the remaking of the Crown?"

Tindolen shrugged. "I don't know. If I had to guess, I would say yes."

"And what about the heir of the royal family?"

"What about the heir?"

"Well, what's the point of locating the other Elf-gems and remaking the Crown if no heir lives to wear it?" asked Evan.

"No point," replied Tindolen. "But that does not mean an heir lives — for precisely the reason I gave before. An heir might have survived the invasion and then died subsequently. It is impossible to know until all these events play themselves out."

Evan felt a cold shiver flow down his spine. The fate of the kingdom now depended on a prophetic spell ... and a fragile one at that. What happened next was anyone's guess, and Evan felt himself powerless to help one way or another.

Powerless? Well, not exactly. As Tindolen suggested earlier, I can do what I came here to do: keep the gem safe and out of Jormundan's hands until Daniel or someone else comes to claim it for the quest that will lead to the reuniting of the other Elf-gems. And then?

He did not know; he'd be expected back at court once the threat from Jormundan was past and the dark mage was captured.

On the other hand, given the importance of finding the other Elf-gems, perhaps I could convince His Grace that I should help find them. Hmmm. Would that force matters in a way that would disrupt the prophecy?

Evan sighed, unable to answer his own question for a second time. *Better keep my attention on the present for now, at least until more of the prophecy plays itself out.*

CHAPTER 15
A THIEF IN OUR MIDST

A small, single-mast sailing ship pulled up to the dock. In the boat, a sailor stood. The seaman had green eyes, pointed ears, and a slender build. His long, dark hair, which hung down to his shoulder blades, was braided into a single column. Despite long hours on the sea exposed to the elements, his skin was fair and smooth. His dark blue trousers and matching jacket fluttered in the breeze.

The sailor lowered the triangular sail and jumped onto the pier to moor his vessel. Surveying his work, he nodded his head with satisfaction; all was in order. He wiped his hands against each other.

Nasty task, he thought. *I wish humans would tolerate the use of magic in their lands; it is so much tidier than manual labor.* He sighed. *Perhaps one day.* For now, he would observe these archaic customs.

Let's go find the Aglari *that is allegedly here. I should be able to slip in and out of town without being noticed.* The elf smiled at the thought.

The sailor walked up the pier toward the harbor's entrance. As he went, up ahead of him he saw a small booth, a line of people, and guards standing on either side of the line. Not sure what to do, the sailor continued walking, having no intention of waiting with the others. One of the guards stopped the seaman before he had taken two steps past the end of the line.

"'Scuse me," the harbor guard said. "Everyone must declare the goods they carry aboard their ships." He pointed to the end of the line.

"But I've nothing to declare," said the sailor. "I am not a merchant importing cargo. I've come for the festival."

The guard's eyebrows knitted. "What festival?"

"St. Sebastian's week."

"Oh, that." The guard rolled his eyes. "Not much of a festival, if ya ask me."

"No?" replied the sailor with disappointment. "I'm surprised. I've heard some good things about it."

The guard's eyes widened. "Have ya? Well, I suppose there may be something of interest for ya. But if ya ask me, it's a waste of time."

"You think so?"

"Certainly."

"Why?"

"Because the whole idea of the festival is to support racial tolerance, and that's pointless."

"I don't follow," the sailor replied, as he scrunched his nose. "How is racial tolerance pointless?"

"Well, it only stands to reason," said the guard, matter-of-factly. "Think about it. If the dukefs really wanted tolerance between the races, all they'd have to do is return Andropolis to human control and go back where they came from."

A faint smirk played on the sailor's lips. "Oh, I see."

"Not that I have anything against elves or dukefs," the guard added as an afterthought.

"No, of course not."

The guard paused for a moment, then scrutinized the sailor more closely. "You ain't one of them dukefs, is ya?"

"Me?" asked the sailor. He laughed. "Not hardly. I'm just a simple elf from Bryford. I heard about the exhibits on display and I wanted to see them for myself."

The guard raised his eyebrows and frowned. "All right. Ya're free to go."

"Thank you." The elven sailor inclined his head and strolled off the wharf and into town. Laughing to himself, the elf was amazed at the human's gullibility. While part of what he had said was true, it was not the whole truth. He had come from Bryford, but that city was not his home. Elvenwood was. The elf had only been in Bryford inquiring about the *Aglaril* at a College of Bardic Lore chapter house.

Images of the merchants from Clearbrook who had been sitting next to him in the Silver Snake tavern flashed through his mind. Up until then, his trip to Bryford had been futile. That all changed as he overheard the merchants mention that several items were on display to celebrate this week of racial tolerance.

The elf remembered and laughed again.

Racial tolerance between elves and humans is absurd. Humans should die as punishment for the death of King Argol. In this, the dukefs were right.

The merchants had continued talking. One of them had asked, "Anything interesting on display?"

Another had answered, "Not really, except a gem on display at the Grey Horse Inn. I've never seen a topaz that small and yet it held my attention as few gems have."

The sailor had stopped laughing at that remark. Only a magical gem would have that effect, and certainly the *Aglaril* were known to dazzle the unwary.

Without another thought, the elf had gotten up, paid his tab, and rushed to the docks. He had set sail for Clearbrook that very afternoon.

And if this topaz is one of the gems I am searching for, I will take it, no matter the cost.

* * *

Daniel sat in the corner of the great hall, his eyebrows knitted together. He wanted to risk another conversation with Aure despite the disorienting effect the first attempt had yielded. He realized that choice might not be particularly wise, but something inside Daniel drew him to the gem. The teen supposed he identified with the gem because, like him, the *Aglari* was alone and looking for its family. However, the risk of becoming disoriented again remained and, as a master of the Art, he could not permit any loss of control. Daniel pondered what to do for a moment and concluded that if he felt bewildered again, he would block the gem's voice as he was doing now.

Dropping the mental barrier he had erected, Daniel listened to Aure talk about the days when the topaz and his brothers had been set into the Crown of Power. Slowly his thoughts drifted and he realized that, for all his study and time living among the elves, he had heard very little about the Elf-gems. As Daniel understood it, there were seven gems of unparalleled beauty created at the start of the world. He assumed they were indeed made by Kaimin when the world began, but he also wondered whether their beauty had not been exaggerated just a bit. Aure did not appear particularly beautiful to him.

Aure continued to weave his tale, and the image of King Argol appeared in Daniel's mind's eye. The elven king had long, dark hair with a slight curl, which cascaded down to his shoulders, and bright green eyes that sparkled fiercely.

The image in Daniel's mind changed:

An open field filled with tents of various sizes arranged in a circle appeared. At the bottom of the formation, guards took turns watching the assembled soldiers come and go. Elves strode about inside the circle wearing mail and carrying long swords and long bows.

Trumpets sounded and the guards at the open end of the circle proclaimed, "The King is coming! The King is coming! Make way for the King!"

Even as these cries were heard, Argol, riding a jet-black horse, thundered into the camp, dust rising all about him. Quickly, Argol dismounted and brushed the dust off his royal purple shirt and his black silk leggings. An elf approached him and knelt on one knee before his sovereign, head bowed.

"Aldandur, arise my son," said Argol.

Aldandur stood up. "Father, how fared you against the winged demons of Dragonor?"

"They are no more."

"And Balodol? Where is it?"

"In my saddlebag."

"I will have it cleaned and made ready for your next battle."

"Very good. In the meantime, assemble the clans so we can assess what other demons still walk the land."

"As you command, my liege."

CHAPTER 16
A LOOK AT THE PAST

Warriors from the three clans gathered in front of the largest tent in camp. Argol stood by the tent's entrance and surveyed the collected hosts. One cluster of elves congregated to the left, another to the right, and the third lay straight ahead, at the far end of the grassy plain. Aldandur, in his princely vestments of purple and blue, stood in the middle of the throng and spoke.

"Assembled warriors, our king has returned. Once more, he has been victorious in battle against the demons unleashed upon the world by human spellcasters. Now, he convenes this council so that he may know what evil still walks over Mirrya."

"Thank you, Aldandur," said Argol. "I would hear from clan Feadil first."

An elf in mail and green silk came forward from the group to the left. He knelt before Argol just as Aldandur had done earlier.

"Arise, Fiemaril, and report."

Fiemaril stood. "As you command, my liege. Our rangers report the land is clean once again in the north and west."

Argol smiled. "Excellent." He turned to the elves on his right. "And what news is there from clan Erendyl?"

An elf in yellow silk and mail stepped up and knelt before Argol.

"Rise," said the king.

The elf, Elsilcel, straightened and said, "Our scouts tell us that no evil walks the land in the south."

"Very good," said Argol, and turned his gaze to the elves at the far end of the field. "And from clan Mealidil, what news is there?"

An elf in blue silk and mail strode before the king. After he completed the ritual of kneeling before the king, the elf named Nolendur, said, "Alas, my news is not as heartening as the others. The demon named Zortan still walks the eastern lands. Reports from our scouts say he has slain the human spellcasters who summoned him and leveled the city of Davenar. What few survivors there may have been were captured and tortured, their souls ripped from them."

Argol grimaced. "It is worse than I imagined." He sighed and then added, "While we cannot save or restore the dead, we can honor their sacrifice and avenge them.

"Zortan will fall or I shall not see another day," Argol concluded, and pounded his left fist in the palm of his right hand.

"Do not underestimate him, my liege," advised Nolendur, cautiously. "He is the most powerful of the demons."

"Yes, but this shall not deter us. He is the last scrap of evil that must be banished, and with Balodol we cannot fail. Where is he now?"

"Still in the ruins of Davenar."

"Very well, we shall ride forth immediately and camp outside the city."

"At once, my liege," said Aldandur. He turned to the assembled host and cried, "To the ruins of Davenar!"

"To the ruins of Davenar," cried the elves. "And victory."

* * *

The scene in Daniel's mind shifted.

The elves were now camped on a flat, desolate plain.

Beyond the camp, rock and rubble were strewn about. Broken and charred trees stood as the last clue that life had once thrived here. All other plants and animals had been blasted clean from the surrounding land, leaving only a bleak and barren tableau where nothing and no one moved.

From the elven camp and out into the ruined city, a lone figure rode a black horse. A silver circlet with seven gems rested on the rider's head. He wore no armor and carried no sword or shield. No other protection was required with Balodol atop his brow. The long, dark hair that blew in the breeze and the rider's green eyes identified him as an elf. His fierce expression confirmed his identity: it was Argol.

The elven king rode quickly and unimpeded through the desolation of the human city. The galloping of his steed was the only sound that could be heard. The land sloped gently toward the center of the devastation where the initial explosion had occurred. Argol rode on for several minutes, barely looking about.

He drew near a large crater and pulled up on the reins of his black stallion. Giant hands with claws half a foot long rested on the edge of the crater. Equally large wrists and arms disappeared into the hole.

Argol's horse snorted. The giant hands moved at the sound. Immediately Argol was off his steed and preparing to summon the power of Balodol. The gems brightened and appeared to come alive. The hands pushed against the ground and the rock underneath each palm crumbled a bit from the pressure. A giant figure emerged from the crater with measured slowness. It had narrow yellow slits for eyes and sharp pointed fangs that looked like spikes protruding over its lower lip. No hair covered the demon's head and large pointed ears moved as a malicious smile crept over its thin, drawn lips. It seemed to be considering Argol's strength when its voice boomed,

"Now you will die."

"No," said Argol. "Only your end is at hand, evil one." He concentrated and the light from the Aglaril illuminated the area.

Lightning bolts struck the ground where Argol stood, but the king remained unharmed. Sheets of flame scorched the land around the crater, but still Argol was unscathed. The gems in the circlet flared and a hole in the air formed, revealing a black void beyond. All the nearby loose rock and debris was sucked into the opening. The demon braced itself against the crater and laughed.

"Is that your best effort? It will take more than this to eliminate me."

Argol knew that Zortan spoke the truth. It was just as Nolendur had said. He must be careful not to underestimate the demon. That meant using the full power of Balodol, dangerous as that was — but there was no other choice.

Argol's jaw tightened with determination and he redoubled his concentration on the circlet he wore. The seven gems sparkled and glowed with the fury of the sun. Zortan was pulled out of the crater and into the air, tumbling head over heels repeatedly.

"No!" cried the demon. "I am Zortan. I am the strongest and the greatest being that has every lived. I cannot be defeated by a mere mortal."

Despite his protest, Zortan was pulled toward the dark void. He struggled against the force that dragged him forward, but he had nothing to push against. He tried to fly away and failed. Some unseen force held him tight and prevented his escape.

Argol, meanwhile, felt the stress of maintaining his concentration mounting. His fatigue was like a physical weight, and beads of sweat formed on the king's brow. Still, he did not relent. Argol could feel Zortan's resistance like a dead weight — the proverbial immovable object — and he pushed against it.

Zortan reached the opening of the void. He peered into the darkness and gnashed his teeth. The pull on the demon was stronger now and it took all his strength not to be swept into the dark hole. Even so, Zortan could not stop his legs from entering the void. Argol saw the demon look about for something and noticed his opponent's eyes shifting from side to side rapidly. The elven king wasn't sure what Zortan was looking for, but it did not matter. In a few more minutes, the demon would vanish into the void and that would be the end of him.

Argol saw a smile come to Zortan's face, a hideous, evil smile. In a single movement, one of the demon's giant hands came up, as if to slap Argol across the face. The elven king saw the maneuver and dodged the blow, but Zortan hadn't been aiming for the elf's face and, a second later, the circlet was knocked from Argol's head.

The effect was immediate. The winds and force that pulled at Zortan turned against Argol. He couldn't concentrate and lost control of the magic that had created the void. Swept up into the air, Argol plummeted into the void, pushing Zortan through as well, just as Balodol struck the ground and shattered.

* * *

Daniel saw a flash of light and then the images in his head went dark. The sudden change startled him and made his eyes pop open. He sat quietly for a few minutes and then he reached out with his mind.

Aure? Are you all right?

Yes. Relating that story has saddened me.

I understand. What happened next?

Immediately after that, it is hard to say. I was very disoriented. When Balodol *shattered, we were separated from each other and came out of the settings that held us. I lost track of my brothers and the events around me for a very long time. Eventually I was found by some dwarves and sold to Tindolen. About the same time, Amelidel prophesied that an heir of the House of Richmond would use* Balodol *and oust the invaders of Andropolis.*

Is that possible?

Yes. The time of reunification is at hand. Soon we will all be united and the prophecy will be fulfilled.

Daniel replaced his mental barrier and sat quietly, thinking about everything Aure had said and wondering how the prophecy could come true.

CHAPTER 17

GATHERING STORM

The sailor gazed at the *Aglari* for a full minute and took in its beauty. He had never seen a gem from the Crown of Power before, and he imagined how magnificent Argol's crown must have been. Inhaling deeply, he let the air out of his lungs slowly and felt pleased.

My search is over, he thought. *I just have to liberate the* Aglari *from its confinement and rendezvous with Jormundan using the shack outside Sapilo.*

The elf narrowed his eyes and thought briefly about opening the display case.

There are guards present and more outside. I doubt I can disable the wards that are bound to be on the glass case and fight off all the guards. No, it would be better to wait until tonight when everyone is asleep. Yes, that will do.

Next, the seaman considered setting some magical traps. Sleep magic with a trigger that only he could release would speed his recovery of the gem later. He glanced sideways quickly to see who was nearby and noticed one of the guards at the far end of the room. The human was handling a ball of flame in his hand.

A mage with hand fire, thought the sailor. *That's no ordinary guard. The humans are more clever than I imagined; I didn't think they'd employ wizards to protect the gem. And that will make my job harder. He'll most likely detect the use of magic if I cast a spell. Better to wait and come back later.*

* * *

Evan ate breakfast at the Grey Horse after talking with Tindolen. During his meal, the Michaeline priest sketched plans in his head for protecting the Elf-gem. Standing guard in the lobby made the most sense because he would not get in the way of the other guards and it would ensure another level of protection.

Evan finished eating and pushed away his plate with a smile.

Frank came over and picked up the plate and utensils.

"That was pretty good, Frank," Evan remarked as he handed his friend a few coins in payment.

"Glad you liked it," the innkeeper said, as he pocketed the money. "Cook is a master with eggs." Frank was about to say something else when he noticed someone in the foyer through the double doors to the lobby, which were now open. He put down the plate and utensils. "Excuse me." He walked off toward the lobby.

Evan, meantime, gathered his cloak. *Time to go shopping,* he thought.

Entering the foyer, Evan saw Frank standing behind the registration counter across from Daniel. They were talking about something, but Evan couldn't hear what they were discussing. Over by the Inn's entrance, Evan saw an elf dressed in the dark blue suit of a seaman. The sailor strode into the lobby and proceeded straight to the great hall where the Elf-gem was on display.

Evan's eyes narrowed. *Odd*, he thought. *I don't recognize the elf and, except for Tindolen and his family, elves usually don't come to Clearbrook. Wonder how far word of St. Sebastian's week has spread and if that has anything to do with this fellow's presence.*

Regardless, this required investigation. Evan stepped toward the great hall when Frank called to him. The priest turned to look and saw the innkeeper waving him closer.

Evan put up a hand. "Just a minute," he said, before following the elf into the great hall. He entered the exhibition room and saw the seafarer coming toward him. Moving to one side, Evan watched the elf leave the Inn.

Maybe the elf meant no harm after all — at least for now. He might have been scouting for weaknesses in the gem's security. I'll deal with that later. Better go see what Frank wants.

"Ah, Evan," said Frank, as the priest approached. "Daniel has some questions about history, and I figured you could answer them."

Daniel shook his head. "Not history. Prophecy."

Evan looked down at Daniel. "Which prophecy?"

"Amelidel's prophecy about the dukefs, the House of Richmond, and the *Aglaril*."

Remembering Tindolen's words earlier, Evan felt his cheeks redden. *Can talking about the prophecy affect it? Maybe, if it affects Daniel's actions. On the other hand, perhaps Daniel knows something; after all, he has spoken with the Elf-gem.*

He looked at Daniel and found him staring, his eyes wide and round, and his mouth open slightly, waiting for Evan's response. "What do you want to know?"

"Will it come true?" replied Daniel eagerly.

Evan sighed with relief; that seemed safe to discuss. "I hope so," he said. "However, none of the royal house is known to have survived. Without them, the prophecy cannot come true."

"But that doesn't mean there isn't an heir to the House of Richmond," Daniel observed. "You just don't know of any."

"Yes, but the odds are not encouraging. If King Leonard had survived, he would have made it known to his subjects so that a new capital could be built or plans could be made to reclaim the old city and exact revenge on the dukefs. If his younger sister, Sandra, had survived, I would have expected her to announce herself too, assuming she even knows her lineage. Since neither event has occurred, the best we can hope for is that Sandra lives, unaware of her heritage."

Daniel listened to Evan, staring all the while. He said nothing and did not react in any way.

"Why do you ask?" queried Evan.

"Well, Aure was telling me about Amelidel's prediction and said it was time for the prophecy to be fulfilled."

Evan's eyes widened in amazement, partially because Daniel had spoken with the gem again and partially because the gem was putting ideas into the lad's head. "It told you the prophecy would be fulfilled?"

"Yes."

"Did it say how?"

"No, but the next steps seem obvious: locate the other *Aglaril* and reunite them with Aure."

Evan smirked. "You make it sound so easy, but assuming the other Elf-gems survived, they'll be nearly impossible to find."

Daniel nodded in agreement. "Aure told me that. But he also said he will know when he is within a few miles of one of his brothers. And if he is placed next to another *Aglari*, both gems will glow."

Evan realized what Daniel was suggesting; perhaps the challenge wasn't as insurmountable as Evan had first thought. It might take years, but perhaps the odds of finding the other Elf-gems were now within the realm of possibility. Of course, if any dukef caught wind of this…

Bending over and lowering his voice, Evan whispered, "Daniel, what you are suggesting is dangerous. The dukefs won't want any of the Elf-gems found unless they are the ones who find them. Therefore, I suggest you keep this to yourself, at least for now. Do you understand?"

"Yes."

"Good," Evan said and straightened. Then he turned away and went into the great hall to talk with the other guards.

CHAPTER 18
A VISIT TO THE GUARD

Evan entered the great hall. He wanted reassurance that the sailor was not a dukef, particularly now that Daniel had been asking about the prophecy and reuniting the Elf-gems. Scanning the area quickly, the priest found only the two wizards standing guard.

He approached Brashani, asking, "Where are James and Iriel?"

"Off duty," replied the wizard, breaking his concentration on the hand fire that floated above his right palm. The flame vanished like a shadow on a cloudy day.

Evan raised his eyebrows. "Oh?"

"Yeah, Jones split us into two groups to have coverage overnight. Molin and I stand guard in the afternoon and evening. Iriel, James, and the boy stand guard overnight and in the morning."

"Did you notice the sailor who came in here a few minutes ago?" Evan asked and gestured with his head toward the exit.

"It was hard not to. I haven't seen many elves in Clearbrook, and he stared at the gem like it was a lost brother."

"Did he do anything unusual?"

Brashani's eyes shifted from side to side for a moment as he recalled what he had seen. "Not that I noticed. Why?"

"Because, as you say, there aren't many elves in town and I suspect he could be a dukef spy."

"Concerned he might steal it?"

"Among other things, yes."

The wizard smirked. "Well, you needn't be."

"And why is that?" asked the priest, raising an eyebrow.

"Because the dukefs aren't going to steal the gem; necromancers from Irenrhod are."

Evan's eyes grew round. "How do you know that?"

"I was living in Irenrhod before coming to Clearbrook and accidentally uncovered their plans."

"Accidentally?" repeated Evan, scratching his head. "How does one accidentally uncover the plans of necromancers?"

Brashani blushed. "By losing control of a magic spell. I was trying to scry for any jobs in town; instead, I overheard their plans to steal the gem."

"Is that why you are here? To stop them?"

The fire mage shrugged. "Yes and no. I had to flee Irenrhod. They found out I had spied on them, and they planned to kill me. There was no way I could fight all five of them."

Evan's brow furrowed. "Then why did you come here? They will still kill you if they learn you are here."

"Well, I didn't know the gem they wanted was here until I arrived. Once I figured that out, I decided it was time to make a stand and put my investigator training to good use."

"Indeed," said Evan.

Brashani squinted, as if in pain. "But it makes no sense."

"What's that?"

"From what I overheard back in Irenrhod, the necromancers are not planning to send anyone to steal the gem. They are going to steal it themselves. I suppose they could have changed their plans, but why use an elf? And what elf would help masters of the dark arts? Elves love nature, art, beauty — all those life-affirming things that people enjoy. Dark mages stand for just the opposite."

Evan considered the wizard's point. "But who better to use than an elf? No one will suspect he works with necromancers. He's probably a mercenary, so it doesn't matter to him who he works for as long as he gets paid."

Brashani shrugged. "I suppose. I've certainly seen stranger things."

"He could also be a dukef," Evan continued. "They will want the Elf-gems too."

The wizard narrowed his eyes. "But if he were a dukef, wouldn't he start killing humans on sight?"

Evan shook his head. "If I were all alone in human lands, I wouldn't; especially if I'd come to steal Tindolen's gem."

"So what's the next move?" asked Brashani.

"Well, dukefs or necromancers, we'll need proof he's a spy or intends to steal the gem," replied the priest, rubbing his chin.

"Sounds about right."

"Did you notice whether the elf cast any spells?"

"He didn't. Molin and I would have noticed the use of magic in the room if he had."

"Good," said Evan. "Then I think I need to find his ship." He smiled at the mage. "If you'll excuse me, I need to talk with a few other people in town."

Leaving Brashani staring after him, Evan bolted from the great hall, out of the Inn, and down the street.

* * *

Standing in the great hall across from the display case that housed a yellow-brown topaz, Brashani thought about his conversation with Evan. Part of the mage wanted to go with the Michaeline priest and part of him didn't.

Running around town and chasing down leads is a job best left to younger men, he told himself. But he didn't believe that statement. Worse still, by staying behind, Brashani knew he would have to trust Evan, and the fire mage wasn't sure he could. Not yet.

And yet I've got no choice. Soon he'll have information about the elf that I don't. And based on what he learns, Evan will come up with a plan to catch the sailor as sure as the sun rises. The only way I can influence those plans is if he consults me first; I doubt that will happen.

The wizard considered leaving his post briefly to chase after Evan. *I can't do that. Jones will fire me and I need the money he is paying me.* He sighed and felt an ache, as if he were pressed against a wall.

Like it or not, I'm going to have to trust him.

Brashani stuck out his tongue at the thought, trying to get the bad taste he felt out of his mouth.

He gestured with his left hand and a small ball of fire appeared in his right palm. He sighed. It was going to be a long afternoon.

* * *

Evan arrived at Clearbrook's seaport and headed straight for the harbormaster's office. He recalled from his childhood that the office was at the far end of the waterfront. Having played all along the water's edge many times as a boy, the priest knew the building on sight. It was a small, shingled, one-story box with a flat roof and a weathered exterior. Looking inside, through the window, he had once seen a desk and a stool. On the desk had been a logbook, a quill pen, and a bottle of ink. Evan had spent several hours one day staring up at the ceiling of his bedroom wondering what was in the logbook.

As he approached the office, Evan saw a sign above the door that had not been there before. It read simply, "Harbormaster." He knocked on the door and heard a voice say, "Come in."

Evan opened the door. A short man with gray hair and a scar across his right cheek sat at the desk Evan remembered. The logbook and ink bottle were open, and the quill was in the man's hand.

The man at the desk, upon seeing Evan, stood and placed the quill in the spine of the book. "Father, what c'n I doo fur you?"

"You're the harbormaster?" asked Evan.

"That I am," replied the man. "Sam Hartshorn." He extended his hand.

Evan shook it and said, "Evan Pierce. Pleased to meet you."

"Glad to be making your acquaintance," Sam replied.

"I'm looking for a ship that came in this morning. I'd like to know who was on it."

"Certainly, Father. I've goot tall the manifests of ships w'th cargo and crew fr'm tis mornin' here in the log." He gestured at the book on his desk.

"And if the ship had no cargo?"

"Ifin it had no cargo a'tall, I'll only have a record that the ship sailed inta the harbor and who be aboard. For more information, you'll be wantin' to talk to the harbor guards at each pier."

Evan sighed. That was going to be a lot more work. "All right. So what can you tell me? Did a single-person ship come in this morning?"

Sam sat down and ran his finger up and down the open page of the logbook. Finally, he said, "Ah, here it be. Aye. A single-mast sailboat docked tis morning w'th one person aboard."

"Where?"

"Pier A."

"Thank you."

* * *

Pier A was located at the seaport entrance Evan had used on his way to see the harbormaster. Walking back, Evan stopped to talk to each harbor guard he saw. He wanted to leave no possibility unexplored. Unfortunately, the guards he spoke with could not give him any information. They had not seen a ship come in without cargo or, if they had, it was a ship loaded with passengers.

"Thanks," was all Evan could say after each disappointment before pressing on. He saw the entrance to the harbor drawing near, and directly opposite it was Pier A.

He looked for the guard who watched over this pier and found him standing near the wharf's entryway. The guard watched the people coming off the ships in the harbor. He was a few inches taller than Evan and broad-shouldered. He also wore a mail shirt and a metal cap that looked too small for his head. At the guard's hip hung a sword with a strip of leather wrapped around the hilt.

Stepping up to the man, Evan said, "Excuse me, maybe you can help me."

The guard looked at him but said nothing.

"I'm looking for information about a ship that came in this morning. It had no cargo and one passenger."

"What do ya want to know?" asked the guard, flatly.

"Have you seen such a ship?"

"Yeah, sure. The fellow sailing the ship wore a dark blue sailor's shirt and trousers."

"That's right," said Evan.

"Only thing was he was an elf, not a sailor in the royal navy."

"Right again."

The guard scratched his head. "Don't know where he got his clothes."

"Has he been back to his ship since then?" asked Evan.

The guard shook his head. "Not that I saw. He told me he was here for the festival."

"Festival?" Evan's eyes narrowed and then his entire face brightened. "Oh, St. Sebastian's week."

"Right. Don't know why an elf cares about a festival for a human saint. Seems silly to me."

"Where's his ship?"

The guard pointed to his left. "At the end of the pier. It's a small, single-mast sailboat."

"Great. Thank you."

Evan hurried down the pier to find it. Now all he needed was a little help from an old friend.

* * *

Eric Brinson, a lieutenant in the town guard, paced along the walk in front of the stores that formed the town square, watching for anyone or anything that might disturb the peace, cause mischief, or commit a crime. At this hour of the day, the local children were the most likely cause of trouble if not for a patrol by the town guard.

He watched the townsfolk come and go, and he listened to his black boots clomping on the cobblestones of the courtyard and his mail shirt chinking softly as he moved. A broadsword dangled from Eric's right hip. On his right arm, the lieutenant wore a small shield of red with a horizontal white stripe emblazoned across the top. A week's growth of beard was plainly visible on the lower half of

Eric's face and ragged ends of dark hair poked out from under his helmet like weeds projecting out of a brick wall.

The lieutenant looked up as Mrs. Johansen came out of the haberdashery with several boxes and immediately began struggling with her bundles. He glanced at the children running and screaming on the far side of the fountain and caught a glimpse of Mr. Colburn sitting by the fountain, whittling. Amid this activity, Evan entered the quadrangle and approached Eric. The sight of the priest brought a smile to Eric's face, but it did not cause the lieutenant to alter his course or change the pace of his patrol.

They shook hands as Evan said, "Eric, I need a favor."

"If I can help," Eric began and came to a stop, "you know I will."

"I saw an elven sailor at the Grey Horse earlier. I'm concerned he may be a dukef or a spy for necromancers."

Eric slid his jaw from one side to the other. "Got any proof?"

"No. But he was staring at Tindolen's gem. If he is a spy, he may be planning to steal it."

Eric scowled at the thought. "The trouble is I have strict orders on the subject from Bigsbee. No guards are to be placed at the Grey Horse. Something about no money in the treasury to pay for such an extravagance."

"I know," said Evan. "And I'm not asking you to disobey. But can't you place a few more men down by the harbor in case something happens?"

"Hmmm," said Eric. "All right. I could post some men at the harbor's entrance."

"Perfect."

"Do you know the name of his vessel?"

"Yes, it's the *Ciryaduin.*"

"Okay. I'll coordinate with Hartshorn and have that boat watched."

"Thanks," said Evan.

Eric said nothing. He just inclined his head to his friend and resumed his patrol.

CHAPTER 19
NAME DROPPING

After speaking with Eric, Evan considered what to do next. *I suppose I could try and find the sailor in town to make sure he is not committing a crime.* He shook his head. *No, Eric and his men can take care of that; it is their job, after all. But I could confront the elf and warn him to stay away.* Evan scratched his head. *I doubt that would do any good and it would tip my hand. No, I should return to the Grey Horse and let the seaman come to me.*

Next, Evan thought about his plans for the evening.

The Grey Horse should quiet down around midnight, assuming Frank still closes the Inn's doors at that hour, the way his father did. So, I should be standing guard by the registration counter a few minutes before midnight and remain on duty until dawn. The cook should have risen by then to start breakfast, and activity among the Inn's guests should have resumed. That only gives me about six hours for sleep. I should have dinner and go to bed by half past five, so I can be alert for the long night ahead.

* * *

The clock tower chimed five in the afternoon as Daniel looked up from his meditation. James and Iriel stood in front of the lad's straw mat in the common area they shared.

"Care for dinner?" the bard asked.

"Yes," replied Daniel. "I am hungry." He hastily put on his shoes and sprang to his feet in a fluid motion.

Stepping out into the lobby, James said, "Iriel and I have been giving some thought to locating members of your family. We couldn't find a wizard in town to help, so I think the next step is to go to Wrightwood. I know a bard and local historian there; she specializes in tracing family lineage. I can write to her and we may be able to visit her in the spring."

"Do you think she can help?"

"I can't say for sure, but I don't see why she shouldn't be able to."

"I will resume my search in Wrightwood then. Thank you." He bowed to James and Iriel.

James pulled open one of the doors to the common room. He gestured to Iriel to proceed. She hesitated; protocol among the elves called for *Qua'ril* masters to lead the way. Of course, they were not in Oldarmare and human customs were different. She shrugged and stepped inside; Daniel followed. James entered behind them.

They walked single file through the maze of tables until they came to an unoccupied one. Sitting down, James waved at Evan, who was seated at the next table. Evan inclined his head in response to James. Frank came out of the kitchen and approached his old friend.

"Dessert?" he asked.

"Sure," said Evan. "Some pie."

"All right," said Frank, and cleared the plates from the table. He glanced at James, Iriel, and Daniel and said to them, "I'll be back in a minute to take your orders."

"No problem," said James. "Take your time."

Evan looked at the bard. "Mind if I join you?"

"Not at all."

Evan got up and sat beside James and Daniel, facing Iriel.

"Enjoying your time in your hometown?" Iriel asked Evan with a smile.

"A little, yes. I've not had time to catch up with any old friends, but I'm sure I will."

James raised an eyebrow. "Why not? What's got you so busy?"

"I've been spending most of my time tracking leads on an elf I saw earlier this afternoon."

The bard wrinkled his nose. "An elf? I didn't think there were many elves in Clearbrook."

"There aren't. And this one seems very interested in Tindolen's gem."

Iriel sat up straighter in her chair. She moved her hands apart and threw her shoulders back. "What difference does that make? Maybe he admires the craftsmanship." She pointed to herself. "I certainly do."

"Maybe," said Evan. "Or just maybe he's a thief come to steal it."

The elf glared at him, her eyes narrowed, and her mouth became almost a snarl. "What is it about humans? Why do you immediately distrust strangers? Or are you just suspicious of all elves? Why is he a thief and I am not?"

Evan heard the edge in her voice. Quietly, and in a level tone, he answered as he pointed a finger at her. "Because you are the niece of a man I've known my whole life." He gestured over his left shoulder with his left hand thumb outstretched. "The elven sailor is not."

Iriel opened her mouth to respond, but no words came. Instead, she just shot him twin emerald spears from her eyes and her nostrils flared.

"Do you really think the elf is a thief?" James asked. His eyes darted to Iriel and then back to Evan.

"It's a distinct possibility," said Evan. "Word that Clearbrook is celebrating St. Sebastian's week has undoubtedly spread to other towns by now, and if someone described the gem to him, it might have piqued his interest. However," he continued, "suspicion is not proof and without proof, there's little more I can do except wait and see what happens."

Frank returned from the kitchen with Evan's pie and handed it to his friend. Then he took Iriel, Daniel, and James's orders. It took a minute for Iriel to calm down enough to order, but she managed and Frank disappeared into the kitchen again.

Daniel cocked his head to one side. "Why does the elf want Aure?"

Evan swallowed some pie before responding. "Hard to say. It depends for whom he works."

James raised his eyebrows. "Are there multiple possibilities?"

Evan placed more pie on his fork. "Yes, he could be, for example, a dukef." He put the fork in his mouth.

"Do the dukefs want to reunite Aure with his brothers?" asked Daniel.

Evan stared at him, raised an eyebrow, and swallowed. "I don't know." He looked across the table. "Iriel, what do you think?"

She thought for a second before answering. "I do not think so. I've never heard any of my people express such an interest. I know

I thought the *Aglaril* were lost ... at least until the beginning of St. Sebastian's week."

"But," Evan added, "I would think the first interest of the dukefs would be to keep us from remaking the Crown of Power so it can't be used against them."

Daniel looked confused. "But if the dukefs find the *Aglaril* first and remake *Balodol*, can't one of them wear it and use it against us?"

Evan and James looked at each other, then James turned back to Daniel. "No, only certain people can use it."

"Really?" said Daniel, his eyebrows knitting. "Why?"

"Because the Crown of Power was given to the elves to fight evil. To prevent abuse, the Makers of the World put safeguards on it so that only the most worthy can wield it," explained the bard.

Daniel tilted his head to the other side. "The most worthy? Who is that?"

"Well," James began, "for starters, the line of elven kings: Argol; his son, Aldandur; and his grandson, Everron. Beyond that I'm not sure. No one has ever said."

"Is the heir to the House of Richmond worthy?" asked Daniel.

Evan broke off more pie to eat. "Yes. The royal heir seeks to correct an injustice done to him or her."

"That explains a lot," said Daniel. "Aure showed me how King Argol used the Crown of Power and how he lost it."

"Showed you? How?" Evan asked with interest.

"I'm not sure exactly; I saw images in my mind. I'm sure I saw Argol and his battle against the demon Zor ..."

"Don't say that name," Evan interrupted and slammed his fist on the table. Iriel jumped and tipped over the empty wine glass in front of her. James sat up and pushed away from the table, his eyes round like marbles. A few people at the tables nearby turned to look at Evan's sudden outburst.

Evan paused for a moment to regain his composure. "Sorry. I didn't mean to startle you; but speaking the names of demons gives them power and that's not something we want to do."

"No, it's not," agreed Iriel, quietly. "But that's no reason to shout or bang the table like an orc."

"I'll remember that for the future," said Evan with a smile.

"Please do," replied the elf with annoyance.

Frank returned with their meals: a plate of vegetables and fruit for Iriel, some roasted chicken and seasoned potatoes for James, and a large chef's salad for Daniel.

They began eating and were quiet for a few seconds when James looked across the table at Daniel. "So you saw Argol's last battle. Remarkable. Can you describe it?"

"Describe it?" repeated Daniel. He stabbed a chunk of tomato with his fork. "Why?"

"It would make a great story."

"Let me think about it," said Daniel. "The images are hard to pin down — like dreams and all jumbled up. I'll need to sort them out first."

"Did the gem tell you anything else?" Evan asked and pushed his empty pie plate away.

Daniel shook his head. "The images spoke for themselves. Argol gave his life to save his people."

"True," said Evan with a nod. "And when the elves subsequently learned that all the humans of Davenar were not dead, they split into two groups: the elves of Oldarmare, who have been our friends, and the dukefs, who hate humans because it was humans who unleashed the demons in the first place. As they see it, all humans are responsible for the death of their beloved king."

Daniel narrowed his eyes and swallowed his food. "That does not sound very elven. Master Alendil always taught me to be tolerant of others."

Iriel smiled. "Master Alendil is correct, Daniel. Tolerance of others is best. As Father Evan said, the dukefs behave as if all humans are the spellcasters who summoned the demons. It is unfortunate; they seem unable to forgive or forget."

Troubled, Daniel sat quietly thinking and staring at his plate for a few minutes before pushing it away, his food only half-eaten.

Iriel, looking somber, also sat quietly. She glanced at James and smiled weakly.

"We'd better get to bed," James said and motioned toward the door to Daniel. "We have to be on duty in less than seven hours."

"All right," Daniel replied and stood. He bowed to Evan and then walked toward the exit.

"Good night," Iriel said to Evan before she followed Daniel out of the room.

"Good night," said Evan. "Sleep well, all of you."

"Thanks," said James.

CHAPTER 20
A THIEF IN THE NIGHT

Brashani stood before the fireplace of the great hall. The fire in the hearth was close to dying. He gestured and the fire flickered out; he gestured again and broke out in a sweat.

Molin narrowed his eyes at his companion. "What are you doing?"

Brashani wiped the perspiration off his face. "Absorbing the heat from the logs so I can rearrange them."

"That's what the fire poker is for," Molin replied with a smirk.

Brashani turned and glared at the other wizard. "Using the poker will hardly let me place the logs precisely for a long-lasting fire."

The senior mage laughed. "But it's faster and less tiring my way."

"Must you argue about everything I do?" Brashani snapped. Anger tainted his voice; his arms flailed wildly about.

Molin's eyes widened. "Just trying to give you the benefit of my experience." Brashani heard sarcasm, but he doubted Molin intended it.

"And I'm trying to tell you about something outside your experience," the fire mage retorted, pointing to himself. "I would think you'd open your mind and try to *learn* from it."

Molin said nothing. Brashani crouched and reached into the hearth; he arranged the logs to his liking and added fresh wood so that the fire, once relit, would last until dawn.

The younger wizard stood and gestured. Fire sparked and played about the wood before igniting it. The embers at the bottom of the pile glowed red and Brashani felt the heat from the blaze.

Satisfied that the fire would keep them warm through the night, Brashani brushed his hands against each other, in an attempt to remove the charcoal from them. He heard the clock tower in the town square ring out six times like a church bell tolling the death of a local lord. The last chime sounded as Frank entered the great hall carrying their dinners.

The two wizards ate in silence while Brashani contemplated the last few days and puzzled out his next move.

Six o'clock and no word from Evan. As I expected. He's doing whatever he feels he needs to while I'm stuck here unable to help.

He chewed a bit of his food and swallowed.

And there's not much I can do about it either. I wonder what he found out ...

He tried to guess what Evan had done this afternoon.

He probably checked with the harbormaster to determine what ship the sailor arrived on. And he's probably having it watched. The harbor guards can surround it and make sure no one boards it. But beyond that ...

His thoughts trailed off as he found himself unable to guess what else the Michaeline priest might have accomplished.

Then he thought about the elf he had seen earlier in the day.

Assuming he's a burglar, I can also assume he came here to see what precautions are in place so he could plan the theft. But he didn't leave any spells behind, so either he's not a mage, which I doubt, or he will use whatever magic he needs, as the situation requires. Given the energy and concentration required to make any spell work, either he is going to use very simple magic or he knows the spells in his repertoire very well, making them easier than normal to execute.

He thought about that for a moment. Simple magic wasn't particularly harmful or useful for incapacitating anyone; its purpose was to help apprentices learn the fundamentals of their craft. *And if I were the thief, I would want something that would take out a guard quickly without raising the alarm. What magic did that leave?*

His eyes narrowed and he rubbed his chin. *Does such a spell even exist? Hmmm … Probably some kind of mind or body control incantation that's a prerequisite for necromancy.* A chill went down Brashani's spine and he shuddered involuntarily. *Well, if that's the case, I never learned it, which is just as well. Those things are best left alone.*

Brashani finished eating and glanced at Molin. The elder wizard had finished his meal too and was drawing out a long pipe.

Good idea. Brashani took out his pipe too.

Both mages stuffed their pipes with tobacco and began puffing.

So where does that leave me? Brashani wasn't sure. He needed to keep his eyes open and monitor the situation. Hopefully, he would be able to stop the thief. If not, it would not be for lack of trying.

* * *

The clock tower tolled eight o'clock. Few visitors to the Grey Horse entered the great hall at that hour. The two mages settled back, ready for an uneventful night, at least for them. From the common room, Brashani could hear people carousing, talking, and laughing. Things in there sounded quite lively.

Typical, he thought. On an average night, Frank usually had the common room full and, from the sound of it, that was the case again tonight. Brashani imagined the activity across the Inn; his mouth watered in anticipation of some beer. The wizard licked his lips, then caught himself and dismissed the thought. As much as he would enjoy an Old Troll ale right now, he had a job to do. He puffed on his pipe some more and created a small ball of fire in his right palm. Idly, he made it float into the air; a small fiery trail extended out behind the sphere as it moved.

"Practicing your act?" asked Molin.

Brashani peered up at him. "Yeah. St. Sebastian's week will be over in three days and we'll all go back to our old jobs."

"Most likely," replied the other wizard.

The night wore on and the crowd in the Grey Horse's common room dwindled until only those staying at the Inn occupied tables. After about an hour of amusing himself with his hand fire, Brashani ended the spell, stood, and stretched. He put away his pipe and went over to the fireplace to see how much of the wood had been consumed.

Molin stood and came over to the fire. "Sorry about what I said earlier. And thank you for setting the fire. Once I get a chill in my bones, it lasts for hours."

Brashani gave the other mage a sidelong glance and wondered why Molin hadn't bothered to keep the fire going. If he had, Brashani wouldn't have bothered to arrange the wood and reignite it. As the fire mage pondered this question, he realized that he had not seen Molin do much of anything for himself. Was that because it was too hard for him to do anything, or was it because, as a court mage, he was used to having things done for him? If the latter, it was possible Molin didn't know how to make a fire.

How sad, thought Brashani, and another idea burst upon him. *It suddenly makes sense why he argues with me. He's probably not used to anyone disagreeing with him. Life outside the King's court must be hard for him.*

"Glad to help," said the younger wizard at last and he smiled.

Molin eyed his companion. "You are?"

"Sure. And if you need assistance with anything else, let me know." Brashani grinned again.

"Thank you." Molin paused and narrowed his eyes. "Why are you being so nice all of a sudden?"

"I owe you a lot. You helped me get a job here and get back on my feet. Why shouldn't I be nice?"

Molin didn't answer immediately. He just stood there glaring at Brashani for a few minutes. Finally, he said, "You're welcome, but you don't owe me anything."

"If you say so."

"Just do me one favor."

"Okay, what?"

"Let the past go."

"Upset over my outburst to Evan this morning?"

"No, but there's no point getting angry over events you can't change. If you could do something about them, then your anger serves a purpose. But you can't and neither can I, so let's just make the best of the situation."

"And resign ourselves to being second-class citizens."

Molin grimaced. "I wouldn't put it that way. We are just doing the best we can."

"I'll think about it," replied Brashani.

"Thank you."

* * *

The clock tower struck midnight as Frank looked around the common room and ran his hands through his hair. He was alone in the room; all the Inn's patrons had retired for the evening. Frank wished he could withdraw to the comfort of his bed too, but he still had to clean up and lock the front doors. He pulled the key to the main entrance out of his pocket and headed for the lobby.

He walked into the foyer and saw James, Iriel, and Daniel coming out of the sleeping quarters the guards shared with Cook. James yawned as he walked. Halfway across the vestibule, he stretched before he continued into the great hall with his companions.

Behind the registration counter, Evan stood watching the scene.

"What are you doing back there?" Frank asked Evan.

"Standing guard."

"Why?"

"Because Bigsbee refuses to have professional guards stand watch and this is the most strategic area of the Inn. There is only one way in and out of the great hall, so if someone wants to steal the gem, he'll have to get by me first."

Frank grunted dismissively. "But there hasn't been a theft in Clearbrook for years."

"I know but I saw an elf in the Inn earlier; I think he's a thief."

"A thief!" Frank chortled. "Here? Ridiculous.

"Maybe," responded Evan. "But he was staring intently at the Elf-gem and that kind of attention concerns me. So I'm standing guard here and watching everyone who passes by."

Frank shrugged. "Suit yourself; but I think you're crazy." Stepping toward the front doors, Frank saw Molin and Brashani emerge from the great hall. Molin smiled and waved at both Frank and Evan before continuing across to the lobby.

"Evening," Brashani said to Frank.

"Pleasant dreams," returned the innkeeper.

Brashani paused for a moment to talk to Evan. "Learn anything interesting this afternoon?"

"A few things," replied Evan. "I'll tell you in the morning."

"As you will," said Brashani. "If there's anything I can do to help …"

"I'll let you know. Best get some sleep now."

Brashani didn't want to rest, but he didn't want to push too hard either. He inclined his head to Evan and then crossed the lobby and disappeared into the sleeping quarters he shared with James and the other guards.

Frank locked the door and went back into the common room to clean up.

* * *

Brashani heard the clock tower strike one in the morning and he yawned. He was tired and wished he had some coffee. He sighed.

Just a few more hours until the Inn opens, then I can go to sleep.

He wondered if Evan had called for him. Was it possible that he had and that Brashani had missed it? He thought about getting up to see but the straw mat was comfortable now and his own exhaustion kept him from moving.

His eyes drooped and his head fell to his chest, but an instant later he was awake again.

Can't fall asleep on the job. Can't. Won't.

His eyes drooped again and stayed closed. He dozed, believing he was still awake and ready for action.

* * *

The clock tower chimed twice as the sailor approached the Grey Horse Inn. Darkness covered many of the Inn's features;

nonetheless, the pale moonlight was just enough for the seaman to see the front doors clearly and the three wooden stairs that led up to it.

Testing the door, he found it locked. The elf rested his hand on the keyhole, ignoring the chill from the late-autumn night air and the cold metal door handle. The sailor concentrated, slowly probing the workings of the locking mechanism. He tried to move the latch; it wouldn't budge, as if the cold air had frozen it into its current position. The elf pushed harder. The lock responded with a resounding click. He turned the knob and opened the door a crack to peer inside.

* * *

Evan was watching the fire in the hearth when he felt a stab of cold air. He turned to face the front door as he silently drew his sword. One of the doors was ajar. More than that he could not discern; the night's darkness seemed to envelop the entryway, making it hard to see beyond. Wasting no time, the demon hunter stepped out from behind the registration counter. Evan's fatigue flared as he moved; his limbs suddenly felt like lead weights. He yawned and felt his eyes close. Shaking his head, the priest inhaled deeply once to throw off the sensation. He took another step toward the door, wavered, and then collapsed on the floor — asleep.

* * *

In the great hall, Daniel sat in one corner while James and Iriel snuggled next to each other in another. Iriel kept stroking James's hair while the bard kept grabbing her hands and putting them back in her lap because he felt this was neither the time nor the place to flirt. If they had been alone, James wouldn't have minded. Hell, he probably would have initiated something and gone a lot further too. But as it was, Daniel's presence was intimidating, and flirting in public was not appropriate in front of a teen; even one who had mastered *Qua'ril*.

A noise from the foyer made Daniel open his eyes and James look up from where he sat.

"Did you hear something?" the bard asked Iriel. Daniel jumped up and assumed a classic *Qua'ril* fighting stance; legs spread and bent slightly, arms raised and bent at the elbow, and body bent forward, ready to defend himself from an attack.

"I did not," she said.

"I'm sure I did," said James after a minute. "And look, Daniel is up, too." Prying himself loose from Iriel, James stood. "I'm going to go check."

Iriel sighed, immediately missing James's body heat. She hugged herself. "Very well. *Faroth mane.*"

James appreciated the elven wish for good luck as he stood. He hoped he wouldn't need it, but he uncoiled his whip just the same. He stepped forward and saw Daniel's eyes flutter and close; the lad collapsed asleep an instant later. Surprised to see his friend crumble to the ground, James ran to him. Iriel stood up, her eyes wide and round. The bard took only one step toward Daniel before he yawned and dropped his whip, collapsing in slumber. Iriel unsheathed a dagger from her boot and peered toward the doorway.

She saw very little. Then she made out the faint figure of someone moving in the shadows. Carefully aiming, she threw her weapon just as sleep overtook her.

* * *

The sailor leapt to the dark corner near the entrance of the great hall when Evan collapsed. He saw Daniel stand and cast a Sleep spell on the lad without hesitating. Even as he completed that spell, the seaman could hear someone else approaching. He froze, peered into the room, and prepared to cast the spell again. As the human came into sight, he cast Sleep once more to eliminate the threat.

The elf crept deeper into the room and saw the form of another guard moving in the darkness. Without a second thought, he cast Sleep once more as a dagger whizzed past his head and buried itself in the wall. If he had been even a second slower ...

He dismissed the thought and scanned the room for anyone else moving about. Satisfied that all the threats were dealt with, he entered the room stealthily, careful to avoid the sleeping forms of the guards.

In three strides, he was standing before the display case at the far end of the room. A small topaz gem rested on velvet inside the enclosure. The sailor gazed at the *Aglari* and then placed his hand on the glass top. He felt several magical wards of protection. They were powerful and expertly set, but they were nothing he couldn't dispel and remove. He set to work.

CHAPTER 21
A RUN IN THE DARK

D aniel sat up groggily and rubbed his forehead. It ached, as if pummeled. He had been dreaming of Aure traveling somewhere when the gem's voice came to him.

I go to my brothers, Daniel.

Realizing his mental block to the gem was down, Daniel re-established it and peered at the display case. It was open and empty. Startled, he jumped to his feet and dissolved the barrier in his mind.

Aure, where are you?

With an elf who has promised to help.

An elf? Then Daniel remembered; he had seen someone in the shadows near the doorway. It could have been an elf — the thief Evan had warned about. He must have come back and stolen Aure.

A cold chill went through Daniel. *Are you sure?* Daniel wondered. *I think the elf has stolen you. He may not help you as you expect.*

Then help me, Daniel. Help me.

He stood and stared at the empty glass case again. He felt his own emptiness now, as if his best friend had died. He needed to help Aure, but how? Daniel glanced around the great hall and saw James sleeping nearby.

Shaking the bard awake, Daniel cried excitedly, "Aure's been stolen!"

James's eyes popped open. "Stolen! By whom?"

"An elf, I think. The one Evan told us about."

"Where's Iriel?" James asked. He scanned the room as he stood.

"Over there," replied Daniel, pointing to the far wall.

James stood up and felt wobbly for a second. He paused as the world around him spun and then slowly settled into place. "Go wake the others," he said finally. "I'll wake Iriel. We'll go after him."

Daniel ran from the room without a word. As he entered the foyer, the dim glow from the lobby hearth provided light for the lad to see by. On the floor, in front of the fireplace, lay Evan sleeping. Daniel saw the priest's idle form and jumped nimbly over the body to avoid tripping. Rousing the priest, Daniel helped Evan to stand.

"What happened?" Evan asked, yawning.

"Aure has been stolen."

"By St. Michael's sword!" cried Evan. "Wake the other guards, Daniel. We're going after the thief."

"James and Iriel are already awake and in the great hall."

"All right," said Evan. "We'll all gather in your sleeping quarters. Go wake Molin and Brashani."

Daniel nodded and hurried out of the foyer.

* * *

Brashani grumbled under his breath when Daniel stirred him from his bed; Molin sat silently, head drooping, arms limp at his side.

"What's going on?" asked Brashani. His eyes were bloodshot; he vaguely recalled trying to stay awake, waiting for Evan's call for help.

Before Daniel could answer, Evan stepped into the room, followed by Iriel and James. The elf appeared to be close to tears and James tried to comfort her. Molin's head came up as Evan and the others entered; he rubbed sleep from his eyes. Brashani ceased his grumbling and realized he had fallen asleep after all.

Evan's face was grim. Heavy circles lined his eyes and his jaw was set tight. "Tindolen's gem has been stolen by an elf, according to Daniel, and we need to get it back."

Iriel began crying. "Uncle is going to be very upset over this and very disappointed in me. I was supposed to ensure nothing happened to it. He'll send me back to Oldarmare for sure once he finds out."

James patted her on the back. "It wasn't your fault," he said soothingly. "The thief put us all to sleep."

"And he removed the protective spells on the display case," said Evan. "But all that is beside the point. Right now, we need to prepare for battle and follow him."

Iriel nodded and wiped the tears from her eyes.

"Battle?" repeated James. Evan saw fear in his eyes as his brow furrowed.

"That's the worst-case possibility. It is much more likely that he won't put up a fight. With six-to-one odds, he'll probably surrender."

"But he's a wizard," observed Molin. "He could kill most of us with a single spell."

Evan shook his head. "If he wanted us dead, we would be. And while he may put some of us to sleep again, we should still be able to overpower him."

Brashani rubbed the grit from the corners of his eyes. "That may be, but if he removed all the wards on the display case, he's very accomplished as a mage. Don't underestimate him."

"Duly noted," said Evan, as he inclined his head.

James sighed and fastened his whip to his belt. "So how do we find him? We don't know where he went."

"Not necessarily true," said Evan. "I have a strong suspicion. If the thief is the sailor I saw early yesterday afternoon, then he is likely to be running back to the harbor to sail out of Clearbrook."

"Do we search every ship in the harbor?" asked Iriel, stringing her bow.

"No. Since elves infrequently come to town, I did some checking. I know where his ship is docked."

"And if the thief isn't this sailor you saw?" asked Brashani, rubbing his face.

"Whether the thief is that sailor or not, we can trail whoever has the Elf-gem with Daniel's help."

Daniel's face brightened at the sound of his name. "Me?"

"Yes, you can talk with the gem. On the off chance that I'm wrong about where the thief is going, we'll need to be able to track the *Aglari*. So tell it that we are coming to rescue it. Hopefully, you can get a direction once you establish contact."

"Okay." Reaching out with his mind, Daniel contacted the dark mustard-colored topaz.

Aure, are you all right?

Yes.

We are coming to rescue you. Send me a signal so we can find you. No response. *Please, Aure, you've been stolen and we want to return you to*

Tindolen. Again, nothing. *Aure? Why don't you answer?* Daniel paused for a moment and realized what was wrong. *You want to find your brothers, don't you? Send me a signal and once we've rescued you, I promise I will help you find them.*

How will you keep that promise?

I don't know, but you have my word as a Qua'ril *master that I will.*

Daniel gazed up at Evan. "I have a direction."

"Let's go."

* * *

Evan and the five people assigned to guard Tindolen's gem ran out of the Grey Horse Inn and down the street; their feet clomping on the dusty road interrupted the quiet of the night. Daniel was in the lead, wearing his white *Qua'ril* uniform and running barefoot, his blond hair shining in the pale moonlight. Despite the cold air, Daniel concentrated on Aure's signal and did not feel the chill.

The others were not as fortunate. "By the Twelve powers, it's freezing," complained Brashani, wishing he had taken time for Warmth magic. Still, the cold air did much to help him shake off the last vestiges of sleep.

Just behind Daniel ran Evan, sword in hand. He wanted to go faster, but the cold air made it hard to breathe and made his lungs ache. As he ran, the priest glanced from side to side looking for town guards. He hoped to see some men standing watch and enlist their aid.

Following Evan were James and Iriel. At his hip, James's whip jostled; he steadied it with one hand as he ran. Iriel had a quiver of arrows slung over her left shoulder and she clutched her long bow in her left hand.

Molin and Brashani trailed last.

"Preparing any spells?" Molin asked Brashani.

"Of course. I've got a Flame Disk ready."

"What's that?"

"It creates a disk of flame and ash that explodes on contact. And you? What are you preparing?"

"I was a court mage, if you remember. I had no real need for combat spells."

"So you don't know any battle spells?"

"I know one, Electric Touch, but that's only effective in hand-to-hand combat."

"Any long-range weapons?" asked Brashani.

"Two daggers in sheaths strapped to my forearms."

"Good, you might need them."

"The signal's getting stronger," said Daniel.

"Which way are they going?" asked James.

"East," replied Daniel.

"Toward the harbor," Evan said, as he sprinted forward.

They crossed the town square and approached the docks. They passed through the gates of the harbor and stopped at the sight of five guards asleep on the ground. Evan examined them quickly; they were unconscious but unharmed otherwise. Iriel looked across the harbor and saw someone moving along one of the piers.

"Father Evan," she said, "someone is moving up ahead." She pointed.

Charging past Daniel, Evan replied, "Then maybe we aren't too late."

* * *

The sailor ran across town as fast as he could; the cold air burned his lungs. He wanted to reach his boat and set sail immediately to avoid capture. All seemed to be going according to plan until he reached the harbor entrance. Five guards stood in the entryway. They wore mail shirts with leather sleeves and leggings.

Fortunately for the seaman, he spotted the guards before they saw or heard him coming, giving him time to slow and crouch in the shadows. The elf rested there for a few minutes, caught his breath, and considered his options. He watched the humans as his breathing slowed. They stood there, occasionally glancing out at the night.

They seem to be looking for something or someone. Or perhaps they have been stationed there.

He grimaced at that thought. That meant the guards wouldn't be moving any time soon, and somehow the elf didn't think he could bluff his way past them.

The sailor rubbed his forefinger back and forth across his chin and thought as his frustration mounted like water behind a dam. Time seemed to fly and crawl in the same instant. No doubt, the guards from the Inn would be waking shortly and would discover the theft. If he didn't act soon, he'd be caught here waiting for these other guards to leave.

He took a deep breath to collect his thoughts and decided he wasn't going to let a few humans stand in his way. He knew he could not fight them all simultaneously and hope to win, but then he didn't have to. A few well-placed Sleep spells should eliminate the risk without raising the alarm.

Carefully he prepared himself. When he was ready, the elf cast three Sleep spells so that each spell enveloped at least two of the humans standing watch. The guards toppled over like empty cardboard boxes that were stacked too high. The sailor sprang forward without hesitation and ran down the dock toward his boat. Two more guards were waiting by his ship. He wasted no time and put these men to sleep with a single gesture before he climbed into his vessel and prepared to cast off.

* * *

As he ran down the pier to where he had last seen the *Ciryaduin* that afternoon, Evan caught sight of the boat hovering over the water. Panic filled him. It looked as if the ship was about to leave the harbor. Evan pushed himself harder to close the distance. He needed to get close enough so he could jump aboard; but even as he increased his speed, Evan saw two dark, oblong objects in his way, which forced him to slow down. The sailboat soared into the night sky and vanished into the darkness.

Evan stood on the pier and cursed himself for his stupidity. *Why didn't I wait for the thief down by his boat?* It was obvious now that would have been a better plan. He should have guessed, too, that the elf would have some sort of magic at his command. *Why didn't I make provisions to defend against it?* He sighed. There was no point in berating himself now. What he needed was a way to follow the thief. He had none.

He looked down at the objects in front of him. *Guards.* He bent over and gave each man a quick examination to make sure they were not harmed. *Only asleep, like the ones at the entrance. Good, at least no one was hurt.* Evan woke the guards and then walked back toward Daniel and the others, not really paying attention to his surroundings.

"He got away," Evan said, flatly.

Iriel looked like she was going to cry again.

Brashani cursed.

Molin's mouth dropped open.

James sighed.

"I know," said Daniel. "Aure is still calling for help. What can we do now?"

Evan shrugged. "I don't know. If there were a shop in town that sold magic items, we might be able to buy or trade for a flying carpet or some sort of tracking device. But there isn't."

"Then Aure is lost to us," said Daniel. He sat down, held his head with both hands, and cried.

CHAPTER 22
FROM THE ASHES OF DISASTER

E van woke the five sleeping guards lying by the harbor entrance and told them about the theft. One of them went to find Eric.

More guards arrived with the harbormaster, Sam Hartshorn, a minute later.

"I seen the trouble the elf caused," said Sam. "So I fetched s'me more men to help."

Evan grimaced. "You're too late. He got away."

Sam placed his right palm against his face. "Blimey. What did he get away with?"

"A good friend," murmured Daniel sadly from his seated position.

"Tindolen's gem," replied James.

Eric came running up a few minutes later and took charge of the scene. He began by questioning Evan and the others.

Evan recapped the events for his friend, describing how the elf put the guards at the Grey Horse Inn to sleep and how they discovered the gem was missing. "We pursued the thief and, as we approached the harbor, we saw the extra guards you had posted here, asleep. Despite the darkness, Iriel saw movement at the end of the pier. I charged forward, but I was too late. He had already put the guards on the pier to sleep and he was aboard his boat ready to leave. Before I could close in and jump into it, the ship flew away into the darkness."

"I see," Eric said. There was no irritation in his voice at the mention of magic, but there was in his eyes. "Continue."

"That's it. We really don't have any way to pursue him."

"Okay, thanks. If I have any other questions, I'll find you."

* * *

They walked back to the Inn slowly. Evan was unaccustomed to losing, and this time was particularly hard because of the value the Elf-gem had — or could have had — to Thalacia. He would also have to explain to His Grace how the elf had eluded him, thereby forfeiting any chance to locate and apprehend Jormundan. Evan wasn't looking forward to that conversation; His Grace would not be pleased by this news.

Perhaps if he had brought along at least one of the Michaeline knights, as His Grace had suggested, the elf would be in custody now. That was a possibility, but Evan had no time for such conjecture. He had to keep his attention on the theft of the Elf-gem and what the loss of it meant.

Perhaps the necromancers are the ones meant to reunite the Elf-gems? No! That can't be right. Then Evan realized he didn't know whether the theft helped or hindered the prophecy.

It doesn't matter either way. I can't let necromancers acquire any of the Elf-gems. The chances of them perverting the jewels into weapons are too great. But what choice do I have? I can't stop the elf who's stolen Tindolen's gem.

He looked to the heavens and prayed to St. Michael for aid.

* * *

They entered the main square. The statue of King Illium and the clock tower cast deep shadows over the cobblestones and the fountain in the middle of the quadrangle. As they walked, Evan was in the lead. Behind him, James strolled beside Iriel and Daniel. Brashani and Molin trailed last.

Daniel trudged along, his head down, as if he had lost his best friend. Iriel frowned and looked ready to cry. The bard tried to think of something to say to cheer them up, but he was tired and nothing came to him.

"I need a drink," murmured Brashani.

That roused Iriel. She stopped walking, turned around, and shot the wizard a nasty look.

Molin came to a halt. Brashani froze where he stood. "What?"

"A drink? At this hour?" she cried with venom.

James stopped walking too and cringed as she spoke. The last thing they needed was to get into a fight with each other. Evan heard the exchange. He turned back to look at the others.

"Sure," said the mage. "It helps me think."

She stared at him and then laughed. James glanced at Iriel and then gazed at Brashani, who shrugged. "Beats me," said the wizard.

Iriel laughed until tears ran down her face. Finally, she stopped. "How utterly absurd. But thank you, Magus Khumesh, I needed a good laugh."

She resumed walking. Brashani scratched his head and muttered, "But it *does* help me think."

They exited the square and approached the Grey Horse Inn. As they drew near, Evan saw Tindolen waiting for them by the hitching post in front of the Inn.

"Uncle?" Iriel said with a quiver in her voice.

Tindolen smiled at his niece. "Iriel, good morning."

"You're up early," observed Evan with surprise.

The merchant frowned. "Yes, well, not by choice, I assure you. I heard Aure's cries for help."

"Then you know the gem's been stolen."

"I do and, judging by your behavior, I'm guessing the thief got away."

"He did and we've no way of following him."

"You don't, but I may know of one."

Evan's mouth fell open. "You do? How?"

Daniel looked up at the jeweler. His face brightened slightly and his blue eyes gleamed with hope.

"Ay?" said James in disbelief. "And what might that be?"

Iriel's eyes grew round and she felt a lump in her throat.

"You're kidding," laughed Brashani.

Tindolen shook his head. "The town inventor, Cornelius Cornwall, has invented a way to fly. You may be able to pursue the thief that way."

Evan considered the merchant's words. He remembered Cornelius from his days as a boy in town. The man had always struck him as absentminded and a scatterbrain. He doubted the man could have invented a way to fly, particularly since he was not a wizard. But if they were going to pursue the thief, they would need to find an answer quickly or the gem would certainly be lost to them forever.

"How did Cornelius invent a way to fly?" asked Evan.

"I don't know," replied Tindolen. "What I can tell you is I had tea with him last week and he showed me the plans he had for a device. He claims it can fly. I didn't really pay close attention since such things bore me terribly. If you are interested, we should pay Cornelius a visit."

Evan nodded his head vigorously. "All right, let's do that and as quickly as possible."

* * *

Evan and James ran inside the Grey Horse Inn to grab their backpacks; if they were going to pursue the thief, they would need all their gear. While they were gone, Iriel approached her uncle. Tears from the corners of her eyes streamed down the sides of her face. "I'm sorry, Uncle. I failed you."

Tindolen smiled at her. "Nonsense, my dear. I'm sure you did the best you could. The important thing now is to find the elf and reclaim my gem. I'm counting on you to help Evan do that."

Iriel smiled weakly. "Then you're not angry or disappointed?"

"With you? Certainly not." He smiled again and she hugged him.

"I won't fail you again."

"I know you won't, my dear."

CHAPTER 23
CORNELIUS CORNWALL

Daniel paced back and forth as he, Iriel, Brashani, Tindolen, and Molin waited for James and Evan.

What's taking them so long? Aure is in trouble and we need to get moving.

The teen realized he was being impatient and stopped pacing. He drew a deep breath and let his concern flow out of him as he exhaled. Daniel smiled. He felt better, but he also felt the need to meditate. It was the only way to stay in control of his feelings.

I don't have time for that though. And besides, it would be another delay when we need action.

His impatience returned, and he realized that helping Aure and staying in control were at odds with each other.

Is this because I care about him? That seemed a reasonable answer. *Then what am I going to do when I find members of my family and get to know them? Will I even be able to continue as a master of the Art?*

A wave of concern sparked a cold sweat over Daniel's body. He paced some more and then stopped.

Maybe I'm worried about nothing. I doubt anyone in my family is going to be abducted. Daniel smiled at that thought only to have his restlessness return.

But that doesn't address my feelings for Aure. I need to master my impatience before it unravels all my accomplishments.

* * *

James and Evan emerged from the Inn, their backpacks strapped on. James carried a third pack in his hands, which he gave to Iriel. Her eyes were red, he noticed.

"Have you been crying?" he asked her.

"I was, but I'm fine now. Uncle still has faith in me."

"Of course he does. So do I."

She gave him a peck on the cheek and put on her pack.

Tindolen waited for her, and then asked, "Is everyone ready?"

Molin groaned and shook his head. "I'm too old to chase after this bauble."

"That's your choice, of course," said Evan. "You can explain to Frank and anyone else who comes looking for the gem, or any of us, what has happened."

"All right," said Molin. "I'll do that. Good luck," he added a moment later.

"We'll need more than luck," Evan mumbled to himself.

* * *

Tindolen set out across town. Daniel walked beside the merchant. Evan and the others followed close behind. In the distance, the first light of dawn was beginning to show in the eastern sky, painting it orange along the horizon and light blue dissolving to dark blue higher up.

They reached the corner of Elm and Maple Streets. Tindolen turned the corner and said, "Here we are." He gestured toward the first house on the left. Evan looked at the place appraisingly. It was a small light blue wooden cottage with white shutters and set back from the road. A thatched straw roof covered the top of the house; smoke curled out of the chimney. A large lawn of brown grass surrounded the dwelling, still showing evidence of the morning frost.

"What is that?" James asked and pointed. No one answered because no one knew what to say.

In the front yard stood four metal poles about twice the height of Evan. Gray metal struts ran between the poles for support. At the top was a platform parallel to the ground and made from the same material as the poles. A metal pinwheel capped the entire structure. The wheel spun in the faint breeze.

Daniel stared at the structure briefly when James spoke, then resumed walking beside Tindolen.

Iriel glanced at the metal poles but did not go near them. She did not even want to look at them. Nevertheless, the elf found herself casting wary glances at the metal poles. She seemed to cower as she walked by them.

"What's wrong?" asked James.

"It gives me a bad feeling," she replied.

Brashani gestured. "I don't sense magic from it."

She gave him a sidelong glance. "Call it intuition."

Evan watched the wheel spin as he approached it. He tapped one of the metal poles and heard a hollow sound unlike anything he had experienced before. It wasn't iron or steel. It wasn't bronze or brass.

What's the purpose of this thing and what is it made of? he wondered. *How could a hollow tube support this frame?*

A path of gray stone blocks ran from the road to the white front door of the cottage, dividing the lawn in two. The surface of the path wasn't smooth but was not as rough as cut stone either.

Iriel eyed the slab cautiously too, tapped it with her foot once, and then walked beside it on the grass instead.

"Is the stone evil too?" teased James.

She shook her head. "Not evil, but not natural."

Evan examined the stone blocks carefully. They appeared to have been poured into square sections like cake batter. But the inventor wasn't a wizard and there were no mages for hire in Clearbrook.

"Brashani," Evan said. "Do you detect any magic from the stone?"

The wizard paused and concentrated for a moment. "No," he replied at last. "Why?"

"No reason," said Evan. "Just wondering how this walkway was made."

"Well, it wasn't shaped by an earth mage, if that's what you were thinking."

"Okay. Thanks."

Tindolen knocked on the front door of the cottage. It creaked open and a thin man with wrinkled skin appeared in the doorway with spectacles perched at the end of his nose. The hair on the man's head was mostly gone; only a few strands of gray were visible across the top and sides of his skull. He wore clothes too big for him, as if he had shriveled up inside them. They hung loosely on his slender frame.

"Tindolen," the man said with a smile. "Good to see you again. Has a week passed already?"

The merchant smiled back. "Cornelius, good to see you too. No, I've not come for tea."

"Oh?" Cornelius's brow furrowed. "Then what?"

"I've come again because my friends can help you ..." He gestured toward Evan and the others. "... and you can help them."

"Help me?" Cornelius squinted, knitted his eyebrows, and frowned. "I don't need help."

"Not even to test your latest invention?" Tindolen asked suggestively.

"My ..." Cornelius trailed off in thought. His face brightened, his eyes widened, and he smiled. "The flying basket!"

"Precisely."

Evan cast a wary eye at Tindolen and Cornelius. "What's a flying basket?"

"Come, come," Cornelius said and waved them inside. "Let me show you."

Tindolen stepped into the house, followed by Daniel, Evan, James, Iriel, and Brashani in single file. The hallway was dark and cluttered with boxes and barrels. Some of the containers had narrow slits along the top and cloth of different kinds had been pulled through the openings. The fabric stood up like wilted, wrinkled pyramids with odd pleats. Cornelius's visitors squeezed between the containers that nearly blocked the front hallway and followed the inventor to the back of the house.

Cornelius led his guests straight through the cottage to the back door. He opened it and stepped out onto the back lawn, which was a large plot of brown grass and weeds cropped short. In the middle of the yard was a wicker basket, just large enough for five people to stand in and about four feet high. Thick, sturdy ropes were tied to the basket at one end and to a large, inflated canvas bag on the other. The bag was the length of ten people lying down head-to-foot and at least that many going around. It lay on its side and rolled about in the breeze.

Evan's eyes narrowed at the sight of the basket. "What is that?"

"The flying basket," said Cornelius with glee.

"That thing flies?" asked James, incredulously. "Is it magical?"

"Certainly not!" replied Cornelius with indignation. "Magic has no place in my inventions."

"Then how can it fly?" asked Evan.

"Well, when you heat the air in the canvas bag, it lifts up into the sky, taking the basket with it. The only problem is, there's no way to keep the air in the bag hot long enough to go anywhere."

"You mean without magic," said Brashani, confidently. "As a fire mage, I can heat anything without too much effort and prolong the effect without getting tired."

"Which is why," noted Tindolen, "I thought they could help you test your invention, Cornelius. In exchange, they get to use your flying vehicle, which they need."

"And the sooner the better," said Daniel.

"Well … I don't know," replied Cornelius, doubtfully. "Using magic with one of my inventions …"

Evan ground his teeth in frustration. At last he understood why Tindolen had brought them all here. It wasn't the best plan for pursuing the thief, but it was a plan and it just might work. Any delay, such as Cornelius equivocating, just widened the distance between Evan and the thief. What was needed was immediate action. Evan was about to open his mouth and say something to Cornelius when the inventor said, "All right. Let's try it."

"Everyone into the basket," commanded Evan.

"Must I?" asked Iriel.

"No, you don't have to come. You can return to the Inn and help Molin."

She looked at Tindolen. "Is this the only way, Uncle?"

"Yes, I'm afraid so, Iriel. But you needn't worry. It won't harm you."

She considered her uncle's words and then saw that Daniel had already strode out across the lawn and climbed into the basket. He was waiting to go. Gathering her resolve, she stood tall and followed the lad.

"Do you think it is safe?" James asked Evan warily.

"It looks sturdy enough," replied the priest.

James looked at the basket and ropes again and then, after a deep breath, he walked across the lawn behind Iriel.

Evan looked at the wizard. "Brashani, prepare your Heat magic."

Brashani inclined his head and trailed after James.

Evan turned to Tindolen and shook his hand. "Thanks for your help with this."

"My pleasure, Evan. Like you, I don't want my gem to fall into the wrong hands."

"We'll get it back."

"I'm sure you will."

Turning to Cornelius, Evan said, "Assuming we can get it into the air, how do you steer the basket?"

The old man shrugged. "I don't know. I've not been able to get it into the air."

Tindolen smiled. "I anticipated this issue and brought you a wind maker." He drew a small stick out of his vest coat pocket. A piece of wood with a single twist in it was attached to the stick by a small peg. Evan saw that the twisted wood spun freely like the arms of a windmill.

"A what?" asked Evan, as he examined the stick.

"A wind maker." He handed it to Evan. "Some elven seamen use these to put wind in the sails of their boats when a weather mage or air mage is not available. You can use it to push you in the direction you need to fly."

"How does it work?"

"Squeeze the handle."

Evan tightened his hand around the stick and the twisted wood spun around, creating a breeze.

"The harder you squeeze, the stronger the wind."

"Excellent." Evan smiled. "Thanks." He approached the basket. Daniel, Iriel, and James were standing in it. Brashani was standing next to it examining the wicker.

"Something wrong?" inquired Evan.

Brashani looked up at him. "No, no. I was just thinking about James's comment about how sturdy the basket is."

"A wicker basket this size can hold all of us."

"Sure, but what if something crashes into us or we're attacked with a flaming arrow? Wicker burns like wood."

"We'll have to take that chance. There's no time to look for anything flame resistant."

"I know there isn't," replied Brashani. "But I can harden the wicker."

Evan gazed suspiciously at the wizard. "What would that do?"

"It will strengthen the wicker and make it act like stone without making it any heavier."

"Will it take long to complete?"

"A minute or so."

"All right. Do it."

Brashani placed both hands on one side of the basket and chanted.

"Wicker, wicker, thicker, thicker
Stone and earth, since the world's birth
Merge and make; cook and bake
A stronger basket; a better casket"

The wicker changed color from varying shades of beige to a uniform gray, as if it had been transformed into stone.

Iriel sighed and smiled. "That feels much better."

"How so?" asked James.

"More magical."

Evan smiled in approval. "Good work."

Brashani tapped the basket a few times, listening to the sound it made. "That should do."

"Get in."

"Right."

Evan climbed in and noticed the wicker didn't squeak. He also noticed that space was tight. Unless he moved in concert with the others, Evan was going to bump into someone or step on someone's foot.

Hopefully, we will only have to be in this contraption for a few hours, Evan thought. Turning to face Brashani, he said, "Whenever you are ready."

The fire mage rubbed his hands together and stared at the canvas bag. The bag began to roll faster from side to side. After a few minutes, it started to bob up and down like a boat on the ocean. A few more minutes went by and the canvas bag rose in the air. The ropes around the basket, which had been slack, became taut.

The basket gave a jolt and everyone fell on top of each other.

"What was that?" asked Iriel.

"I think the basket lifted off the ground," replied Brashani. He scrambled to his feet and looked over the side. The basket was indeed a few inches off the ground. He resumed heating the canvas bag and the basket climbed higher.

On the ground, Cornelius jumped for joy. "It works! It works! My God, it works."

Tindolen smiled at the inventor and waved good-bye to Evan and the others.

* * *

The basket rose high in the air, frightening several pigeons in the vicinity. Fortunately for all, the birds flew off leaving the basket unscathed. Once the basket was above the trees, Evan turned to Daniel.

"Which way do we go, Daniel?"

The lad pointed toward the sun, which was just clearing the treetops too. "East."

Evan squeezed the wind maker hard and propelled the vehicle forward.

Brashani stood in the middle of the basket and reduced the heat to keep them at a consistent altitude. The wizard wondered how heat-resistant the canvas and ropes were. He did not want them to catch fire because it would be a long way down to the ground. Once or twice, as they ascended into the sky, Brashani made sniffing noises; the odor of something burning had caught his attention. Carefully, he examined the canvas overhead and the ropes but saw no flames.

All the while, Daniel, standing on the east side of the basket, did his best to concentrate on the signal being sent by Aure. It was faint and intermittent but it was there. Daniel tried to guess how far away it was but without a reference, was unable to tell.

Evan's right hand started to hurt after he had been squeezing the wind maker for a few minutes. He switched hands and flexed his fingers to relieve the pain.

Iriel looked out over the southern edge of the basket and clapped her hands in delight. She jumped up once with excitement but when she landed the entire basket shook.

"Don't do that," said James. His eyes darted around to make sure the ropes still held. His hands gripped the edges of the basket tightly and all his muscles tensed.

Iriel blushed and lowered her head, a little embarrassed. "Sorry, I have not been flying before. It's so exciting. And the view from up here is marvelous." She looked over the edge again. Farmland and brown tilled soil, now barren after the autumn harvest, stretched out in all directions like a patchwork quilt. Occasionally a barn or a farmhouse dotted the landscape and, on the horizon, Iriel saw a small copse of trees and a small town.

She waved to James to join her. "Come and look."

The bard relaxed a little and went over to her. He looked over the edge and felt his hands go clammy. Sweat beaded along his forehead and cheeks. The back of his neck became wet and a small army of butterflies hammered at his stomach. The world started spinning and he fell back, landing in the bottom of the basket with a hard thud. As he landed, the flying contraption shook again.

Evan eyed him with concern. "Are you all right?"

"Yeah," replied James, putting his hand to his head. "Just dizzy. Guess it's vertigo. I've never been up this high before." He tried to stand but his legs kept buckling and would not support him. Then he felt queasiness in his stomach and he decided to stay down. Iriel knelt beside him. She felt his forehead; it was cool to the touch and wet.

"Keep still. These feelings will pass."

James hoped so, but up to this point it seemed to him that coming along had been a bad idea.

CHAPTER 24
THUNDER AND LIGHTNING

Daniel turned to face the others. "We're slowing down."
Evan nodded his head. "Sorry. My right hand is badly
cramped so I've had to switch hands. My left hand just
doesn't have the same strength as my right one."

"Let me hold it," offered Daniel.

"All right." Evan and Daniel swapped positions, squeezing
past Brashani in the process. Daniel tightened his grip on the wind
maker and the basket zoomed forward.

Iriel reached into a pocket of her trousers and pulled out a few
nuts. They looked like small almonds. She crouched down next to
James and handed him the nuts. "Eat these."

The bard looked at them. "What are they?"

"Leingo nuts. They will ease your dizziness."

James shrugged and took the nuts from her. He chewed and
swallowed them. "Yuck. These taste awful."

"Sorry, love. Give them a few minutes to start working."

Evan tapped Iriel on the shoulder. "Iriel, a word please." The elf stood up and went over to him. "We are going to need to take turns using the wind maker. Since James is ill and Brashani is busy keeping us in the air, Daniel, you, and I will need to keep the basket moving."

"I understand. When will you need my help?" Iriel asked.

"Fifteen minutes, maybe less; it depends on how long Daniel can hold out."

"Very good. I will comfort James in the meantime."

On the west side of the basket, Daniel stood staring east and trying to keep the connection to Aure from dissolving. *We're coming, Aure. Don't give up hope. We're coming.* He got no response.

The teen held on for half an hour, using *Qua'ril* techniques to mitigate the pain. In the end, he had to admit he couldn't operate the wind maker any more. His hand was too badly cramped. The basket slowed and then stopped.

"Father Evan," said Daniel, "you can have the wind maker back."

"Give it to Iriel," he said. "She'll take over."

The lad handed the magic stick to Iriel and moved to stand near James. Iriel slipped past him to stand along the west edge of the basket. Applying pressure to the handle, Iriel pointed the wind maker due west and the basket sped off to the east.

Daniel stared eastward and pointed. "What are those dark clouds?"

Evan glanced in the direction Daniel indicated. Dark gray clouds stretched across their path. "Looks like a storm. Rain most likely." He faced Brashani. "I don't want to fly through that. Can we go higher?"

"Probably, but I don't know how much heat the canvas and the ropes will take. Going over the storm might not be safe. If something were to catch fire ..." Brashani trailed off.

"Understood," replied Evan. "But if there is lightning in that storm, we could be just as dead. Let's try going over the storm first and watch for signs of overheating."

Brashani grimaced. There didn't seem to be a good solution to their situation. "All right," he said at last and increased the heat to the canvas bag. The basket rose higher in the sky. Tendrils of smoke reached Brashani a few minutes later.

"Do you smell smoke?"

Evan sniffed. "Yes."

Brashani looked up into the canvas bag and saw some of the fabric smoldering. He reversed the flow of heat to cool the canvas and the basket dropped a little in the sky. Then he resumed heating the bag at the same rate he had before.

"I don't think we can go over the storm," he said to Evan.

Evan looked at the dark clouds ahead. Thunder roared in the distance. He ran his hand through his hair and narrowed his eyes. "Then we have no choice. We have to go through it."

* * *

The flying basket pierced the rain clouds and a light rain began to fall. Thunder echoed in the distance followed by flashes of light.

The rain had a cooling effect on the hot air. Brashani felt the basket descend almost immediately upon entering the cloud bank. He increased the intensity of the heat he provided and hoped it was enough.

James sat curled up in the southwest corner of the basket. His eyes were slits.

Iriel gazed at her lover worriedly. "How are you feeling, James?"

The bard spoke without moving. "Nauseous. And wet, thanks to the rain. All I want is to feel the solid ground under my feet."

"The leingo nuts are not working?"

"Not yet."

"They should soon."

"It won't be soon enough."

They flew in a murky, thick sky for several minutes, the dark clouds acting like fog. Streaks of lightning could now be seen in the distance and were coming closer, followed by rolling thunder that punctuated the silence.

The noise gave James a splitting headache on top of everything else.

Why can't the weather be quiet? he thought. The thunder sounded again; the lightning grew closer. *What have I done to deserve this? Is my relationship with Iriel offending an elven sky god?*

James couldn't think of any elven sky gods, but his throbbing skull only served to muddle his thoughts.

No, he concluded at last, *no sky god should care about Iriel or me. So why am I suffering so badly?* Thunder boomed again, louder, and James groaned. His head felt as if it were splitting open.

Be quiet! he screamed to himself. The thunder replied by crashing again above them, as if to taunt him. It sounded a little like laughter too.

That's it, he thought, and he stood up. He withdrew his whip; it uncurled and the bard lashed out at the storm. As he raised his arm with the whip, the weapon struck the side of the canvas bag.

Evan pushed past Brashani and Daniel, and grabbed James's forearm. "What are you doing?"

James yanked his arm free and looked directly at Evan, whose narrow blue eyes bored into the bard like daggers. James stared back, in an attempt to convey his anger. He wasn't convincing enough, however, because Evan didn't move. *I'm too wet, nauseous, and dizzy to give a good performance. And my head is pounding too.* He glared at Evan. *Now Evan is mad at me.* Tendrils of fear surfaced. Would Evan call down some Michaeline plague upon him? No, Evan wasn't nearly as frightening as the masters of his order.

"Nothing," the bard said at last. "I don't feel well. I just want some peace and quiet."

"Well, slicing open the canvas bag with your whip won't help," Evan pointed out.

James realized what he had just tried to do. "Oh, sorry," he said. "It's hard to think straight with this headache."

"I understand," said Evan. "But you need your wits about you. Any one of us could kill us all if we make the wrong move."

James put his hand on his forehead and rubbed it. "I know. It's just ... my thoughts are all tangled up."

A bolt of lightning streaked past them and brightened the sky for an instant like a flare. Thunder crashed above and the rain became more intense.

* * *

James dropped his whip and nearly jumped out of the basket when the lightning bolt slashed across the sky. Iriel grabbed him with her free hand and he clung to her like a scared newborn clutching his mother. The basket rocked violently in the sky and Evan was sure that, if the basket had been a boat in the ocean, it would have capsized.

Evan suspected he knew how James felt — how they all felt. Nerves were frayed and tempers were short. Evan counted to ten and forced himself to relax. They needed to get out of the clouds. Evan began to brainstorm for a less hazardous path than where they were now.

Bright light once more illuminated his surroundings and a lightning bolt struck the corner of the basket. It caught fire briefly then fizzled, emitting some smoke and the odor of charcoal.

That was too close, Evan thought. *If lightning had punctured the canvas bag or sliced through one of the ropes, we'd all be dead now.*

James leaped up, broke free of Iriel, and stood on the basket's southern edge. The ropes groaned at the disproportionate weight applied to them. Evan, Brashani, Iriel, and Daniel tumbled forward, and slammed into each other.

"What the …," said Brashani.

"Ouch!" cried Evan, as his knee hit the transformed wicker.

Lightning struck near the canvas bag and wicker basket, missing both by inches; if James hadn't moved the lower end of Cornwall's flying invention, Evan was sure another corner of the basket would have caught fire.

Evan and Brashani pulled James back toward them, and the bard landed in the bottom of the basket again. The entire flying machine rocked back and forth like a pendulum for a minute before settling down.

"Stay there," commanded Evan. He wanted to say more, to chastise the bard, but he had more immediate issues to deal with. Addressing the fire mage, he ordered, "Brashani, stop heating the air."

"We'll fall."

"Yes, and maybe we'll be less of a target for the lightning."

The wizard considered this. It couldn't be any worse than their current predicament. "All right," Brashani replied after a minute.

The flying basket descended slowly. The thunder grew softer and the lightning became distant flashes of light. The rain increased, then slackened, and finally stopped. The sun came out. Evan looked behind them. The line of dark clouds was receding.

"A blessing from Elas," said Iriel.

"Thank God and St. Michael," said Evan, smiling.

Brashani smiled too and shook Evan's hand.

"About time," said James.

Evan peered out over the northern edge of the basket to see how far they had fallen. They were much lower than they had been. The copse of trees Iriel had spied earlier was now directly under them. Small figures with sickly green skin moved about. Evan was sure they weren't human.

Goblins, maybe? he wondered. Whoever they were, they were no concern of Evan's. Turning his attention to the ropes, Evan inspected them for damage. They seemed fine.

"Brashani, I think we need a little more heat," said Evan.

"All right," replied the wizard as he heard a thud.

Evan had heard it too. "What was that?" he asked.

"I don't know," replied Brashani.

Daniel pointed to the floor. "I think it came from underneath the basket."

James jumped up as if his trousers were ablaze. "Daniel's right. I felt something strike from underneath us."

Evan looked out over the basket's edge again. Below them in a clearing surrounded by trees, five small figures stood next to a catapult. The figures appeared to be of the same race as the people he had seen earlier, and these five all carried spears. They were pointing at the basket in the sky and aimed the catapult accordingly. Two of the figures loaded a large boulder into the device.

"How fast can we gain altitude?"

"Not very," answered Brashani, "judging from my earlier attempts."

"Well, do what you can. I'm not sure we can withstand too many of those boulders."

CHAPTER 25
FLYING IS FOR THE BIRDS

Wasting no time, Brashani increased the heat to the canvas bag. In response, the basket rose higher. The figures on the ground released another boulder from their catapult. It flew through the air, grazed the bottom of the flying machine, and fell back to earth. Evan watched as the figures fired their weapon a few more times. Each attempt bore the same result: the rock they launched sailed high into the air but it never reached the flying basket. The flying contraption was higher in the sky now and out of range. Evan breathed a sigh of relief.

James wiped his brow. "Phew! That was a close call."

"Yes," said Evan. "How do you feel?"

"Surprisingly good. The unexpected attack from the ground seems to have done the trick. Or maybe the nuts Iriel gave me are finally working."

Evan hoped it was the latter. He had seen it before: a sudden fright helped cure an ailment for a short time only to have the symptoms return later. But if James's issues were resolved for the moment, Evan wasn't going to say anything to spoil it. He pushed past James to stand next to Iriel.

"How are you holding out?" asked Evan.

"I am well," said Iriel. "I know a few *Qua'ril* techniques to control the pain. But I could rest now."

"All right. Rest your hands." Evan took the magic stick from her.

"Thank you," she said, and moved to the south side of the basket as Evan stepped over to the western edge. He squeezed the wind maker and propelled the craft forward.

Iriel put a hand on James's arm. "Are you well? You worried me more than once."

"Sorry, love," the bard replied. "I didn't mean to, but I wasn't feeling myself."

"Stay away from the edge of the basket."

"That's hard to do. It's tight quarters in here."

"I know, but ..."

James smiled at her. "If you are worried about a relapse, don't be. I don't plan to look over the edge until we land."

Iriel hugged James and whispered into his ear, "I hope we never experience an ordeal like that again. I love you too much to think about losing you."

James kissed her lightly on the lips. "I love you, too. And I'm not going anywhere."

Iriel smiled at James and hugged him again.

They flew on for several minutes, peaceful for the first time since setting a course east. James picked up his whip, coiled it up again, and affixed it to his belt. In the distance, they heard honking. Evan turned to look, but he recognized the sound before he even moved: geese were approaching.

Daniel confirmed Evan's assumption a minute later. "There's a large gaggle of geese coming this way."

Now Evan saw them too. They were in a classic V formation and were pointed directly at them. Evan felt like cursing. Hadn't they had enough obstacles to overcome so far on this trip?

"Increase the heat, Brashani," said Evan. "Let's try to go over them."

"Okay, but I can't add too much or the canvas will smolder again."

"Understood."

Brashani concentrated and the basket rose higher in the sky. "That's the best I can do," claimed the wizard.

"Let's hope it's enough," replied Evan.

* * *

They heard the geese flapping their wings and honking as they passed underneath the basket. James sighed in relief when the entire basket began to shake. Iriel and her companions fell on top of each other. Evan lost his grip on the wind maker; he heard it clatter onto the transformed wicker floor as he collapsed on top of Brashani. The flying basket came to a stop, hung in the air, and swung back and forth like an inverted metronome. Feathers sprayed up and into the basket next to Daniel. The teen pulled himself up using the side of the basket and looked over the edge. There, on the other side of the wicker, was a bloody smear and the carcass of a goose falling toward the ground. Hearing something above him, Daniel crouched down. Two geese had flown into the basket and were caught in the ropes.

The flying machine shook violently as the birds tried to free themselves. Evan and Brashani tried to stand and failed. The basket was shaking too much. Evan tried again and frustration turned his face red. Concern that the ropes might break grew in the wizard's mind.

Iriel reached up from her position in the bottom of the basket and grabbed one of the geese. It turned its head and bit her hard. Instinctively, she snatched her hand back and rubbed it for a minute. She gritted her teeth and narrowed her green eyes on the bird before she tried again; this time she aimed for the goose's neck. The goose squawked as Iriel seized it; she rose to a crouched position and tossed it out over the side. It floundered for a moment before it recovered and flew after its flock.

The other goose flapped its wings a few times and sprayed feathers over James, who withdrew into the southwest corner of the basket. Daniel, still crouching, moved past Iriel, Brashani, and Evan, grasped the goose from underneath, and stood up in a single, fluid motion. In response, the goose flapped harder and hit Daniel a few times in the face with its wings. However, the lad was not deterred. He pivoted, forced the goose out into the open sky, and then released his hold. The goose continued to flap its wings and, as soon as Daniel loosened his grip, it flew away toward the other geese.

The basket's gyrations diminished and the goose feathers settled. Daniel returned to the eastern side of the basket.

Evan spit a few feathers from his mouth and stood. "Nice job, Iriel and Daniel. Let's get moving again."

"Yes, please," said Daniel.

Evan grabbed the wind maker from the basket floor and squeezed it.

James brushed goose feathers from his shirt and trousers. "Now I know how a pillow feels."

Brashani stood and examined the ropes for fraying. "I should have strengthened the ropes too."

"Are they intact?" asked Evan.

"They appear to be. Guess we were lucky," the wizard replied.

"You call that luck?" James asked. He spit out some feathers and eyed the fire mage.

"Nothing else but. These ropes have held despite all we've been through. They might have snapped."

"Well," replied Evan. "Lucky or not, let's hope that other flying creatures will avoid us."

"We're high enough to avoid most birds," observed the wizard.

"What about dragons and rocs and other large-winged monsters?" asked James.

"Dragons are extinct," said Brashani.

"And most of the other creatures roam and hunt among the mountains northwest of here. They haven't been seen in this area for centuries," said Evan.

"Good," said James. "I've had enough excitement on this trip for awhile."

Evan agreed with that sentiment.

A wind from the east began to stir.

"We're slowing down," reported Daniel.

Evan noticed it too. Squeezing the wind maker harder didn't help much. He needed a different approach.

Sailors, he realized, had the same problem when they tried to sail into the wind. Their solution was to sail at an angle to the wind. Evan didn't know whether that would work, but it was worth a try.

"James, let me stand in the corner."

"Sure," replied the bard.

As Evan moved, the basket's direction shifted and its forward movement increased. Soon they were flying along, heading northeast.

"You did it," said Daniel, smiling. "We're moving again."

"Yes," said Evan. "Until the wind shifts again."

The priest tried to gauge five minutes and then he moved into the northwest corner of the basket. The basket slowed briefly and then flew off to the southeast.

Back and forth, from one corner to another Evan moved, tacking against the wind for half an hour; then, unable to hold the wind maker any longer, he let Daniel take over. The lad continued to use the same tacking maneuver until the east wind finally stopped. Then he resumed his position on the west side of the basket.

"Should we be sinking?" Daniel asked Brashani.

"No. I'm maintaining a constant heat flow."

"Then why is the ground getting closer?" Daniel pointed.

Brashani and Evan looked over the edge and saw that Daniel was right. The ground was closer than it should have been.

"What do you think is wrong?" asked Evan.

"Well, since I'm heating the air at a constant rate, my first guess is there's a leak."

They both paused and looked up at the inflated canvas bag above them. It appeared to be as full of air as before. Brashani closed his eyes, concentrated for a moment, and listened intently. At first he heard nothing unusual; only a bird's cry and the faint whirl of the wind maker. Then a faint hissing sound reached him.

It stopped. Then it repeated. Then it stopped again.

Looking up, Brashani examined the seams of the canvas bag and said, "Some of the stitching isn't holding." He pointed. Evan followed the mage's finger and saw that some of the threads in the canvas stitching were loose.

"We are slowly leaking air," said Evan.

"And if we don't do something about the leak," said Brashani, "we'll crash."

Evan heard the concern in his voice and shared it. "What can we do? There's no way to stitch the canvas back together again while we are in the air."

Brashani nodded his head in agreement. "True, but we could try to mend the fabric together."

"Magically repairing the canvas would be better," offered Iriel.

"Better, how?" said Evan.

"It's permanent," replied the elf. "Mending items lasts ten minutes. Twenty with luck."

"But I don't know how to repair items magically," said Brashani. "I can only fuse things together so we'll have to make do."

"Can you repeatedly fuse the fabric together?" asked Evan.

"Of course," replied the wizard.

"Then if the bag leaks again, mend the canvas again. We have to keep going or the gem is lost."

"Understood," acknowledged Brashani. "But each time I use magic, it weakens me. The more magic I use now, the less use I'll be later."

"That can't be helped. If we crash, there won't be a later."

While they spoke, the ground loomed closer. They were near the treetops. Brashani concentrated and willed the canvas to stick together, as if glued. Then he began heating the air in the canvas bag again. Slowly they rose.

Evan looked doubtfully at the canvas bag above him and prayed that this repair would last long enough to find the gem.

CHAPTER 26

LOSING THE TRAIL

D aniel peered east for a few minutes, then he turned and faced his friends. He smiled. "We're getting close. The gem is on the ground again, I think."

"Good," said Evan. "Where are we?"

James surveyed the countryside. "Judging by the terrain, near Sapilo."

The town of S, Evan thought.

Daniel snapped his head around, he glanced west, and then back to the east. He let go of the wind maker and slowly slid into the bottom of the basket. He looked pale and stared straight ahead in disbelief. "In Kaimin's name, it's not possible."

The basket drifted to a halt. "What's wrong, Daniel?" asked Evan.

The lad looked up at the Michaeline priest. "The gem is not in front of us any more; it's behind us. We've come all this way for nothing."

Iriel's eyes widened. "What?"

"That's impossible," said James.

Brashani rubbed his chin. "Hmmm, sounds like it was teleported."

Evan agreed with that assessment. "Where is the Elf-gem now?"

"Back the way we've come and deep in the earth now," said Daniel.

Evan sighed and ran his fingers through his hair repeatedly. His jaw tensed briefly and his hands, sore as they were from the wind maker, clenched into fists. He wanted to hit something hard to ease his frustration. Instead, Evan sighed again and let his anger go. "If what you say is true, then we have two options: go on without a firm guide or go back."

"Going back means facing God-knows-what in the sky," said James.

"Agreed," said Evan. "And there is no guarantee we could even reach the gem in time to prevent whatever plans are unfolding. On the other hand, if the thief teleported himself somehow, we should still find his boat somewhere up ahead. When we do, we'll know where to set down."

"He couldn't know how to teleport himself," said Brashani, "or he would have teleported way back in Clearbrook."

"True," said Evan.

"So there's probably a device of some kind near his boat," the wizard concluded.

"But not out in the open," noted James. "Or lots of people would know about it and would be using it."

"Good point," replied Evan. "Let's keep a lookout for the boat."

"Look for a rundown shack and a swamp too," said Brashani.

"Why?" asked Evan.

"Humor me. Call it a vision."

Daniel stood, squeezed the wind maker again, and propelled them forward. Minutes passed and Evan grew tense. Had he made the right decision? There was no way of knowing until they searched the lands around Sapilo.

And what if we find no boat? he wondered. *Perhaps the thief concealed his ship or hid it extremely well.*

Turning to Brashani, Evan said, "Bring us down a little."

"All right."

"Ease up on the wind maker, Daniel," Evan continued. "I want to search for the boat."

The basket sank in the sky and slowed. More minutes flew by, although they seemed like hours to Evan. He scanned the land to the east, and saw the town of Sapilo and a small swamp just to the west of it. He ground his teeth in frustration until he spotted something.

Evan stared intently at the swamp below them.

"What do you see?" James asked.

"I don't know," said Evan. "I thought I glimpsed something man-made. Hard to tell what it is at this distance. Brashani, take us down so we are just above the tops of these trees." He pointed to the trees in the swamp.

The wizard complied and the flying machine descended further.

"There!" said Evan, pointing. "Isn't that a white sail?" A wave of relief swept through him. He had guessed correctly. He permitted himself a moment of elation.

James and Brashani looked. Listing to one side in a small clearing of the swamp, a sailboat was resting in the mud.

"It appears to be," Brashani said and nodded his head in satisfaction.

"We found it!" James said and grinned.

Daniel and Iriel smiled too.

"Then that's where we are going," said Evan.

"What's that next to it?" asked James.

Evan looked. He hadn't seen it before, but a few yards away from the boat was an old shack. The wood of the shack was gray and weathered. Odd bits of wood were stuck onto the building or pegged in place. From what Evan could see, it appeared as if someone had tried to cover holes that had been created from natural deterioration or made by swamp creatures that had tried to make the shack a home.

Evan looked at Brashani. "How'd you know there'd be a shack here?"

"As I said, it was a vision."

"Have any other visions?"

"Yes, but I'm not sure they make sense at the moment."

"Well, let me know if you figure them out. This one was spot on." Evan addressed Daniel next. "Can you position us over the clearing?"

"I will try," replied the lad. The flying basket crept forward a few feet in one direction and then a few feet in another.

Once they were in position, Evan turned to Brashani. "Remove heat from the canvas bag slowly. We don't want to hit anything on the way down."

Brashani inclined his head and they descended into the clearing. Daniel made small adjustments to their position as they drifted down from the sky. Evan scanned the scene below as they approached.

"The sailboat still has its sail up and does not appear to be moored to anything," observed Evan. "Apparently, the thief wasted no time going wherever it was he went."

"Any idea where that might be?" asked Brashani.

"No, but we're going to find out."

"Are we searching the boat first?" inquired Iriel.

"No," Evan replied. "We already know from Daniel's connection with the gem that it isn't in the boat or the swamp. It is wherever the thief went; we're going to follow him."

In the soft mud, Evan saw a line of footprints leading from the sailboat to the shack. *So either the thief is in the shack waiting or he has teleported away. Given Daniel's information, I'm guessing it's the latter.*

Finally, they came to rest on the marshy ground.

"At last," said James. "Solid ground." The bard looked again. "Well, sort of."

It didn't feel solid to Evan. He felt the basket settle into the mud and his jaw tightened again. Looking at Brashani, he said, "I hope you can get us off the ground and out of the mud later."

"So do I," said Brashani.

Evan examined the land around them. It looked wet and slimy but there didn't appear to be any sinkholes or quicksand.

Daniel gave the wind maker to Evan. The priest pocketed it and drew his sword. James readied his whip. Iriel loaded an arrow into her bow and examined the quiver slung over her shoulder. It was full of arrows fletched with blue feathers.

"Everyone ready?" asked Evan.

"I am," said Daniel.

"Yes," said Brashani.

"Ready when you are," said James.

"So am I," said Iriel.

"Good," said Evan. "Let's go, but be careful. We don't know what we're walking into."

Daniel vaulted out of the basket and landed lightly in the mud.

"Don't get too far ahead of us," Iriel called out.

Daniel made no motion to acknowledge Iriel, but he waited for the others nonetheless.

Evan climbed out next. The heels of his boots sank into the mud, but, aside from this, the ground around the basket seemed solid enough. He motioned for the others to follow.

Feeling the ground under him for the first time in hours, James smiled. It was a wet squishy ground and he sank a little with each step. "Never thought I'd live to walk on the ground again," the bard said idly.

"You almost didn't," observed Brashani and clambered out of the basket.

"Say, that's right. And come to think of it, this entire ordeal would make an excellent ballad. I bet I could write something about the whole experience."

"Probably," said Evan. "But let's stay keep our attention on the current task, please. Now is not the time for such things."

"No, of course not," replied James, as he helped Iriel out of the flying vehicle.

They approached the shack with caution, and Evan tested each step to determine if the mud would hold him. The smell of wet, dank soil and decaying, rotting leaves was heavy in the morning air; strange birdcalls, which Evan had not heard before, echoed in the distance.

As he came up to the shack, Evan signaled James to one side and Brashani to the other. Iriel stood back with a clear shot of the door. Daniel stood next to her. Evan examined the ground in front of the door for tripwires. When he did not find any, he asked, "Brashani, sense any magic in the area?"

The wizard concentrated for a moment. "Yes, but it is faint. I don't think it is out here."

"So, no wards or protection spells on the shack?"

"No. The magic is inside, I think."

"What about traps? Can you detect them?"

"I can."

"Sense any?"

"No, none."

Evan stepped up to the door, pushed it open, and jumped back in case an arrow or crossbow quarrel came flying out when the door moved. The door swung open and Evan landed in the mud with a definite squish. He looked down and saw the mud was up to his ankles.

"Brashani, look inside," Evan said, as he struggled to free his feet from the goopy ground.

* * *

Brashani stepped in and to one side of the shack's doorway with a fireball and a magic shield ready, just in case. Looking about, he saw nothing of interest, only some dead leaves scattered across the muddy floor. The sense of magic was definitely stronger now but not well defined.

Where is it coming from? the mage wondered. He was about to leave when something caught his eye. A small yellow stone was stuck in the dark brown mud. It looked like the corner of a ceramic tile. He bent over to pick it up but it wouldn't move.

Odd, thought Brashani. Clearing away the dead leaves around the stone and some of the surrounding mud, Brashani understood why the stone would not budge. The yellow stone was the corner of a large ceramic tile set into the ground. On the face of the tile was a seven-pointed star painted in brown.

His eyes widened. *Well, I'll be a sorcerer's apprentice.*

Brashani straightened and stepped out of the shack to talk with his companions.

"What did you find?" asked Evan; he shook the mud off his boots.

"The magic. You'll never guess what it is." Evan shot him a pained look. Brashani got the point. The priest was in no mood to play games.

"It's a portal stone," the wizard said after a moment. "I'm surprised to find one here. They're very rare, but it explains how the elf teleported."

"Yes," said Evan. "And it confirms what you told me yesterday. The thief is working with necromancers."

"Necromancers?" repeated James. Iriel and Daniel looked at Evan, as their eyes grew wide. Iriel's mouth opened as she gasped.

"Yes, I've been fighting them for months. They seem to have an endless supply of resources. If not for the efforts of His Grace and the men at his command, this duchy would have fallen to them some time ago."

"This portal stone probably goes to the necromancers' lair," observed Brashani.

"One of them, yes," said Evan.

"One of them?" asked Iriel.

"Yes. Necromancers organize themselves into groups of five; if some are captured, the others are not at risk. Each group has a lair of its own."

"Does anyone coordinate the mages?" asked the elf.

"It is hard to know," said Evan. "Because we capture so few and they generally do not answer our questions even under intense interrogation. They usually die first."

Brashani cleared his throat. Everyone looked at him. "Evan, I'm sure you are a fine demon hunter and do the best you can against the necromancers; however, I was fighting them back in Marngol when you were just a boy. I can tell you that they do not have endless resources, just magic to make whatever they need. Most serve one demon or another and these fiends resurrect their most faithful subjects. So you end up fighting the same people over and over again. They look different, but they are the same people."

"That explains a lot," said Evan. "Thanks."

"My pleasure," said Brashani. "Now let's kick some dark mage ass."

Evan smiled but Daniel looked distressed and went pale. "In Kaimin's name, it cannot be."

"What cannot be, Daniel?" asked Iriel.

He looked up at her. Tears welled up in his eyes. "I've lost Aure's signal. I think he's dead."

CHAPTER 27
CAPTURING THE THIEF

Evan didn't understand how a gem could die, but he wasted no time and prepared to enter the shack, his sword drawn. As he stepped up to the door, he heard a noise inside the shed. Immediately Evan moved to one side and motioned to the others to move back so they could not be seen from the doorway. He put his finger to his lips and waited.

The door opened and a man in a dark blue shirt and trousers stepped through the entryway. Evan grabbed the man and threw him to the ground. The stranger tried to resist, but only managed to sink a little into the mud. Evan pressed his advantage and pushed the tip of his sword into the man's chest. It was only then that Evan noticed the man's long dark hair, sparkling green eyes, and pointed ears.

"You're the elf we've been chasing," Evan said. "Where's the gem you stole?"

The elf did not answer. A whisper of a grin played on his lips.

"Where is it?" Evan roared and pressed down on his sword a little more.

"Killing me won't help you," the elf sneered.

"Who said anything about killing you?" There was a trace of sarcasm in his voice. "Torture will do. You'll be maimed and disfigured if I don't get the information I want."

"Ppppf, you're bluffing," the elf replied.

"Try me," Evan snarled. His eyes were like ice.

The elf paused. His eyes shifted back and forth and the faint grin on his face faded. He swallowed hard and perspiration beaded on his face.

"It's gone," said the elf.

"Gone?" Gone where?"

"I don't know exactly. I sold it."

"To whom?"

"A mage."

"His name?" Evan asked insistently, teeth clenched.

"Jormundan."

"Is he still around?" asked Brashani.

Evan looked up at the wizard. "You know him?"

"We've crossed paths before. A long time ago."

Turning back to the elf, Evan asked, "What's your name?"

"Ebalin."

"What is Jormundan planning to do with the gem?"

"I don't know. I was hired to find the *Aglaril* and give them to him. That's all."

Evan didn't like the sound of that. "And how many have you found?"

"Just the one."

Evan gestured with his head toward the shack. "Where does the portal stone go?"

"To Jormundan's workshop."

Evan grabbed Ebalin by his shirt and pulled him to his feet. "Show me."

"I can't."

"Why not?"

"The portal stone knows who is permitted into the workshop and who is not. If you are not permitted, you end up outside the underground complex that houses the workshop."

"A dungeon?"

"A series of caves. Each one has a trap or a creature in it to discourage the curious and the greedy."

"So, you'll guide us."

"No," Ebalin answered, as he grew pale and his lower lip quivered. "I don't know how to get through the traps. No one ever has. It's suicide." He tried to pull away from Evan but the priest held him tight.

"Tie him up and gag him," the priest said to James.

James took some rope out of his backpack.

As the bard started to restrain Ebalin, Iriel eyed the sailor. "How could you consort with necromancers?"

"And why shouldn't I? Human necromancers are trying to kill human demon hunters and vice versa. It's just like Davenar all over again; and it's great sport to watch too." He smiled broadly. James pulled the rope tight around his wrists. "Ouch," cried Ebalin. He turned his head toward the bard. "Not so tight."

"But they're evil," implored Iriel. "Working with undead, causing strife? Elves are better than that."

Ebalin raised an eyebrow and turned back to face her. "Oh, really?" he said with scorn. "Tell that to Queen Emeriel and her minions who now occupy Andropolis."

Iriel blushed and walked away. James found a rag and stuffed it into the elf's mouth.

Evan released his grip on the sailor and lowered his sword after surveying James's work, satisfied that it would hold his prisoner. He went over to Iriel.

"Don't let Ebalin upset you," the priest began.

"He didn't," she replied curtly and then added, "But I was taught to believe in values that elves hold dear — truth, justice, honor — and to shun the negative, such as hatred, anger, and intolerance. It is unsettling to remember that not all elves share those values. The dukefs certainly don't and apparently neither does Ebalin." She glanced over her shoulder at the sailor. "I wonder what makes him ignore our most cherished values and side with necromancers?"

"He probably wasn't taught the same lessons you were growing up."

"But to be cruel to another elf ..." she trailed off.

"He is just trying to undermine your morale."

Iriel raised an eyebrow and smiled at him. "It won't work."

Evan smiled. "Glad to hear it." He turned to face the others and said, "Let's go. Brashani, be ready to detect traps."

"Sure."

"What do we do with him?" James asked and gestured at Ebalin.

"Leave him in the boat."

"Won't he escape?"

"Not when I get through with him," said Brashani. "I can enchant those ropes of yours to entangle him. He won't be able to move, let alone escape, after that."

"Perfect," replied Evan. "Do it."

CHAPTER 28
INTO THE FIRE MOUNTAINS

E van stepped on the portal stone and watched the shack dissolve around him. The top of his head felt like it sank into his feet and when that sensation eased, he felt as if he were being stretched back into shape slowly, like taffy being pulled. The world reassembled itself and he was standing in the mouth of a cave on the side of a mountain. From this altitude, he could see a large forest to the south. There was flat land covered by dry grass to the east and north.

A hint of sulfur was in the air. Evan peered up at the top of the mountain and saw it smoking. Immediately, he knew where he was.

The Fire Mountains, he thought. *Hope the volcano doesn't erupt in the next few hours.*

Evan looked into the cave. It was dark and he could not make out very much. Iriel appeared, her bow ready to fire. She saw Evan and stepped over to him.

"We'll wait for the others," he said to her.

Iriel put up her bow but she held onto the arrow. Glancing south, she asked, "Is that Oldarmare?"

"Yes, I think so."

She studied the ground. "I see no portal stones here. How do we get back?"

"We'll walk if we have to. But something sent Ebalin back to the swamp so there must be a portal stone somewhere around here."

James and Daniel arrived in quick succession. James appeared wide-eyed and patted himself down. "I guess I'm all here," he mumbled. Daniel just looked around.

"Any signal yet, Daniel?" asked Evan.

"No, none." His lower lip trembled and his eyes were bloodshot.

"No worries. We'll find the gem," Evan reassured him.

"Yes, of course we will," Daniel replied without enthusiasm. Evan wondered if he meant what he said. The priest knew that the lad cared about Aure, but Evan hadn't appreciated how deeply until now. Daniel was an orphan and alone in the world, like the gem; they had become friends, apparently very close ones. Now that the Elf-gem was gone, Daniel probably felt lost without it. Or worse, as he had said earlier, the gem might be dead. Daniel probably felt like mourning. It certainly looked as if he had been.

Brashani appeared and saw the others waiting. He glanced about and then said to Evan, "Let's go."

Evan, James, and Daniel lit torches and entered the cave. Iriel loaded her bow and followed them; Brashani created a small ball of hand fire and brought up the rear.

The walls were rough and colored pale brown. Dust and sand covered the floor and some rocks and stones were scattered about.

The ceiling was high enough for them to stand upright, and in the distance Evan heard the sound of water running.

After a few minutes of searching the caves, James said, "So, where's the exit?"

"It's probably concealed so people can't find it," said Evan. "Brashani, sense any traps or magic in use?"

The wizard concentrated. "Traps, no. Magic, yes. I think I can dispel it." He walked back into a deep corner of the cave and placed his hand on the wall in front of him.

Iriel gasped as the wall dissolved away like a ghost and revealed a narrow passage into the mountain.

"Nice job," said Evan. He turned to the others and said, "Ready your weapons and be prepared for anything."

James uncoiled his whip.

"Brashani, keep checking for traps."

"Will do."

"Let's go," said Evan. He started down the passage. Iriel followed, with James, Daniel, and Brashani close behind.

CHAPTER 29
THE ANIMATED DEAD

The passageway curled and turned like a piece of kinked hair.

"This reminds me of the summers I spent spelunking in Rockborough," James whispered to Iriel.

"You intentionally spent time exploring caves?"

"I did. And climbing up the sides of steep cliffs, too."

"Why?"

"It was fun."

Iriel shook her head. "How dwarven of you."

James smirked. "Yes, it was, actually."

They followed a few bends in the tunnel; when the passageway straightened, Evan signaled for them to stop and be quiet. He listened and heard shuffling in front of them.

"I hear something," he whispered. "Iriel, scout ahead, but don't let yourself be seen."

She stepped past Evan and crouched. Slowly, she crept down the passage a few more feet, pausing every few inches to listen before resuming her way forward. A few minutes later, she returned in much the same fashion.

"What did you see?" asked Evan.

The elf stuck out her tongue and squeezed her eyes shut. She shook her arms and torso, as if trying to shake off an insect or small crawling forest creature. "Ick. The necromancers have animated some dead bodies. They are pacing back and forth across the entrance to the cave up ahead."

"Zombies," said Evan with a frown. "The necromancers use them as guards. They will attack if we get too close. See anything else?"

"No, I saw nothing else," replied Iriel. "But I only glanced into the cave quickly so I wouldn't be seen."

"Understood."

"What's the plan?" asked Brashani.

"Well, the simplest way to deal with zombies is to hack them to pieces."

"Ick," said Iriel again and scrunched her nose.

"I know," agreed Evan. "It's disgusting, but I don't want to be detained here. There are likely to be worse and more time-consuming things up ahead. So we charge in and engage them."

"I could fire bomb the room," offered Brashani.

The priest's face brightened. "That's a better idea. Let's start with that and engage whatever's left."

Brashani stepped forward to the spot in the passage he had seen Iriel use as a scouting position. He saw the zombies with their dull eyes with no pupils, the tattered clothes, and their pale — nearly white — skin. He lobbed three small red points of fire into the cave ahead of him, took a step back, and detonated each point. Fire exploded all around the mouth of the cave and enveloped the zombies. Brashani held up his hand and prevented the flames from swarming into the passage where he and his companions waited.

The flames burned for several minutes. When Brashani saw the zombies collapse, he extinguished the fire and waited for the flames to subside. Then he lowered his hand and examined the zombie remains. Charred flesh and broken bones littered the front of the cave entrance before him.

He turned back to the others and said, "All clear."

Evan and the others moved up and peered into the cave. As they did, the broken bones of the zombies started to fuse together.

Iriel's eyes bulged. "What is this?"

"The magic that's animating them is still at work," said Evan. "Looks like we'll have to fight them, after all."

Even as Evan spoke, a newly formed skeleton stood up and grabbed a torch from a nearby sconce. It approached them.

Evan stepped up, swung his sword, and broke off the arm with the torch. Using its fist, the skeleton caught Evan by the side of his arm. He stumbled to one side. Other skeletons were assembled now and approaching the others with torches. Daniel grabbed one and slammed it against the wall; it shattered like glass. James cracked his whip and broke his opponent's arm. Brashani hit a third skeleton with a jet of flame and blackened its rib cage. Iriel fired her bow, but the arrow hit the skeleton's hip and fell to the ground with no effect.

The skeleton fighting Evan turned to face him. Evan swung his sword and snapped a rib. In response, the skeleton swung at Evan again and missed.

Daniel pivoted on one foot and turned his attention to the skeleton Iriel had fired upon. He picked it up and threw the animated creature into the skeleton approaching James. Both skeletons broke apart into a pile of bones.

Brashani threw a fireball at his opponent. It dipped a little and then swung into the rib cage of the skeleton, where it exploded and sent shards of bone in all directions. One fragment hit James.

"Watch what you're doing," snapped the bard.

"Don't stand so close to my opponent next time," returned the wizard.

Evan took another swing at his assailant and severed the skeleton's head. The skeleton's frame continued to move forward and the headless creature swung at Evan again. Evan ducked. Daniel stepped up next to Evan and grabbed the skeleton's arm. Rotating on the ball of his right foot, Daniel rammed the monster's body against the wall; it splintered.

Evan surveyed the area of combat to see if the bones would reassemble, but they did not move. Satisfied they could proceed, Evan signaled to his comrades to proceed toward the rear of the cave. Upon reaching the back wall, they found a small opening. It was too small to walk through, however, and from what Evan could see, it led nowhere. Following the wall a few steps more, they found another exit. Turning to his companions, Evan asked, "Ready?"

"Yes," replied Daniel.

"All set," said the fire mage.

"Lead on," said James.

"I am," said Iriel.

Evan proceeded out of the cave and down another twisting passageway.

CHAPTER 30

THE PIT

As they followed the tunnel, the ground trembled. Dirt from the ceiling rained down on them in a fine spray.

"Is the volcano inactive?" asked James.

"I don't know," replied Evan. "I've heard there was a fire giant living at the base."

James gulped at the thought. "Yes, I've heard those stories; according to legend, he has a nasty temper but no one has ever seen him. He's supposed to be a myth."

"Let's hope he is," said Evan. "Dealing with a fire giant on top of everything else will be a bit much."

"Amen," said James.

They continued down the passage another forty strides when Brashani said, "Slow down, there's a trap around the next curve."

Evan slowed and peered around the bend in the path. Just ahead, he saw a deep pit. Its width filled the entire passage, and it was twenty strides across to the other side. He approached it with caution. Large, sharp, iron spikes were set in the bottom of the pit.

He waved the others forward. James and Brashani glanced into the pit and then turned back to face Evan.

"I don't think we can jump across," said Evan. "It's too far, especially with the added weight of our weapons and gear."

"We could climb down into the pit," said James.

"Perhaps," said Evan. "But we'd have to avoid the spikes and make sure they aren't coated with contact poison or something equally lethal."

"I can melt the spikes to make it easier," said Brashani. "That might burn off any poison or other substance they might be covered with."

"All right," agreed Evan. "That sounds like the best plan."

Brashani stepped up to the edge of the pit and sprayed the spikes along the left edge with fire. As flame touched the first spike, it erupted in a ball of fire that filled the pit and the passageway.

Without blinking, Brashani gestured, his hands positioned as if they held an invisible sphere in front of him. Instantly, the approaching flames halted and formed a large ball of fire. The wizard pressed on the invisible sphere and brought his hands closer together. The ball of flames responded, shrinking.

Brashani repeated the gesture until his hands touched and the sphere of fire shrank to the size of an orange. He squeezed one hand into a fist; the flame globe vanished, snuffed out and left only the faint acrid odor of charcoal.

The wizard turned and faced the others. "That was a surprise. They must have coated the spikes with oil. Not a trap, per se, but dangerous nonetheless."

"What happened to the spikes in the pit?" asked Evan.

Brashani glanced down behind him. "The heat of the fire has melted most of them. We should be able to get across now."

"Good," replied Evan. "Let's go."

* * *

Evan climbed into the pit and then helped Daniel and Iriel down. James and Brashani climbed down by themselves. They started across the pit and the ground shook again.

"This is starting to annoy me," said James.

"Just hope the shaking doesn't get any worse," said the wizard, "or we could be buried alive."

"Thanks for the cheery thought," returned the bard, sarcastically. "You're a real comfort."

They reached the other side of the pit and Evan pulled himself up and threw down a rope. James caught it.

"Daniel first. He's the lightest."

They tied the rope around Daniel and Evan pulled him up out of the pit.

They repeated the process for Iriel, with Evan and Daniel on the rope. Iriel's footing slipped more than once and it took James and Brashani pushing from underneath to get her out of the pit.

Evan threw the rope down for James. The bard climbed up with ease, as if he had done it all his life.

Evan smiled. "Part dwarf, are you?"

"No, just a good climber," replied the bard. "Spelunking in Rockborough has its advantages."

Finally, it was Brashani's turn. He did his best to climb up but, like Iriel, he had a hard time getting a good foothold; so in the end the others had to drag him out of the pit.

Once everyone was back in the passageway again, James said, "Let's rest a moment. That was hard work."

CHAPTER 31
CROSSING LAVA

They resumed their trek through the volcano after resting for a few minutes. The ground shook again. This time the left wall split open and a large chasm formed in front of them. Lava gushed into the opening, splashed against the side of the crevasse, and hit James and Daniel.

James screamed in pain as the magma seared his forearm through the gray sleeve of his tunic. Daniel felt a sting where the magma pocked the back of his right hand, but he did not cry out.

Evan watched the lava to see if it would exceed the confines of the fissure. When it appeared that it wouldn't, he turned to his companions and took out his first-aid kit.

"These aren't serious wounds, fortunately," noted Evan.

James winced. "But it hurts like a bee sting."

Iriel opened her pack. "I have a salve for burns."

"Let's use it on James. He's got the more serious wound," commented the priest.

Iriel pulled out a small round container from her pack. "Daniel, have you no pain?"

"No, I channeled the pain away," replied the teen.

"That's a *Qua'ril* technique, isn't it?" asked the bard.

Daniel nodded his head. "Yes. I control the pain and focus to stop the ache."

James stroked his chin thoughtfully. "Sounds like something everyone should learn."

Iriel opened the container to reveal a white cream. She applied it to James's burns and Evan wrapped the wounds with cotton gauze. Then, turning to Daniel, the priest took the teen's hand and covered the back of it with a bandage.

When Evan was done, Daniel flexed his hand.

"Something wrong?" asked the priest as he put away his first-aid kit.

"No, I'm just testing my hand's range of motion."

"The bandage shouldn't interfere too much."

"How long do I need to leave this on?"

"A few days, at least. I can apply a new bandage tomorrow."

Looking around, Evan saw Brashani standing by the edge of the gorge; he approached the mage.

"Know any way to get across?"

"Yes, I think so. I can cool the lava so that a strip of it hardens, essentially creating a bridge for us to walk across."

"Won't that act like a dam and cause the lava to overflow the chasm and flood this passageway?"

"It might. But I don't think we have any other options — unless you want to wait for the lava to cool on its own."

"No, I want to keep going."

"Thought so. Then I've given you your choices."

Evan ran his right hand through his hair. Neither option Brashani had outlined was ideal, and Evan did not want to risk everyone's safety in the interests of getting to Jormundan's workshop as quickly as possible. But the sad truth, Evan realized, was that risk was part of his job. He was always taking risks when confronting necromancers, and this time was no different … with one exception: his companions this time were not Michaeline knights or priests; they were civilians and unused to this type of danger. But given the options Brashani had proposed, there was really only one choice.

"All right," agreed Evan. "We'll try your plan. Let me know when you are ready."

* * *

Evan explained to the others what he and Brashani had discussed.

"Sounds dangerous," said James.

"It could be," conceded Evan. "But if we move across to the other side quickly, the lava shouldn't overflow the fissure. If I'm wrong, though, be prepared to run; we should be able to outpace the magma."

"And if other traps wait for us ahead?" asked Iriel.

"We'll face them and figure out something when we reach them."

James frowned. "I have to say, I'm not thrilled with this idea. We could die."

"That's true," Evan acknowledged. "But I don't see another way. If you've got any better ideas, I'll listen to them."

James shrugged. "Sorry, I don't."

Evan looked at Iriel. "I don't either," said the elf.

The priest gazed at Daniel. "I have no preference. I just want to reach Aure as soon as we can," the lad added.

"I understand, Daniel," said Evan, smiling. "We're doing the best we can."

"I know, but it feels as if we are moving in molasses."

Evan was about to respond when the wizard said, "I'm ready."

"All right," said Evan to the others. "Get ready. We'll proceed single file and go as quickly as we can until we reach the other side of the passageway."

Brashani concentrated, raised his arms, and then lowered them so that they were parallel with the river of molten rock. Evan watched and saw no change in the lava at first. Then the river's speed seemed to slow. A thin black line appeared on the surface of the lava. The line widened to form a crust, which hardened and solidified.

Evan looked at the fire mage. Perspiration covered his face. Through clenched teeth Brashani rasped, "Go!"

Instantly Evan bolted across the blacktopped lava. It didn't feel very sturdy, but it held his weight; for that he thanked St. Michael.

Daniel, Iriel, and James followed Evan over the magma, while Brashani moved slowly, lowering his arms completely as he began his journey atop the bridge he had created.

Evan reached the far side of the chasm and, as he did, he glanced at the lava. It was higher now, and rising. He turned back and saw James, Daniel, and Iriel approaching. Brashani, however, was only a portion of the way across and walking slowly. If he didn't start running soon, the lava would envelop him. Then Evan realized that Brashani probably couldn't maintain the spell and run at the same time. Perhaps giving thanks to a supreme power had been premature.

Iriel, James, and Daniel stepped off the magma crust. As they did, Evan pulled Iriel aside.

"You probably know more about fire magic than I," he said.

"I might, but I only studied the most basic fire spells."

"Am I right in guessing that if Brashani loses his concentration, his spell will collapse, the magma will soften, and he'll fall into the river of lava?"

"What you say is true if he breaks his concentration on his spell."

"Will the lava kill him?"

"I would think so."

"But you don't know for sure. As a fire mage, he might be able to withstand the heat of the lava or he might even be immune to the types of burns James and Daniel suffered."

"I've heard tales about fire mages being immune to fire. But won't the flow of the lava sweep him downstream and separate him from us?"

"Probably," replied Evan. "But he'd be alive and so would we. That might not be true if he maintains the spell much longer."

"But we'll need Magus Khumesh. Who knows what other obstacles are in front of us?" the elf pointed out.

"I realize that and I don't want to split us up, but there may not be any other way."

"But you are only guessing that the lava won't hurt him. If you are wrong, he could die."

"And if he maintains the spell much longer, we could all share that fate."

"Evan," cried James. "Look!" He pointed at Brashani.

The Michaeline priest followed James's finger. Out in the middle of the lava bridge, Brashani stood, wobbling, as if he were dizzy. The stress of maintaining the spell for so long appeared to be catching up to him. A portion of the bridge behind him broke away, and the force of the trapped lava behind the hardened magma swept it away.

Evan racked his brain trying to think of a way to help his friend, but before he could devise a plan, the remaining surface of the bridge became shiny and slick. At the same time, the section of the magma Brashani stood upon rose higher in the air so that it became a ramp, which the wizard promptly slid down. As the fire mage moved, the blackened lava broke up and only Brashani's momentum kept him ahead of the disintegrating stone.

James and Evan saw the wizard approaching fast and braced themselves to catch him. But it wasn't necessary: Brashani glided to a halt just before colliding into them.

"Did you do all that?" asked James.

"Yes," replied the fire mage, panting. He wiped sweat from his face. "I could feel myself losing control of the magic I used to hardened the lava and realized I needed a quick way to get across. So, I made the magma slick so I could slide across it and then elevated my end of the bridge to create a slide. It worked perfectly."

Evan smiled and clapped him on the back. "Nicely done. I was afraid you weren't going to make it across."

"Who, me?" asked the wizard. "It takes more than a little lava to slow me down."

"Well, let's move on," said Evan. "There's no telling how much farther we have to go and there's no point delaying here."

"Actually," said Brashani, still breathing hard. "If you could give me a moment, I'd appreciate it. Maintaining that spell was very draining."

"All right," said Evan. "Let me know when you are ready."

"You'll be the first to know."

CHAPTER 32
SWINGING SUCCESS

Brashani rested for ten minutes before standing up and stretching. "My bones ache," he said.

"I know the feeling," said Evan.

"Any chance of sleeping for a few hours?" Brashani asked.

"I'd love to oblige you, but we really need to keep going."

The wizard sighed. "More's the pity. But I figured you'd say something like that." He paused and stretched again. "Okay, I'm ready."

"Good. Do you have enough strength to resume detecting traps?"

"Yes, I think so."

"Then do it and let's move out."

They continued along the tunnel, which turned and twisted, first one way and then the other. A few times, Evan thought he was walking up an incline but he wasn't sure.

The passageway opened into a large cave. The cavern's floor was finished and smooth, made from the same stone as the cave walls. The ceiling was unfinished; stalactites hung down like round, blunt fangs. Directly opposite the entrance, on the far wall was an exit.

As they stepped into the cave, Brashani held up a hand and said, "Something's wrong here."

Evan stopped and put his arms out to either side to block the others behind him. "A trap?" he asked.

"Yes, I think so. Just up ahead. The floor is trapped somehow."

"Can you be more specific?"

"Hmmm. I wouldn't put weight on it."

"So we have to get across without walking on the floor."

"That seems to be the case."

James's face brightened. "I could swing across on a rope and see if there's a way to disarm the trap on the other side."

"And what will you attach the rope to?" asked Evan.

"One of those things." He pointed at the stalactites.

"Are you any good at throwing a grappling hook?"

"Actually, I am. As I told Iriel, I spent summers climbing the caves outside of Rockborough while I was training as a bard. That's how I got to be a good climber."

"How's the burn on your arm?"

"Fine. It still hurts, but it shouldn't be too much of a bother climbing rope."

"All right," agreed Evan. "Who has grappling hooks we can use?"

James raised his hand. "I do."

"I do, too," said Iriel.

"That's enough," said the priest. "But instead of swinging across, use the grappling hooks to climb across. We'll tie rope to each one. You'll have to throw one from here and then climb up, then throw the other one and swing over. The hard part will be pulling the first hook out of the rock so you can reuse it to repeat the process."

"It shouldn't be too hard," said James. "I've done this sort of thing before."

"Okay, the rest of us will wait in the tunnel. Once you are over the middle part of the floor, drop something on it. That should trigger the trap and make it safe for the rest of us."

* * *

James swung the grappling hook around a few times and let it go. It sailed through the air and lodged into the side of a thick stalactite. Testing the rope to see if it would hold him, James started climbing the rope. He went up twenty feet then took the other grappling hook and threw it at another stalactite deeper into the cave. It landed squarely at the base of the stone fang. James swung out on the second rope and pulled on the first rope. It wouldn't come free; James tried again as he swung back, pulling harder this time.

The hook came away and flew out of James's hands. It landed on the floor with a clank and, in the same instant, a volley of spears soared out from the walls along the sides of the cave, grazing James's legs in several places and tearing his trousers.

The bard broke out in a cold sweat as panic gripped him. He screamed.

Evan heard the grappling hook hit the floor, saw the spears crisscrossing the cave, and heard James's cry. Iriel rushed to stand beside Evan. Looking up, they both saw James holding on to the second rope. Concern played in the elf's eyes and her brow furrowed.

"Are you all right?" called Evan.

"I'm not sure, but I think so. Those spears startled me."

"Well, you can come down now," said Evan. "I think you've disarmed the trap."

CHAPTER 33
FEAR AND WIND

Evan confirmed with Brashani that the trap in the cave was no longer a threat and James climbed down. The bard freed the second grappling hook from the cavern's ceiling and handed it to Iriel. After putting his climbing gear away, James examined his legs and clothes. Red scratches covered his calves. They didn't hurt but they were sore to the touch.

"Look at me. The ends of my trousers are all ripped and my tunic has burn marks from the lava earlier. It looks like I've been in a fight." He shook his head. "I'm going to need a new uniform to perform in when we get back to Clearbrook."

Evan smirked. "Let's hope that's our worst problem for the next few hours."

James looked at him, realizing that ripped clothes were a petty concern at the moment. He blushed a little and went silent.

They continued on, out through the exit and down another narrow tunnel.

The passage turned right and then immediately left and widened into a cavern. Wind howled through the space like a tortured dog and Evan felt the first stabs of fear. He speculated: *Is there a banshee living here?*

"I sense magic," said Iriel.

"I feel it too," said Brashani.

"That explains the fear," commented Evan.

The wizard glanced about the roof of the cave. "And the wind too. How else would the air howl? I don't see any opening to the outside."

"Regardless, Fear magic will be difficult to overcome," noted the priest. "Can you remove it?"

Brashani tensed a few stiff muscles and then relaxed them. He sighed. "Not right now. I'm still pretty weak."

Daniel stepped up. "Let me go. I'm not afraid."

"You're not?" queried Evan, raising an eyebrow.

"No. It's like the lava burn; all I need to do is focus on walking through the cave and control my fear."

Evan considered this for a moment. "All right. We'll tie a rope around you that the rest of us can follow."

"We should put wax or cotton in our ears too to block the sound of the wind," said James. "That may help."

"Good idea," said Evan. "There's cotton in my first-aid kit."

* * *

They secured a rope around Daniel's waist and put cotton in his ears. Calling on his training as a *Qua'ril* master, Daniel closed his eyes to meditate. A minute later, when he could feel inner peace beginning to grow within him, Daniel opened his eyes, bowed to everyone, and then started across the cavern.

His progress was slow; he had not gone more than a few steps when the wind intensified, which forced him back. Daniel stood still and fought the wind. He remembered the trial by air he had endured to become a *Qua'ril* master. It had been very much like this experience except it had not been in a cave, just a special grove in the forest.

He thought about his goal and reminded himself that Aure needed him. His fear melted away like thin ice on a warm spring day. He took a step forward. Then another. Slowly he trudged across the cavern to the other side.

* * *

Evan watched the rope uncoil and fastened another section of cord to it. After a few minutes, it stopped moving and Evan assumed it was time to follow after their comrade.

Giving the others some cotton for their ears, he said, "Try to ignore anything you see or feel. Just follow the rope until you reach Daniel."

They put the cotton in their ears, took hold of the rope, and set out.

The wind picked up strength a few feet from the entrance and with it came fear, an unbridled urge to flee from the scene back the way they had come. Evan fought it with all of his being. He prayed to St. Michael for guidance and protection. He chanted a verse of scripture to himself and slowly the fear became more tolerable.

He turned to see how the others were doing. James was helping Iriel, who did not want to go any further. Tears stained her cheeks and ran down her face.

"James, take me home! I can't go forward. I just can't!"

James saw Iriel's distress and removed the cotton from one ear.

"James," Iriel repeated. "Please, I can't go forward."

"You must. Daniel needs us."

"I know, but I can't help him now. I'm too scared."

"Nonsense. You are one of the bravest women I know. Fight it. Use your *Qua'ril* training. It got Daniel through this, maybe it can help you."

"My training. Yes. I had not thought of that … I will try," said Iriel.

James waited a few seconds and Iriel began to move forward again. He followed her, ignoring the thought that if he delayed, he would lose Iriel forever.

Brashani followed up behind. Fear raked at him. He was sure that the necromancers from Irenrhod had found him and it was time to run again. Maybe he should find a bottle of ale and hide somewhere. Then his old confidence resurfaced and he realized that drinking was not the answer. He had come to kick their asses and he was prepared to walk into a necromancer's workshop and do whatever he needed to do to stop them. He smiled and his fear faded. "I will have my old life back," he murmured, "or die trying."

It took several more minutes for the group to cross the cavern and find Daniel. When they did, the fear, the wind, and the howling faded away.

Iriel kissed James. "Thank you for helping me. I was afraid you might leave me to fend for myself."

"The thought crossed my mind, but then I remembered how much I love you." He kissed her.

Evan cleared his throat. Everyone looked at him. "Well done, everyone. That was a particularly hard obstacle to get past. We must be getting close to the workshop. So be ready and stay alert."

CHAPTER 34
SNORRI FLAMETONGUE

They continued down the passageway and followed the bends and curves of the tunnel. After several turns, the passage opened into another cave with a high ceiling. Evan expected some sort of trap.

"Sense any trouble ahead?" he asked Brashani.

"No, nothing," replied the wizard.

Nonetheless, the Michaeline priest signaled a halt and stood listening. In the distance, he heard water dripping and felt a presence of some sort.

The ground shook. "That wasn't the volcano," observed Evan. "Something caused the cave to shake. Iriel, do you hear anything?"

"I do," replied Iriel. "I hear someone breathing. Over there." She pointed to the right.

"All right. Scout that section of the cave and stay hidden."

Iriel disappeared for a few minutes among the rocks and stone debris in the cave and then returned.

"There's a large child chewing on some bones on the other side of the cave."

"Describe him," said Evan.

"He's tall, like an ogre, big and muscular, but his skin looks like bronze, and his hair looks like fire."

"That sounds more like a fire giant," commented James.

"Yes," agreed Evan. "And fire giants have children."

Everyone looked at him. "But if that's the child of the fire giant," Brashani began, "what's he doing here?"

"Good question," replied Evan. "I'd also like to know where the child's mother is. If she's anywhere nearby, she might come after us if she thinks we are threatening her youngling."

"And if he's lost?" asked Iriel.

"Then there's not much we can do about it. None of us can tolerate the heat of the volcano to lead him back to his home."

Iriel frowned. "But we can't leave him here."

"Well, we can't take him with us, can we?"

The ground shook again and the sound of something sniffing the air could be heard. The child giant stood and Evan saw him just as Iriel had described him. Three times Evan's height, the child's eyes were scarlet; his teeth were yellow and crooked, and his face looked round and soft like that of a babe. He wore trousers made from animal hides and no shirt.

"Who's there?" the giant asked, looking about.

Evan put a finger to his lips and motioned the others to hide behind some nearby boulders.

The giant sniffed the air again. "I smell an elf, and a human boy, and a man." Another sniff. "And a magic-man, and ..." *Sniff.* "Something else." He raised a large club and struck the ground. The entire cave shook. "Where are you?"

Evan crouched behind an outcrop of rocks with Brashani beside him.

"He's looking for you," whispered the mage.

"I know, but I doubt showing myself will help. If it would, I'd do it. On the other hand, I could create a diversion so the rest of you could get away."

"Don't be silly," said Brashani. "The giant is as likely to eat you as look at you, and if we run into necromancers up ahead, we're going to need you."

"True," Evan agreed. "But we aren't going anywhere with this giant looking for me, and we really can't afford this delay. Plus, if we don't stop him from shaking the cave, his mother is likely to come running. Then we'll have two giants to deal with instead of one."

"Maybe we can sneak away."

"It's worth a try," said Evan.

Gesturing to James and the others to be quiet, Evan motioned the direction for them to go. The group moved as quietly as they could. They crept along for a few steps before Evan's foot kicked some pebbles that went skittering across the cave floor. The Michaeline priest froze, hoping the giant had not heard the noise. But even as Evan wished for the best, he heard the giant say, "There you are."

Evan looked up and saw a huge hand coming toward him. He swung his sword but the giant caught it and grabbed the priest around his chest. Lifting Evan off the ground, the giant sniffed his catch.

"You are what I've been smelling." *Sniff.* "What are you?" asked the giant.

"I'm a man," replied Evan.

"You don't smell like a man."

"What do I smell like?"

The giant sniffed Evan again. "I don't know." He paused. "Medicine. I don't like medicine. It tastes bad and screws up your face. Maybe I should crush you." The giant began to tighten his fist and Evan found it hard to breathe.

"But I look like a man, don't I?"

"I s'pose, but you could be trying to trick me."

"Why would I do that?"

"Maybe you are mean."

"But I'm not. I'm a priest. I help others."

"Says you."

Evan did not seem to be getting anywhere. He had hoped that reasoning with the child would resolve the potential conflict, but the giant was having none of it. He appeared to have taken a dislike to Evan for some reason; the priest would have to try a different approach.

On the ground, Iriel shot arrows at the giant. They lodged in his shin and after a few minutes the giant brushed them away with a sweep of his free hand.

James cracked his whip and lashed the giant's foot. The giant responded by using his other foot to rub the spot struck by the whip.

Daniel studied the giant for several minutes and then sighed. "He's too big," he said softly. "*Qua'ril* requires the combatants to be about the same size so that leverage can be applied and the opponent's momentum can be turned against him."

"Do the best you can, lad," urged Brashani, holding out his right hand where a small ball of fire was growing.

The giant squeezed Evan again when a voice from the right side of the cave called out.

"Snorri! Snorri Flametongue. Where are you?"

The child said nothing.

"Snorri, answer me this minute or so help me, I'll whip your hide when I get my hands on you."

The child sighed and looked for a place to put Evan, but the animal-hide trousers the giant wore had no pockets.

"Snorri! There you are."

Snorri turned around to face his mother, instinctively hiding Evan behind his back. Evan only got a quick look at the giantess; she was slightly taller than her son but had the same eyes, hair, and skin coloring. She wore a one-piece dress made from animal hides. Her eyes narrowed and her mouth was twisted in a snarl as she regarded Snorri. She marched right up to him.

Snorri forgot about Evan momentarily and the giant's grasp eased enough for the demon hunter to get one hand free. He waved to his companions and gestured for a rope.

"What are you doing out here?" demanded Snorri's mother. Then she saw the cracked bones he had been chewing on. "Snacking between meals? What am I going to do with you? Wait 'til I tell your father. He'll blow the roof right off this mountain."

Snorri said nothing, but cast mournful glances at the stone floor.

James, meanwhile, tossed Evan a rope. Evan caught it and tied it around one of Snorri's fingers. Then he threw his sword to Iriel, who caught it with one hand. Slowly Evan wiggled out of Snorri's grip and started climbing down the rope.

Snorri's mother shook her head. "Why do you insist on making trouble for yourself?" No answer. Then she noticed he was hiding something behind his back.

"And what have you got in your hands?"

Snorri looked up. "Nuffin'."

"Don't lie to me."

"I swear. I got nuffin' in my hands."

"Then show me. Put your hands where I can see them."

Snorri hesitated, for which Evan was grateful. He had climbed down almost the entire length of rope, but now hearing this exchange, he decided to jump the rest of the way.

"Snorri! Show me your hands now!"

Snorri complied just as Evan jumped. The Michaeline priest rolled as he landed to minimize the impact.

Snorri showed his mother his hands.

"What's that piece of string on your finger for?"

Snorri looked at it and scratched his head.

"Well?" prodded Snorri's mother.

He shrugged. "I don't know."

"You tied a string on your finger for no reason?"

"No, I d'int."

"Then who did? A cave fairy?"

Snorri didn't answer immediately, but his eyes grew round and he looked at his mother.

"There's elfs and humans here," he whispered. "I caught one, but he is tricketty and escaped."

His mother looked around at the floor then back at Snorri.

"Even if there are elves and humans in the cave, you can't go snatching them up."

"Why not?"

"Well, for one thing, you know how your father and I feel about pets. You're not old enough to have one."

"I don't want 'em as pets. Just to eat."

His mother shook her head. "Not worth the trouble, dear. They are mostly bone unless you find a really fat one. That's why your father hunts ogres, rocs, and hippogriffs. Much more meat there. Now come along and untie that string."

Snorri untied the rope and let it fall. Then, with his head hanging low, he marched off to the right side of the cave, his mother close behind.

CHAPTER 35
FLYING KEYS

Evan and the others did not move until they were sure the giants were gone. When he was certain it was safe, Evan stood up and brushed himself off.

James walked up to the priest and gathered the rope he had thrown. "This is one for the books. I've never seen a giant up close before. It will make a terrific tale."

"I'm sure it will," agreed Evan. "But let's get what we came for first and go home."

"Of course," said the bard.

"Are you hurt?" asked Iriel.

Evan patted himself down, and flexed his arms and legs. "No, I don't think so," he said at last. "But my ribs will be sore for awhile."

Brashani nudged James "You think that giant was something? I once fought a fire elemental."

"Really?" James's eyes narrowed and he slid his jaw to one side. "Or are you pulling my leg?"

"It's the truth. It was guarding a shipment of items tainted with dark magic. I had to fight the thing and then deal with the criminals that had summoned it in the first place."

"I'd love to get those details for a tale some time."

"Okay. Maybe after St. Sebastian's week ends."

* * *

They continued walking through the cave for a few minutes until Evan finally spied the exit. As they left the cavern, they stepped into a hallway of finished stone, wide enough for two people to walk abreast. The corridor had a ceiling of average height and went straight for forty strides, with a door at the end.

"The workshop could be behind this door," said Evan. "So look sharp, everyone. Are there any traps on the door, Brashani?"

"No, I don't sense anything special."

"Good." Evan cracked the door open and peered inside. The room had an eerie, dim light.

"Something's moving inside," said Iriel softly. "I can hear it."

Hazarding a more substantial look, Evan poked his head into the room. At first, the chamber appeared to be empty; on the far wall was another door. Then something whisked by him. He followed the motion and saw an odd bit of metal flying through the air. It was roughly cylindrical and about a quarter of an inch wide and half an inch tall. A metal wire, eighteen inches long, ran from the top to the bottom of the cylinder to form a large, crude handle.

Evan saw no purpose for the handle since the metal cylinder flew so fast it was nearly impossible to catch. The cylinder arced up toward the ceiling, stopped, and hovered in the air. Next to it were five more metal cylinders with similar handles. They hung in the air for a few minutes, then one dipped down and flew around the room, eventually returning to its starting position.

Pushing the door open, Evan waved everyone forward. The metal cylinders seemed harmless enough, which concerned him. So far, the necromancers had employed obstacles that were designed to deter the curious, with the obvious exception of the weight trap in the cave; those spears had been meant to kill. So, were these metal cylinders harmful or simply a deterrent of some sort? Evan didn't see how they could be either. He ran his right hand through his hair and watched the flying objects for a moment.

James, Iriel, and Brashani also stared at the metal bits suspended in the air. Daniel ignored them and continued toward the door on the far wall.

"Are they harmful?" asked Evan as he turned to Brashani.

"No," replied the wizard, after a moment. "I don't think so. I can't be sure without a full analysis, which I don't quite have the strength for, but I'm not sensing any traps."

Evan scratched his head. "All right, then let's take a look at the other door."

As they approached the far end of the room, Daniel said, "The door's locked."

Brashani stepped up. "I might be able to unlock it magically. I think I have enough strength now for that."

"Good," said Evan. "Try it."

Brashani placed his hands on the door and concentrated. After a few seconds, he lowered his hands and stepped back from the door.

"How ingenious," said the wizard.

"What is?" asked James.

"The magic in this room."

"I don't follow," said Evan.

"Well, obviously the metal cylinders flying about are part of a spell. The door is locked magically, too."

"So how is that ingenious?"

"They are both part of the same spell."

Evan glanced at the door and then at the ceiling. "Does the door have a keyhole?"

"Yes," said Daniel. "But we have no key for it."

Brashani smiled and pointed to the metal cylinders suspended in the air. "Yes, we do."

Daniel's eyes grew round as he realized what the wizard was suggesting.

"You think you can make a key out of those bits of flying metal and open the door?" asked James.

"If we can catch them, yes," responded the fire mage.

"Exactly what I was thinking," said Evan.

"How do we capture them?" inquired Iriel.

"Wait until they fly by," suggested James.

Evan shook his head. "They move too fast. I doubt any of us can snatch them out of the air unless someone has a net."

No one spoke up and Evan took the silence as confirmation of his assumption.

"I could shoot an arrow through the space between the cylinder and the metal wire. If we tie a rope to it, we should be able to pull on the rope and capture it," Iriel suggested.

Evan tapped his right forefinger against his lips while his mind was deep in thought. "Yes, that seems like a possibility. I'm guessing it will be like bringing down a kite on a windy day, but if James and Daniel help me, we should be able to manage. Let's try it."

CHAPTER 36
INTO THE NECROMANCER'S LAIR

They tied several pieces of rope together, fastening one end to an arrow. Iriel loaded her bow and waited for a metal cylinder to swoop down. As soon as one of the cylinders moved, she followed it briefly and then fired. The arrow went through the space between the cylinder and the wire and fell to the ground, threading the rope through the opening.

Evan pulled on the cord. The cylinder changed direction temporarily; but it quickly adjusted to Evan's interference and resumed its original flight path.

He tugged on the line again and said to James and Daniel, "Help me bring it down." They ran over. All three yanked on the rope and slowly forced it to the ground. The cylinder finally stopped fighting them when it touched the floor.

Evan ran up to the metal flotsam and took a closer look. The cylinder had a pin at one end and a matching notch on the other.

Brashani had been right; it should be possible to assemble the object by fitting one piece into another.

Iriel retrieved her arrow and got ready to fire again. Another piece of the key came flying across the chamber. The elf aimed and fired. The arrow sailed through the air carrying the rope with it, but missed the target.

"This one is moving faster," said Iriel. "I'll have to track it as if I were hunting deer."

She tried again; this time she anticipated the motion of the cylinder and when it was in position, she fired. The arrow and rope sailed through the handle. Immediately Evan, Daniel, and James pulled on the rope. The cylinder fought back harder, but they slowly managed to reel it in.

By the time Iriel aimed at the fourth cylinder, it was speeding through the air too fast for Iriel to follow it. She tracked it, fired, and missed. She tried again and missed again.

"It's moving too fast," she said.

"Know any magic to slow the cylinders down?" Evan asked Brashani.

"Hmmm," said the fire mage, "not exactly. I could thicken the air. That should make it harder for the cylinders to fly."

"Thicken the air? How?" Evan asked.

"By absorbing heat."

"That thickens the air?"

"Yes, I saw it done once years ago. Before the air even thickens though, frost should form on the cylinders, which should affect their ability to fly."

"Will it affect the air we're breathing?"

"I don't think so. I should be able to contain the effect."

"All right, try it."

Brashani closed his eyes and gestured with his hands. Nothing seemed to happen for several minutes; the cylinders kept zipping through the air too fast for Iriel to follow them.

"It's hopeless," Iriel said. She shook her head and placed her arrow back in her quiver.

"Look," James said, as he pointed.

Evan glanced in the direction that James indicated and saw frost forming on the walls along the room's ceiling. He looked at the cylinders; they had frost on them too.

"Try again," said Evan.

"All right," Iriel sighed. She pulled an arrow out, aimed, and followed the flying metal. She fired; the arrow hit the edge of the handle and bounced through the loop. Evan, James, and Daniel pounced on the rope. The cylinder fought back hard, yanking the rope out of James's hand at least once. Evan, too, almost lost his grip. Daniel felt the rope dig into his hands, but he focused on holding the cord tightly and controlled the pain. After struggling with the rope for about a minute, the cylinder was close enough for Evan to reach out and grab it.

Encouraged, Iriel tried again and succeeded on the first shot. Bringing down this bit of metal was easier, and soon Iriel aimed at the one remaining cylinder. It was more like a vibrating snowball hanging in the air, as if trying to move but unable to.

She loaded an arrow into her bow and released it. The arrowhead buried itself in the frost around the cylinder. Evan, Daniel, and James pulled on the rope and the snowball crashed to the ground.

"You can stop your spell, Brashani," said Evan.

The wizard opened his eyes and lowered his arms, then wiped sweat from his face. "Good. Give me a minute to cool off too."

They waited for the frost on the metal bits to melt and for Brashani to cool down before they tried to assemble the parts. One of the pieces was clearly the part that would be inserted into the lock to open the door. Another piece had a flat circular end; it was the key's head, used to turn it in the lock. The remaining four pieces made up the shaft of the key.

As they started to put the pieces together, they found that each piece fit only a specific pin or notch. So, it took a few minutes and several attempts to determine the exact order in which the pieces fit. But once they had assembled the key correctly, it shimmered and fused together into a solid single object.

Evan put the key into the lock of the door and tried to turn it. It wouldn't move. He struggled and tried again. Slowly, it yielded … until he finally heard a click and the door opened just enough to see inside.

The chamber beyond the door was large like the audience hall of a king or duke. The air smelled stale and musty.

Evan opened the door wider. The walls were rough-hewn stone and the Michaeline priest saw no windows, only small rocks set into the ceiling every few inches glowing with a soft warm light. *Stones enchanted with Light magic*, thought Evan.

Along the left and right walls hung long wooden shelves holding old leather-bound tomes covered in dust. Three long tables filled much of the chamber. One table stood along the left wall and another along the right wall. The third table was at the far end of the chamber, perpendicular to the others. On the tables to Evan's left and right, potions boiled or dripped into glass vials from copper tubing.

The floor was dusty and hard, as if sand had been thrown over a stone floor. To Evan's right was a portal stone identical to the one that had brought him and his companions to the Fire Mountains.

Finally, a way home, he thought.

He moved into the room and doused his torch; the others followed behind him and extinguished their torches too.

Brashani gazed around the room and whistled softly in amazement. "Maybe I was wrong. Maybe they do have endless resources. Look at all this stuff."

"Yes, and any of it could be dangerous," replied Evan. "So let's remember why we are here and what we are after. Touch nothing unless you have to."

"Fine by me," said Brashani.

"To start, are there any traps, magical or otherwise, that we need to avoid?"

Brashani scanned the room, careful not to touch anything on the tables or the bookshelves. After a minute he said, "No, I don't see anything."

"Good," said Evan. He turned to Daniel. "Do you sense the gem?"

"No," Daniel answered, sullenly.

"Okay, well, lets see what's on the far table and examine the other two tables as we go. With luck, it is here and we'll find it. If we can't find it, we'll wait for someone to show up and interrogate him or her about it."

* * *

They moved cautiously up the chamber to the table at the front of the room. As he scanned the paraphernalia on the tables to the left and right of him, Evan saw a wide assortment of copper tubing and liquids of every imaginable color in flasks bubbling away without the benefit of fire. The flasks and tubing were held in place by metal clips attached to a wooden frame. Evan counted at least twenty work areas of flasks and wooden frames on the tables and realized the necromancers were working with alchemists on a grand scale. He would have destroyed them all but he knew that mixing strange potions together could be dangerous; the resulting concoction could easily explode, killing them all. Best to ignore the potions for now. He could always come back and deal with them later.

About halfway up along both walls were two portal stones. They each had the same seven-pointed star, similar to the one Evan had used, but on these stones the star was white and the ceramic dark green.

Evan could see, as he drew near the front table, that it was covered with various articles of clothing and weaponry. Cloaks, gloves, boots, shields, swords, and helmets of different styles were spread out. James reached out to turn over a pair of gloves when Evan put his arm out to block him.

"Let's have Brashani examine these first," said the priest.

"I can't do a detailed analysis of each item," said the wizard. "It would take hours and I don't have the strength."

"Understood," said Evan. "But these are all magical, right?"

Brashani concentrated for a moment before responding, "Yes, and that helmet ..." He pointed. "... is particularly strong."

Evan looked at it. The helmet was cylindrical with a thin metal strip, like the fin of a great shark, running from the top of the headpiece down the back. Set into the helmet at the top, just under the metal fin, was a small, perfectly round topaz. It looked like a dark mustard marble.

Daniel's heart jumped when he saw the stone.

Aure? he thought, but got no reply. His lower lip quivered.

"That gem looks like Tindolen's," said Evan. "Is there anything else on the table with a gem set into it?"

Everyone looked, and after a few minutes, they all shook their heads, seemingly in unison.

"There doesn't appear to be," said Brashani.

"I don't see one," said James.

"No," said Iriel.

"Brashani, examine the helmet carefully. Is it safe to take?"

The wizard gazed at the helmet; he looked away and blinked several times after about minute, as if he had been staring at a bright, intense light. "Amazing," he said. "The helmet is being powered by the gem. Somehow, they've tapped the power of an *Aglari* and used that power to create a magical helmet. It's one of the most incredible adaptations of one item into another I've ever seen."

"Is it safe to take?" Evan repeated.

"Yes, I think so."

"And you're sure this gem is an *Aglari*?"

"Absolutely. The power level alone gives it away. So does the cut of the gem. It is perfectly spherical. No other gems are cut like that."

"Why doesn't it talk to me?" asked Daniel.

"The enchantment on the gem prevents it. That's why you suddenly lost the signal. The thief had to get the gem back here so that the gem could be enchanted."

"Can we remove the enchantment?"

"I don't know," replied Brashani.

"We'll need to deal with that later," said Evan. "Right now, let's take it and get moving."

Daniel grabbed the helmet and tried to pull the gem off. It wouldn't budge.

Evan prodded the lad forward, but he didn't move. "Time for that later, Daniel. We need to leave now. Before anyone shows up."

The others agreed and began to move toward the back of the room. Evan waited with Daniel.

"Daniel, please," Evan said. "We must be going. There will be time to figure out how to remove the gem from the helmet on the way back to Clearbrook."

"And if we can't?" asked Daniel.

"Then there's no point waiting here to be caught."

Daniel sighed and nodded slowly. He ran after James and Iriel; Evan followed.

* * *

Daniel stepped out of the shack and looked around. The swamp looked much the same as it had before. By the sun's position in the sky, he could tell it was past midday but otherwise nothing else had changed. As he examined the flying basket, Daniel noticed that the canvas bag had deflated completely and the basket had sunk into the mud a little more. He doubted the basket would fly again but that was of little concern. They would find another way home. Perhaps they could take the sailor's ship.

Daniel looked down at the helmet and pulled on the topaz stuck to the front of it. It didn't move. *How am I ever going to free Aure?* he wondered.

Iriel came out of the shack. Her intense gaze softened and she gave Daniel a little smile.

"The gem could be attached magically," she said. "Pulling on it will not detach it."

Daniel looked at her. "But I've got to free Aure."

"We will. Magus Khumesh might be able to dispel the enchantment that was used."

Daniel sighed and waited for the others. James strode out of the shack a second later, followed by Brashani. They waited a few seconds for Evan, but he did not appear.

"Where's Father Evan?" asked Iriel with concern.

James pursed his lips in thought. "Maybe he found something important to take back with him."

The elf nodded her head. "That might be."

"Give him another minute," said Brashani. "If he's not back by then, Iriel, we'll both go back for him."

"How can you?" asked James. "The portal stone won't take you back to the work room and it will take too long to go through all those caves again."

"Now that we've used the portal stone to come back here, it should know who we are and allow us to go directly to the work room," Brashani explained.

"It had better," said Iriel. "Father Evan could be in big trouble."

CHAPTER 37

SHOWDOWN

Standing next to the yellow portal stone, Evan watched Brashani disappear. He was relieved his companions had returned to the swamp and took the gem with them. Hopefully, they were safe and they would get back to Clearbrook in the same condition. With luck, they would find a way to free the topaz from the helmet so that they could return it to Tindolen.

The Michaeline priest sheathed his sword and was about to step onto the portal stone when he heard a noise behind him. His eyes widened with surprise as a bald man stepped from the green portal stone that was halfway down the wall behind him. The man wore black boots and a workman's trousers and tunic.

Evan recognized him immediately. "Jormundan!" the priest rasped.

The bald man looked up at the sound of his name and saw Evan. The dark mage's brown eyes widened then narrowed. His mouth became a sneer. He raised his arms and stared intensely at the demon hunter.

Evan started to draw his sword as he ran toward his opponent. After only two steps, a wave of pain wracked his body. Evan stumbled and caught himself on a table.

Pain stabbed at him again, more intensely this time. Evan dropped his sword and collapsed. Every nerve was on fire. He had never felt anything like this before.

"Die, Michaeline scum," screamed Jormundan.

Tears welled up in Evan's eyes. He wanted to scream, but he wouldn't give Jormundan the satisfaction. The pain increased. Evan felt his legs go numb and then his arms. He was helpless.

Jormundan slowly moved closer. He had expected the priest to scream. *Stupid pride*, Jormundan thought. "Beg," he said to Evan. "Beg for death."

"Go to Hell," Evan choked out. His mouth was becoming numb, too.

Jormundan laughed. "I've been there and back. The great dark lord, Zortan, restored me and gave me knowledge and power to serve him. And now I shall by killing you in his name. You will serve him and know agony for eternity."

Evan didn't answer. There was no need. His power and support came from His Grace and ultimately from God and St. Michael. If Jormundan destroyed his physical body, Evan would ascend to Heaven and rest, having served St. Michael long and well. He would never serve Jormundan's master. Never.

Jormundan ended his spell and drew a dagger. Evan heard him mumble a few words and saw him place his hand on the dagger's blade. It glowed a sickly red, and a slow evil grin spread across Jormundan's face. He approached Evan and stepped over him. Lifting Evan's torso, Jormundan crouched and put the blade to Evan's throat.

Evan braced himself for the death stroke.

It didn't come.

Evan heard Jormundan cry out in pain as his weapon clattered to the floor. The wizard looked at his arm and saw an arrow shaft piercing his forearm. He turned and stood; Evan dropped to the ground. Iriel stood by the yellow portal stone. She had another arrow loaded into her bow.

"Move and you die," she said. Jormundan froze.

Brashani suddenly appeared next to Iriel, his hands raised and ready to cast a spell. Instantly he recognized the necromancer.

"Jormundan? This is a surprise," said Brashani.

The necromancer raised an eyebrow. "Do I know you?"

"I doubt you'd remember me. I was an investigator for the town guard back in Marngol trying to shut down your business in items tainted with dark magic."

Jormundan thought for a moment and then smiled with recognition in his eyes. "I remember you. You're that mage who tried to raid our warehouse, who killed our fire elemental, and set the warehouse aflame."

"You remember me," the fire mage said with sarcasm. "I am touched." He clasped his hands over his heart.

"Burned off all my hair, too."

"A shame," replied Brashani in a mocking tone. "I see it still hasn't grown back. Tsk, tsk."

Jormundan glared at him. Iriel signaled with her bow and arrow as Jormundan started to stand. At Iriel's motion, he froze again.

"Nice and slow," said the elf. "And keep your hands where I can see them."

Jormundan stood slowly, his hands at his side.

Evan, meantime, began to feel strength return to his arms and legs. He had heard Brashani's conversation. *Keep him distracted,*

Brashani, he thought, *I need the time to recover.* He wiggled his fingers, rotated his hands at the wrist, and tensed and relaxed his arms a bit to get the feeling back in them. As he moved his right hand, he felt the hilt of Jormundan's dagger next to it. He grabbed it.

"You can't stop me with a bow and arrow," Jormundan said to Iriel. This time it was his turn to mock. "Because even if you kill me, I will be reborn."

"I don't think so," said Iriel. "I have special arrows that negate Rebirth magic."

Jormundan's eyes shifted from side to side. "You're bluffing." He smiled.

Gritting her teeth, Iriel said, "Try me." Her voice was hard and Jormundan's smile faded.

"I'll tie him up," Brashani said and produced a coil of rope from his pack.

Jormundan made a sudden pushing gesture with both hands and Brashani and Iriel were forced back against the wall, unable to move.

Evan heard Iriel cry out. He moved, and pain shot through him again. Gnashing his teeth and anticipating the pain, Evan struggled to stand.

Jormundan heard a noise behind him and turned. His eyes widened and his brow furrowed as he saw the demon hunter on his feet.

Evan, dagger in hand, lunged at Jormundan before the wizard could react. The blade impaled the necromancer, and he staggered back.

Collapsing from the exertion, Evan gasped, "I'm spent."

Jormundan saw a dark stain envelop his chest. His eyes grew round; he shrieked in agony and aged visibly in a matter of seconds. His skin fell away from his frame and his skeleton turned to dust before it collapsed onto the floor.

Brashani could barely watch the transformation, but forced himself so he would have a reminder that the power of necromancy was not something to trifle with.

Iriel couldn't watch and closed her eyes when Jormundan screamed. She only knew the event was over when she felt the force that held her against the wall vanish. Opening her eyes, she saw the wizard's bones dissolve to dust. Her stomach heaved, but she forced the vomit back down and raced over to Evan.

"How do you feel?" she asked.

"Awful," replied Evan, with a grimace. "I ache in places I didn't even know I had. But I'll recover."

"What happened to Jormundan?" the elf inquired.

"I don't know. I used the blade he had prepared for me. He enchanted it with some kind of magic; I can only hope that it was deadly enough to stop even him."

"It was," declared Brashani, stepping away from the wall. "Judging by the effect, I'd say his soul was eaten."

Iriel held her stomach again. It churned, but it did not heave. "Ick," she said, scrunching up her face.

Evan agreed. It was an awful way to die but he had no remorse for Jormundan. He deserved it. "Let's go home," he said. "We have a gem to return."

CHAPTER 38
THE WAY HOME

Evan stepped out of the shack, moving awkwardly and wincing in pain every few steps.

James ran over to take his arm and steady him. "What happened to you? You've got dust all over your clothes and you look awful."

The priest smiled weakly, as pain mixed with the sudden absurdity of the situation. "I met an old friend."

James looked at him blankly. "Did I miss the joke?"

Evan shook his head. "No, sorry. I'm just a little punchy." He paused to collect himself and then said, "It's a long story. I'll tell you on the way back to Clearbrook."

Iriel came out of the shack and saw Evan. She smiled, then looked around for Daniel. She spotted him sitting on the bow of the sailboat. Her grin deepened.

"Why do you sit up there?" she asked.

"I wanted to meditate ... and wait for you all out of the mud."

She noticed the ship was no longer resting on its side; it was now sitting levelly in the mud.

Brashani strode into the swamp.

Seeing the wizard arrive, Iriel turned to Evan. "I would think we can leave."

Evan tilted his head and smiled. "I'm more than ready."

Iriel glanced up at the sailboat again. "Daniel, climb into the basket. We will fly it home."

"I don't think the basket will fly again," said Daniel.

"Why not?"

Daniel pointed. "Look at it."

She looked. The canvas bag was deflated and half the basket had sunk into the mud.

"He's right," agreed Evan. "Anyone know how to sail a boat?"

Brashani shook his head.

"I do not," said Iriel. "But Ebalin is our prisoner. We could force him to help us, or he might even help willingly."

Evan frowned. "He might, but I'm in no mood to make a deal with him. He committed a crime; now he must answer for it."

"I can't sail a boat," said James, "but I know how these boats work. There are many old elven tales about flying ships and sailing them is easy. You sit at the helm and steer with the rudder."

"All right, then," said Evan, smiling. "Everyone get aboard. We're going home."

* * *

The sailboat was a single-mast vessel with a triangular sail. A small seat was positioned aft and behind it was a lever, which moved horizontally to operate the rudder. In front of the seat was the helm and steering wheel of the craft. Along the port and starboard sides of the ship were low wooden benches.

James took the helm and sat down. Evan dusted himself off and sat directly in front of the helm on the starboard side; Iriel sat opposite Evan on the port side. Daniel and Brashani sat near the bow of the ship.

Ebalin was in the bottom of the boat still tied up, although the bonds around his hands were a little looser than before. Evan tightened them again and placed him next to Iriel.

"Watch him," he said. "If he gets free, there's no telling what he might do to himself or to any of us."

"He appears desperate to you?" asked Iriel.

"Very. If he can escape, he will."

Iriel gave her kinsman a sideways glance then drew a dagger from her boot.

"Do not make me hurt you," she said.

Ebalin's forehead furrowed and he looked at her with wide innocent green eyes.

"Save it," said Iriel flatly. "You've caused us a lot of pain, grief, and heartache."

Evan smiled and sat down.

Swiveling in his seat, James touched the lever behind him. Instantly, the boat began to quiver. James moved the lever to his right with one hand and moved the steering wheel clockwise slightly. The boat responded and rose up out of the mud slowly. The bard turned the wheel more and the boat took off, soaring into the sky.

Once they were above the trees, Evan related to James the events of the battle with Jormundan. The bard listened and made mental notes in his head for later. This would be another great tale.

At the front of the ship, Daniel spoke to Brashani.

"Iriel told me that Aure might be attached to the helmet magically and that dispelling the magic might restore Aure. Is that right?"

"The helmet is using the Elf-gem's power. I got that from my initial examination. But exactly how that is working and what can be done to separate it from the helmet will take more investigation."

Daniel's lip quivered a little. "So you don't know."

"No, I don't. But I can find out." He held out his hand for the headpiece.

Daniel gave it to him. Brashani concentrated, as he placed his hands on either side of the helmet. He became still and appeared to go into a trance.

They sailed for an hour free of incident. No birds attacked, no storms erupted, no one shot rocks at them. Daniel stared at Brashani and hoped Aure would be all right.

As they approached Clearbrook, Daniel looked out along the port side of the boat and saw the town's clock tower in the distance. He heard a noise and saw Brashani stir.

"Well, I'll be a sorcerer's apprentice," said the wizard, with a half smile.

"What is it?" asked Daniel.

"The way they wove the enchantment around the gem and the helmet. I'm pretty sure, if I can dispel the magic on the helmet, the gem will return to normal."

Daniel's face lit up. "Really?! That's great."

"I said *if*. The mage who put this enchantment on the helmet was quite accomplished. It's going to be hard to remove. Plus I'm still tired from casting all those spells in the Fire Mountain caves."

Daniel's optimism visibly diminished. He felt a lump in his throat, and tears threatened to obscure his vision. "But you'll try, won't you?"

The wizard straightened in his seat and looked a little indignant. "Of course, I'll try."

"Now?"

Brashani sighed. "Now." He concentrated again and closed his eyes. This time perspiration formed on the fire mage's forehead and his hands tensed. Seconds stretched out unbearably for Daniel.

After a few minutes, Brashani sat back and slumped a little in his seat. He didn't move and Daniel wasn't sure if the exertion had killed the man or not. Tentatively, the lad began to reach out to Brashani with his hand when the wizard spoke. "Done," he said simply.

Daniel jumped back, startled at the sudden sound. The topaz brightened and slid off the helmet. Daniel caught it before it hit the deck.

Aure? he thought.

Daniel. I am Aure, Giver of Light. Help me find my brothers.

I will, Aure. I promise.

CHAPTER 39

BETRAYAL

James slowed the boat as it flew over the entrance to Clearbrook harbor. He spun the steering wheel a quarter turn counterclockwise and the vessel moved closer to the surface of the water.

James nudged Evan. "Do you see a pier we can dock at?"

"Yes," Evan said. He pointed. "Over there."

James glanced in the direction Evan indicated. The pier was the same one the vessel had left from earlier in the day. He slowed the ship to a crawl and lowered it until the hull skimmed the water. As soon as they were close enough to the pier, Evan jumped out of the craft and moored it to the dock. James released the rudder and the ship rocked a bit as it sank into its berth.

Evan helped his companions out of the boat and together they walked up the pier. They met Sam Hartshorn at the end of the dock. With him were Eric and some of the town guards.

Eric raised his eyebrows as he saw his friend. "Evan, this is a surprise."

Evan smiled. "I'm sure. We've had a time of it."

Eric glanced at the ship. "Is that the thief's sailboat?"

"It is. You'll find the thief tied up in the boat."

Eric furrowed his brow. "How did you ...?"

Evan put up a hand to interrupt the questions. "It's a long story. Perhaps James can tell it. Right now, I think we all need to get back to the Grey Horse and put Tindolen's gem back in its display case."

"You mean you got it back?" asked Eric in disbelief.

The priest grinned with satisfaction. "Yes. Now if you don't mind, we should be getting back. They have jobs to finish and I need to rest."

* * *

Eric ordered the town guards to escort Ebalin to jail. Sam went back to his office to record Evan's arrival. Nearby, harbor guards looked on and when Evan and his companions proceeded toward the harbor entrance with Eric, they let them go.

"Must have business with the cap'n," one guard murmured to himself.

Evan and his companions strolled back to the Grey Horse slowly. Eric, walking beside Evan and James, joined them.

"So who is going to tell me what happened?" Eric looked from Evan to James and then back again. "You or James?"

Evan laughed. "All right. I'll do it." He related the story as well as he could. They entered the main square as Evan finished the tale. Eric looked up at the clock tower; it was late in the afternoon — later than he realized.

Turning back to Evan, the guard lieutenant said, "The town has been in an uproar ever since the theft of the gem became common knowledge. Mayor Bigsbee has been especially upset and he ordered me to go over the harbor with a fine-toothed comb to make sure no clue had been missed."

"Bigsbee realizes the theft occurred at the Grey Horse, doesn't he?" Evan asked as they exited the quadrangle.

Eric shrugged. "I assume so. But as I understand it, Tindolen told Bigsbee that he searched the Inn for clues."

In the distance, Evan could see a crowd in front of the inn. As he got closer, he saw the people were standing in an S-shaped line that stretched out of the double doors and into the road.

James's eyes widened. "Are all those people waiting to get into the Grey Horse?"

"It would appear so," said Evan.

"How do we reach the entrance?" asked Iriel, her eyes round and her brow furrowed.

Eric smiled. "Leave that to me." He waded in to the crowd. "Coming through. Official guard business. Coming through."

Slowly the throng parted. Evan and his companions followed the guard lieutenant and made their way to the great hall. The top of the display case was still up and Tindolen and Molin were standing next to it answering questions from the local townsfolk. When Evan and the others pushed into the room, Tindolen interrupted Molin, who was explaining how the gem had been stolen.

"A moment, Molin," said the gem merchant. "I believe there's been a development in the story." He pushed into the cluster of people nearby and gestured for them to move aside. The townsfolk complied and Evan and the others made their way to the front of the hall.

Tindolen smiled at his old friend. "Evan, good to see you again. Were you successful?"

Evan gestured to Daniel. The lad reached into his pocket, pulled out the topaz, and held it between his thumb and his middle finger. It shone a bright yellow, as if alive.

A big grin spread across Tindolen's face and his eyes sparkled like emeralds. "Marvelous," he exclaimed. Taking the gem from Daniel, he placed the topaz back on the velvet lining in the display case and closed the glass lid.

Turning to face his fellow citizens, Tindolen addressed them, "If you'll excuse us, I'd like to talk to Evan and the others in private."

"We have to leave?" asked one man, an annoyed expression on his face.

"If you don't mind."

No one moved. Evan sighed and glanced at Eric. The guard lieutenant shook his head and stepped up. "You heard the man. He's just recovered his lost property; give him a few minutes alone with the people who retrieved it."

Eric motioned to the other guards and together they slowly prodded the townsfolk out of the room. Once the townsfolk were out in the foyer, Eric closed the door behind him, as he left the great hall too.

Tindolen placed a hand on the shoulder of each mage. "Molin, Brashani, if you would assist me for a moment." The mages looked at the merchant quizzically.

"How can I help?" asked Molin.

"You need me?" Brashani asked.

Tindolen nodded his head. "Yes, a bit of strength from each of you will help me reset the wards on the display case and make them stronger than before."

Molin inclined his head. "All right, proceed."

Brashani sighed. "Very well. You can have what's left, but I'm pretty weak from all the spell casting I've been doing."

"Thank you," replied Tindolen. "I'm sure it will be enough, Brashani, and I'll try not to drain you too severely." He waited for the two mages to place one hand on his shoulders and then complete the circuit by doing the same with each other. Once that was done, Tindolen prepared himself for the warding. But before the merchant could begin, electricity enveloped the elf and fire mage, sparking and illuminating the room. They collapsed on the floor a moment later. Molin raised the lid of the display case, reached in, and seized the gem.

Evan had his back to Tindolen, but when he heard the electricity spark, the priest turned, drew his sword, and stepped forward.

Molin turned to face Evan. His eyes were slits and his mouth a snarl. "Stop where you are. I've got the gem and I'll use it. So, no sudden moves."

Evan frowned. "What's the meaning of this?"

"Money," said Molin. "The necromancers will pay lots of money for this jewel; enough so I can retire completely."

Evan raised his eyebrows and his eyes became ovals. "You'd side with them?"

"Why not? Who else is there?"

"We can restore the House of Richmond."

The wizard laughed. "Ppfff! The House of Richmond isn't worth spit. I gave Kenilworth thirty years of loyal service and Leonard dismissed me without a second thought. I should've been able to retire in the peace and dignity that I earned from all those years of faithful service. But instead I'm forced to work here, doing parlor tricks and hoping I don't run out of money before I die. It's degrading. If an heir lives, we'll all be better off leaving him where he is."

Evan narrowed his eyes and set his jaw. "That's your opinion, but as a member of His Grace's court, I must act for the benefit of the kingdom and it needs its king or queen back."

"The kingdom," Molin scoffed. "Bah. Better to let that die too."

"I can't let you have it," declared Evan and tightened his grip on his sword.

Molin raised an eyebrow. "Let me?" he said, incredulously. "I don't think you have any choice. I have the power and I'll use it if you force me to."

"You can't escape. There are too many of us; you can't take us all on at once." Evan hoped he was right about that. The sad truth was that few really knew the full power of an *Aglari*. If Molin could tap it, he might be unstoppable.

"But I have the gem." He held up his hand with the jewel in it. "I outpower you all," he boasted.

"Perhaps individually, but not as a group."

"Care to test that theory?" the wizard asked, mockingly.

"And where will you go? Even if you kill me, others will come after you. You'll never have the peace you claim to want."

"We'll see about that."

* * *

Daniel had watched and listened to the exchange between Molin and Evan and decided it was time to act. He had promised Aure to help, and he couldn't stand by and witness someone else walk away with him again.

Aure, are you all right?

Daniel, I am fine.

I can't let you be stolen again.

If you move against him, he will kill you. I can't permit that.

Then how do we stop him?

There is only one way: he must take possession of me; otherwise, he will kill you all.

* * *

James eyed the door to escape; but he was afraid that if he moved, Molin might use the gem to kill him. He glanced at Iriel. She still carried her bow in one hand, but she had not nocked an arrow.

Is she too close or is she just scared?

Meeting her eyes, he saw her looking at her uncle. *She's probably concerned for his well-being. Hope he's not dead.*

Electricity crackled around Molin's raised hand and James looked at the wizard.

Evan raised his sword and prepared to strike.

Lightning shot out from Molin's fist and stunned Evan, Iriel, and James; they collapsed. A second lightning bolt crackled and struck the side of the great hall that faced the street; it blew a hole in the wall large enough for Molin to step through.

"Hello?" said a voice from the other side of the door. "What's going on in there? Is everyone all right?"

Ignoring the question, Molin emerged onto the street through the opening he'd just made. He laughed and lifted himself into the sky.

CHAPTER 40
AURE'S WILL

D aniel woke Evan, James, and Iriel.

James groaned and held his head with his right hand. "What happened?"

"Molin knocked you out with a lightning bolt," reported the lad.

Evan moaned. "We're lucky we aren't dead," he said and rotated his right arm at the shoulder to work out the stiffness that he felt.

James struggled to his feet; Evan did the same.

"Did you see where he went?" Evan asked Daniel.

The teen nodded his head. "He flew off into the sky." He pointed through the large hole in the wall.

Evan sighed and picked up his sword. He sheathed it. "All right, we'll have to go after him in the elf's sailboat. James can fly it, and once Molin lands, I can confront him."

"He'll kill you," James said, helping Iriel to her feet.

"We should all go," said Iriel. "He can't attack us all at once."

Evan considered the suggestion, concerned for the others' safety. *Yet they seem to be prepared to do whatever is necessary regardless of the cost to themselves.* Evan smiled to himself and felt the pride he normally reserved for his men after a successful campaign. "All right," he said at last. "But let's wake Tindolen and Brashani first. We can use their help too."

* * *

Molin circled Clearbrook twice and took in the sights. He had always wanted to fly but he had never had the power before. With the *Aglari* in his possession, power was no longer a consideration. He could feel it and tapping the power was easy. But there was something else there; a presence. He tried to block it, but he couldn't.

Molin Black, hear me. I am Aure, Giver of Light. You have used my power to hurt others and to take what is not yours. I cannot permit this to continue.

You can't stop me. I have the power.

But I am the power. Only people who submit to the Tahteem, *the Test of Purity, and are judged worthy may use my power or that of my brothers.*

You're bluffing. Trying to scare me with some made-up story.

I speak the truth. If you use my power without passing the Test, you will go mad. Others will come and hunt you down. You will die.

Bah! Let them come. I will kill them all.

* * *

Evan heard Brashani cry out in pain as he helped the wizard to stand. Iriel ran forward to help her uncle.

"How do you feel?" asked Evan.

Brashani rubbed his face with his hands. "Like a pin cushion."

The priest glanced at the merchant. "Tindolen?"

"No worse for wear," replied the jeweler as he stood. "What happened?"

Evan sighed. "Molin's stolen the gem. Daniel says he flew away but we can follow in Ebalin's sailboat."

Brashani felt the need for a drink, but he suppressed it. "All right, let's go."

Tindolen raised an eyebrow. "He's using the gem?"

"Yes, I think so," said Evan. "Why do you ask?"

Tindolen shut his eyes tightly, as if in pain, and sighed. "Then he'll be tainted by the power unless he passed the Test."

Evan narrowed his eyes. "What test?"

"The test that the *Aglaril* conduct before they let anyone use them. It is a test of character called ..."

"... *Tahteem*, the Test of Purity," said Daniel.

"Yes," Tindolen agreed, then looked at the lad and smiled.

Evan didn't like the sound of this. "What does this test entail?"

Tindolen shrugged. "I don't know, but remember that only the most worthy can use the *Aglaril*. This is how the gems ensure the person wielding them is worthy. If he does not take the Test before using the power, he will increasingly crave the *Aglari's* magic and ultimately go mad. He must be stopped, possibly killed."

Evan's jaw tensed. Maybe the Elf-gems were better off lost. He dismissed the idea almost as quickly as it had occurred to him. The dukefs had to be driven from Andropolis and the House of Richmond needed to be restored. The Elf-gems were the best hope of achieving both goals.

Tindolen stood with Iriel's help then brushed off and straightened his clothes.

Evan sighed. "Tindolen, will you come too?"

"Me?" asked the elf with a furrowed brow. "Why me? I'm no fighter."

"You know the most about the *Aglaril*. We may need this knowledge."

The gem merchant considered this for a moment. "All right. I'll come."

They turned to leave as Eric climbed into the hole left by Molin. "What happened here?" he asked.

"It's a long story. Suffice it to say the gem's been stolen again and we were just leaving to pursue the thief."

"Who stole it this time?"

"I'll tell you later," said Evan.

"All right." Eric surveyed the damage. "Frank is going to be livid."

Evan and his companions dashed out of the great hall through the hole in the wall to avoid the crowd in the lobby. They made their way across town once more and down to the harbor; they climbed into the single-mast sailboat. James got behind the wheel and Tindolen magically severed the moorings. A moment later, the boat zoomed into the air.

"Which way, Daniel?" asked James.

Daniel concentrated for a moment. He looked up and pointed above them. "There!"

CHAPTER 41
DEFYING FATE

Molin drew on Aure's power. It coursed through him like an electric charge. He felt stronger, younger, and more alive than he had in many years. He embraced the feeling and the power grew more intense.

A malicious grin spread across his face as he cast his gaze on his surroundings. Below him, Molin saw a single-mast sailboat approaching from the harbor. He waited for it to get closer. He laughed when he saw Evan, Tindolen, and the other Grey Horse guards in the ship. They were pursuing him.

Fools.

* * *

Evan saw Molin hovering in the air. "We need to knock him out of the sky or at least force him back to the ground. Options?"

"A fire strike," said Brashani.

Iriel gasped.

Tindolen's eyes widened for an instant. "A rather severe course of action, don't you think?"

"What's a fire strike?" Evan asked. He looked from Brashani to Iriel to Tindolen.

Brashani cleared his throat. "It brings a column of flame down onto the person I direct the spell at."

Evan raised his eyebrows. "I agree with Tindolen — that is severe. I don't want to kill him, just get the gem back."

"I doubt it will kill him," said Brashani. "Not with that gem in his possession. And I doubt you'll be able to pry the gem away from him unless he is stone-cold dead."

Evan considered the wizard's words. "Do you agree with that assessment?" he asked Tindolen.

The elf blushed and avoided Evan's eyes.

"Do you?" he pressed, his eyes narrowing.

Tindolen sighed and met Evan's eyes. "Yes."

Iriel's eyes grew round and her jaw fell open. "Uncle!"

The merchant turned toward his niece. "I'm sorry, Iriel, but look at the situation. Molin has stolen an *Aglari*. That very act makes him unworthy. Which means he hasn't submitted himself to the *Tahteem*. If he had, he wouldn't be flying. And that means he will go mad; it is just a matter of time. In that context, a fire strike isn't really lethal force — not when he has an *Aglari* for protection."

Iriel did not answer but a tear ran down her cheek and she turned away from him.

Evan turned back to Brashani. "All right. Do it."

* * *

Molin watched the sailboat for a moment.

Time to fly away and find a place where I can sell this gem to the necromancers who want it.

He flipped that thought around in his head. It began to rankle him.

Why should they get the gem? No, I will not sell it; I will use it ... to build a tower and destroy any who would oppose me.

He turned his attention back to the sailboat. They would be the first to die. Molin smiled at the thought. His fist began to crackle with electricity again when a column of flame shot through the sky, struck him, and knocked him back. He resisted the flames and struggled to stay afloat as he pushed against the blazing column; but it was no use. Molin lost altitude and fire seared away his clothes and hair.

Moments later, the wizard found himself on the ground in a large field, smoldering. A few tatters of cloth clung to his otherwise naked form. He felt old and fragile once more. The gem lay next to him. He seized it and lay there conserving strength. He would wait; Evan would come and, when he did, the wizard would kill him.

CHAPTER 42
CHECK AND MATE

Evan had James land the ship a short distance from Molin. The elder wizard saw the vessel descend from the sky and lay there without moving. Once the ship had come to rest on the ground, he closed his eyes and waited.

As he stepped out of the boat, Evan scanned the area. They were in the middle of an empty field. Tall brown grass bowed in a gentle breeze. He saw no one moving about and no birds in the sky. He turned back to Iriel and said, "Cover me."

"*Faroth mane*," returned Iriel; she nocked an arrow into her bow.

Evan drew his sword. "Brashani, come with me. The rest of you stay here. I don't want to risk your lives; if Brashani and I fail, you four will need to come up with another plan."

Tindolen raised an eyebrow. "What can we four do?"

"Warn others, at least."

Evan waited for Brashani to climb out of the boat. Together, they approached the fallen wizard slowly. As they approached, they noticed the grass around the elderly mage was black and scorched. Small fires burned and smoldered around him in several places.

Brashani gestured and the flames died out. "No sense starting a wildfire," he murmured to Evan before he formed a ball of fire in his right palm.

Molin popped an eye open when he heard Brashani's voice. He watched the pair advancing on him briefly and then closed his eye again.

Brashani and Evan came closer, stopped, and stood over the prone figure for a moment.

"Think he's dead?" asked the fire mage.

Evan considered this but noticed the other wizard's shallow breaths.

"No. He's playing opossum." He turned to their quarry and asked, "Where's the gem, Molin?"

The wizard said nothing; he sat up slowly and held his head with his left hand. He moaned. A faint smile played on his lips and an opaque dome ten feet in diameter sprang up out of the ground and enclosed them.

"Wha ...?" sputtered Evan. He looked at the enclosure; it shimmered like polished steel.

An electrical charge shot out of Molin's hand and knocked Evan back. He hit the magical barrier and slumped to the ground.

Brashani threw the ball of fire in his hand. It exploded on Molin's chest but left him unharmed. Molin laughed and threw a stream of electricity at Brashani. The fire mage gestured for a shield but the electrical flow shattered it and struck the wizard. He collapsed.

Molin laughed again as he approached Evan and kicked the priest's sword to the other side of the dome. The wizard concentrated and electricity sparked around his hand.

Evan opened his eyes and saw Molin standing over him. He wanted to groan; he felt awful. He looked for his sword and once he failed to find it, Evan realized he needed a plan of action fast. He smiled and hoped he would be able to thank Sir Ahlan, who had taught him the trick he was about to use.

He kicked out with his legs and hit Molin behind the knees.

Molin cried out as his legs buckled, his concentration broke, and the electricity in his hand evaporated.

Evan stood up and saw his sword on the other side of the dome. He started for it, but only got halfway across the space when Molin tackled him from behind.

They wrestled on the ground, rolling in one direction and then another. Finally, Evan broke his opponent's hold and began hitting Molin repeatedly about the face and shoulders. Blood oozed from the wizard's nose and the corner of his mouth.

Evan stopped his assault. Molin didn't move; his breathing was shallow. He stood and glimpsed his sword where it lay. He turned back, faced his adversary, and asked, "Where's the gem?"

Molin did not answer.

"Where is it?" Evan screamed.

Molin opened his right hand.

Evan glanced at Brashani, who still lay unconscious on the ground. He hoped his friend wasn't dead. When he looked back at Molin, he saw the wizard hadn't moved. The topaz was still in his right hand.

As he bent over to take it, Evan watched Molin carefully. He suspected treachery and glanced at the gem. As Evan gazed upon the jewel, Molin struck him with another electrical blast. The charge knocked him back off his feet.

Molin stood and smiled. He stumbled forward and held onto the dome to steady himself.

Evan shook his head to clear it. *Enough is enough*, he thought. He rolled to his feet and ran at Molin, slamming him against the magical barrier before the wizard had time to complete another spell. Evan saw Molin go limp and eased the former court mage to the ground. In the old man's right hand, Evan saw a faint yellow glow. He pried his opponent's right hand open and saw the *Aglari* resting there, no worse for its ordeal.

He took the topaz from Molin, placed it in his pocket, and stood. He went over to retrieve his sword. As he grasped the hilt, Evan heard Molin stir.

"It's mine, you fool," the wizard murmured. "Give it back. It's my gem."

Evan watched as Molin slowly crawled toward him.

He's like a mad dog. I guess what Tindolen said was true. He'll never stop craving the gem.

Evan tensed his jaw and tightened his grip on his sword. He contemplated killing Molin to end his craving for the jewel. He raised his sword and then lowered it. He could not kill the man, not in cold blood and not in the middle of an empty field. There was not a soul around for miles. At the same time, he couldn't leave Molin here either. He'd die of exposure.

Molin reached Evan's boot and stopped moving. Evan felt for a pulse and found one.

Brashani moaned and the priest went to him. "How do you feel?"

"Lousy," said Brashani. "He shattered my shield and then stunned me with that electrical blast of his."

"Can you do anything about this magical dome he created?"

"Yes, give me a minute."

Evan helped Brashani to stand. The fire mage placed one hand on the magical barrier and concentrated. It wavered and then dissolved. Evan saw Tindolen and James standing on the other side of it. The gem merchant was scratching his head.

"What happened?" asked Tindolen. Evan told him and concluded the tale by saying, "Molin's not dead, just unconscious. Let's tie him up and take him back with us. Eric can put him in jail for theft."

"All right," James agreed, as he took some rope out of his backpack.

CHAPTER 43
THE PROPHECY TAKES HOLD

Once James had bound Molin's arms and legs, he lifted Molin's body by the shoulders; Brashani picked up the elder mage's feet. Together, they carried Molin's unconscious form carefully toward the sailboat.

Tindolen walked up to Evan.

"Here," Evan said, and thrust the topaz into the gem merchant's hand.

Tindolen took it and looked at his old friend. He noticed bruises on Evan's face in several places and it seemed to him that Evan's countenance was grim and unforgiving. "Sorry for all the trouble my gem has caused."

Evan paused, sheathed his sword, and sighed. "I'm sorry too. I shouldn't take it out on you. It's not your fault." Evan turned away and followed James and Brashani toward the sailing ship.

Tindolen watched Evan walk away then he gazed at his jewel and examined it carefully. Finding it undamaged, he smiled and placed it in his vest pocket. He patted it, felt the slight bulge, and was satisfied.

James and Brashani reached the flying ship and lifted Molin into it. Iriel and Daniel, who had been sitting in the vessel the whole time, helped ease the wizard into the bottom of the craft.

"We should be getting back," Evan said as he stepped aboard.

James took his seat at the helm. Brashani sat down across from Iriel. Evan turned back and saw Tindolen approaching. Once he was aboard, James maneuvered the boat into the air and set course for Clearbrook.

As they flew, Tindolen looked at Evan. "Now tell me, how did you recover the gem originally?"

Evan looked at James, who cleared his throat and told the story. Tindolen listened, marveling at not only the obstacles that Evan and the others had overcome, but also at James's style in telling the story. When James had finished, Tindolen said, "So death mages and dukefs want my gem. There's an unholy alliance."

Evan rubbed his forehead with the tips of his fingers. "Indeed. Although Ebalin may not be a dukef. He may be an unhappy elf from Oldarmare or a rogue element in the kingdom. On the other hand, it may be that the dukefs are supporting various groups of necromancers to undermine the entire kingdom. I don't know."

Tindolen shrugged. "Regardless, since necromancers tried to steal the gem once, they may try again. I need a better way to protect it."

"Any idea why they want it?"

"Judging from what James has said and the way the gem was enchanted to the helmet you found it on, my guess is they are trying to create different types of magic weapons powered by the *Aglaril*. Exactly what these items would be and would be able to do is anybody's guess, but any weapon of sufficient power in the wrong hands is dangerous."

Brashani rubbed his forefinger across his chin as he pondered the discussion. "That makes sense. Such items would be more powerful than other similar types of items because the Elf-gems are inherently more powerful than other magic gems."

Tindolen considered the fire mage's words. "And that bodes ill."

"I should say so," agreed Evan.

"I don't understand, Uncle. What is so bad about making magic items from the *Aglaril*?" asked Iriel. "Isn't *Balodol* a magic item?"

"Yes, of course, my dear. But think for a minute, Iriel. If necromancers create magic rings or amulets, say, from the *Aglaril*, the resulting items could ignite whole cities in fire or encase entire armies in ice. Or they could set a pestilence upon the land. It is hard to say; it all depends on the spells placed into the item. But regardless of the item created, it all suggests the necromancers mean to wage war. But that's not the worst of it."

Iriel's eyebrows knitted. "It's not?"

"No, what's worse is that when you bind an *Aglari* to a wand or a helmet or anything, you suppress its individuality. It appears to be like any other gem. Only it isn't; it is much more powerful, as Brashani noted."

A look of realization swept over Daniel's face. "That's why Aure stopped communicating with me."

"Yes, it had been enchanted by then. It is also why there are rules about who can use the Crown of Power, so that only the most worthy wield it. But the necromancers, by creating a separate magic item from Aure, circumvented these rules, allowing anyone to use the power without the risk of failing the *Tahteem*. In short, they are fomenting war and anarchy."

Iriel's mouth fell open and her eyes nearly jumped out of her head. She shivered and hugged herself, as she tried to restore warmth to her body.

James grimaced. "I suppose it is a good thing the locations of the other Elf-gems are not known."

Tindolen looked at the bard with sadness in his eyes. "Only for the time being. Assuming I can protect my gem adequately, they will go after the others."

Evan ran his hand through his hair. "But isn't that where Amelidel's prophecy comes in?"

Tindolen thought for a moment, then his face brightened. "Oh, I see what you are suggesting. Because you cannot force the prophecy to come true, you are wondering if the prophecy's magic will guide events so that the necromancers and dukefs cannot find the other *Aglaril*."

Evan nodded his head. "Something like that, yes."

"I'm afraid it does not work exactly like that. They still have free will."

"So they are free to search for the Elf-gems using whatever method is available to them, regardless of the prophecy?"

"Yes, except the prophecy's magic is guiding them too. So they may not be able to find any gems because they are forcing events. Or it may be that they will find some of the *Aglaril* by accident in much the same way I found Aure."

Evan didn't like the sound of that, but he wasn't going to try to fight magic so subtle that it guided events all across the kingdom.

Daniel pulled on the merchant's sleeve. "Mr. Tindolen, sir?"

"Yes, Daniel?"

"Are you saying we can't search for the *Aglaril*?"

"Not if we want to find them and have the prophecy come true. We cannot force those events."

"But Aure wants help finding his brothers."

"I know, Daniel. But there's no other way." Daniel's upper lip trembled a little.

"But I promised Aure earlier today I would help him find his brothers. If we cannot search for them, I don't see how I can help him."

The elven gem merchant was silent for a moment as he considered Daniel's remarks. "That would certainly solve both problems we are facing."

Evan scratched the back of his head. "I don't follow."

"Think, my boy. It will be harder to steal my gem if it is constantly moving about and changing location. And, if Daniel can locate the other *Aglaril*, we needn't worry about anyone else locating them or using them for evil purposes."

Evan's eyes grew wide. "But you just said we can't search for them."

"True. We'll need another reason for Daniel to be wandering about the kingdom."

"And Daniel can't do it alone," replied Evan with concern.

"No, you are quite right. There'll be many dangers and he'll need help. I can certainly pay for his expenses but that alone is not enough."

James cleared his throat. "Perhaps we could help him. Daniel and I were planning to search for his family anyway once we saved enough money to do so. If you can finance us, we could do that and look for other Elf-gems at the same time."

Tindolen studied the bard closely for a moment. "And whom do you mean by 'we'?"

"Me and ..." He looked at Iriel, who gave a slight nod of her head, "... and Iriel."

The merchant smiled. "Excellent. That works perfectly. You, Iriel, and Daniel searching for his lost family. And in the process the prophecy will work through you. Before you know it, I'm sure you'll have found five or all six of the missing jewels.

"But be careful," Tindolen continued. "You cannot force events by searching for the *Aglaril*. Doing so only delays the prophecy. Your purpose must be to locate Daniel's family. Only then will the prophecy be able to guide you down the paths needed to find them."

"If you say so," offered James.

Tindolen gestured toward Brashani. "What of the mage in your group? He could be a great help."

"That depends," answered the wizard. "What happens once all the gems are found?"

"You would return them to me so that the Crown of Power can be remade."

Brashani shook his head. "You've misunderstood me. What will we get in return?"

"Oh," said the merchant. "You mean like a reward."

"Exactly."

"Well, I will pay for your supplies at the start and give you enough money for several months. I will also give Iriel a sack of gold and a bag of gems that you can sell as you need to, so you should not want for money. Beyond that, you will be paid for your time once all the *Aglaril* are found and given to me. The specific terms will have to be discussed, but I'm sure we can come to some arrangement."

Brashani raised his eyebrows and inclined his head, impressed. "All right. That sounds like the best job offer I've had in a long time. I'll go."

"Good," said Tindolen. "Four people traveling together should not draw too much attention, so you should be able to search discreetly."

"Is that so important, Uncle?"

"Absolutely. In fact, it is critical that you travel as inconspicuously as possible. If the dukefs learn that you are searching for the *Aglaril*, I'm sure they will send assassins to kill you."

"And if necromancers want the gems too," said Evan, "they are likely to abduct and torture you so that you reveal what you know, or worse, so that you turn over any gems you do find."

"Therefore," said Tindolen, "Speak to no one about this."

Daniel cocked his head to one side. "What about Father Evan? He should come too."

Tindolen smiled at the thought and regarded his old friend.

Evan smiled at the lad, pleased that he should think of him. "Would that I could, Daniel, but I have many matters waiting for me back at court."

"And yet without you," noted Tindolen, "I'm sure they would have all perished on your journey to reclaim my gem."

Evan shrugged. "Perhaps, but that doesn't change my duty to His Grace or his court."

"Then perhaps they might be accompanied by someone from His Grace's court — a friend of yours, say?"

"That may be possible." Evan rubbed his chin as he considered this idea. "It will take some convincing by me and it would mean they would all have to come with me to Wrightwood."

"Do what you can," said Tindolen. "Frankly, I think they would benefit from your knowledge and experience on the open road. At least for the first part of their journey."

"All right," said Evan. "I'll help get them to Wrightwood."

"Excellent," said Tindolen, smiling. "You can all leave town together once St. Sebastian's week is over."

The sailboat glided over Clearbrook harbor and settled back into the berth it had left less than an hour before.

Evan and his companions walked up the pier after mooring the boat. Eric was standing there talking to one of the harbor guards. Two of the town guardsmen stood behind Eric, awaiting orders. As Evan reached the end of the pier, Eric noticed him and went to talk with his friend.

"I was just asking about you," said the guard lieutenant. "Welcome back, again. Care to enlighten me about what happened?"

"We've only just returned," said Evan. "As to what happened …" He trailed off and scratched his head, not sure where to start. "Well, Tindolen was about to set wards on his gem when …" began the priest, and he proceeded to describe the events of the last few hours, summarizing their pursuit of Molin. In conclusion, Evan said, "Once I had the gem, it seemed wrong to kill him. So, we loaded him in the boat and brought him back here. You can put him in jail for theft."

"All right," said Eric. "Where is he now?"

"Trussed up in the sailboat."

Eric motioned to the guards behind him. "Take Molin to the jailhouse. He can stay there until a magistrate can hear his case."

The guards nodded in acknowledgment and scurried down the pier to find him.

CHAPTER 44

FRANK'S IRE

"**G**oing back to the Grey Horse?" asked Eric after the town guards hauled Molin off to prison.

"Yes," replied Evan. "You?"

Eric shook his head. "No. I need to report to the Mayor. See you later."

Evan and his comrades all felt tired and walked slowly across town. Evan, especially, was bone weary and needed some rest. They were all glad that the gem had been recovered once more and that they could resume their normal routines.

They crossed the main square and approached the Inn.

James whistled when he saw the amount of damage Molin had done. He also saw Frank standing on the other side of the hole surveying the wreckage. Brashani blushed; he recognized the image from his vision, days earlier.

"What in the name of goodness happened here?" Frank asked.

"Molin stole Tindolen's gem. He made the hole in his escape," James replied.

"Where is he now?"

"Jail," said Evan.

"I see. And how am I going to repair this … mess?" Frank gestured at the hole and the debris around it.

No one answered immediately, then Daniel's face brightened. "By mending it magically?"

"What?" inquired Frank.

Iriel raised an eyebrow and smiled. "Good idea. If Mr. Jones has fresh wood, Brashani can use it to patch the hole … at least for now."

"I suppose," said Brashani. "But that won't repair the damage permanently."

"True," agreed Tindolen. "Perhaps if I assist you, we can mend the hole in an enduring and lasting way."

The fire mage gave him a sideways glance. "Is that possible?"

"Yes. I know a few tricks that might help."

"Great. You should probably lead then; I'm still tired. I've been in more fights and have cast more spells in the last twenty-four hours than I have in the last twenty-four years."

"All right, let me put my gem back in its display case first and set the wards needed to protect it."

"Good," said Frank. "And while you are doing that, I'd like a word with Evan."

Evan heard the acid tone in his friend's voice and felt himself break out in a sweat. As many times as the priest had faced necromancers or demons, somehow explaining the day's events to Frank seemed worse. Slowly he, Tindolen, Brashani, Daniel, James, and Iriel made their way into the Inn through the crowd and entered the great hall where Frank was waiting. The innkeeper's face was somber and showed no expression, but Evan knew that was the calm before the storm.

"Where do I start?" Frank began. He raised his eyebrows and ears. "I know." He smiled maliciously. His voice took on a mocking tone. "Let's begin with this morning when I found out that all my employees-turned-guards had disappeared without so much as a good-bye and then returned without even bothering to tell me, only to leave again, this time leaving a hole the size of a small wagon blasted through my place of business."

Evan felt his face grow hot. "Didn't Molin tell you where we went?"

Frank nodded his head. "He did, but you were already gone. I had to send one of the chambermaids over to that crackpot Cornwall's house to find out that you had flown off in one of his contraptions two hours earlier.

"Then you came back … and look what I find when I come to find you." He gestured at the hole in the wall.

"It's my fault," said Evan contritely. "I needed their help."

"Damn right, it's your fault," barked Frank. "What were you thinking, Evan? They're my employees and I've got a business to run. They can't just go running off on a whim."

Evan looked sheepishly at his friend. Guilt beat on him. "Sorry. It won't happen again, Frank. I promise."

"It had better not," said the innkeeper angrily. "Now back to work, all of you." He stormed out of the room.

Eric appeared in the doorway and caught Evan's eye.

"Want some good news?" asked the guard lieutenant.

"Please," said Evan.

"I've just informed Bigsbee that Tindolen's gem has been recovered."

"Really? What was his reaction?"

"He assigned eight town guards to stand watch over it."

Evan laughed. "You're joking."

"No. I think he's rethought his original position."

"Interesting," remarked Tindolen. He placed the topaz back on the velvet lining of the display case, closed the lid, and turned to face Eric and Evan. "Still, it would be good if Brashani could remain on watch during the day. Likewise, since Daniel can talk to Aure, he should remain on guard. However, I think Iriel can go back to work for Mr. Jones."

"What about me?" asked James.

Tindolen smirked. "I think you'll have your hands full telling the tale. People will want to know what happened. But you might want to clean up first."

James looked down at his clothes and grimaced. "I know. I look like I've been in a fight."

Iriel nodded her head. "We both do. Let's wash and change our clothes."

"Good idea," agreed the bard. They left the great hall as Eric motioned to several guards in the lobby. Eight men marched into the hall. The guard lieutenant pointed at the glass case on the far side of the room. Four of the town guards took up positions along the back wall behind the display while the remaining four men paired off and flanked the left and right sides of the case.

"I'll station more men outside," Eric declared. "That should stop any more thefts."

CHAPTER 45

AFTERMATH

Tindolen and Brashani spent much of the remainder of the day repairing the Grey Horse. It was slow work, because each piece of wood had to be cut to size and, between them, they had only so much strength to cast spells. Much of the time was spent resting to recover the needed strength to fuse the next board into place.

Iriel washed up and went back to work for Frank, as her uncle had suggested. James, on the other hand, doused his face in water and changed his clothes; he put on a white shirt and a pair of tan trousers, before he returned to the great hall. As he entered the room, the bard found dozens of townsfolk waiting for him. They barraged him with questions and wanted to hear the story — both stories — of the gem's theft and recovery.

James glanced about the hall looking for assistance from his fellow guards, but Daniel sat in his customary corner meditating and Brashani was outside mending the hole in the wall. *No help there*. He raised his arms and held out his hands for silence. The crowd quieted down and James cleared his throat.

"It began early this morning," the bard said, and began to tell the story as slowly and simply as he could. When he had finished, some of the locals left the hall; others came in and asked the same questions he had just answered. So, he told the stories again, adding details and refining the tale each time he told it. Brashani, while resting, provided other little bits to the bard's tale until the simple retelling became grander and more heroic.

Evan, meanwhile, was pleased. Professional guards assigned to watch the gem meant he did not need to stand watch any more. And with Ebalin apprehended and Jormundan slain, the priest's mission was complete. He could return to court any time now. But before he did, he needed to let the residual pain from Jormundan's spell fade away completely. That would probably take a day or two and he was in no hurry. After all, how often was he able to visit his hometown?

His stomach growled and he realized he'd not eaten all day. When had there been time? He headed over to the common room. As angry as Frank was with him, he wouldn't turn down Evan's patronage.

As the day wore on, James grew tired of telling the story; Brashani, tired of hearing it. James tried to take breaks, but the crowd clamored for more. Some wanted other stories. Some wanted to hear the first tale of the theft once more; others, the second tale. By dinnertime, James was mentally exhausted.

Evan was exhausted too, both mentally and physically. After eating, he had gone upstairs to rest; however, the growing commotion in the great hall woke him several times. The last time was just after the clock tower struck six in the evening. He sighed, realized he would not be able to sleep soundly until the crowd was gone, and decided to go back down to the common room.

He stood. The pain in his limbs was gone but he felt his fatigue like a dead weight. *I need coffee,* he thought. He felt his face. It was sore in places from his fight with Molin.

Lethargically, Evan tromped downstairs, waded through the crowd, and made his way into the common room. He settled in at a corner table with some coffee and a bowl of stew, and hoped the throng would disperse soon.

Tindolen came in and sat down across from Evan. "The repairs are complete," he reported. He wiped his forehead.

Evan smiled. "Good, Frank will be pleased."

"Yes. You'd never know anything had happened."

The priest gestured at his food. "Care to join me for dinner?"

Tindolen shook his head and stood. "Thank you, my boy, but no. I've been neglecting my business far too much today. I need to get back."

"All right," Evan said, waving good-bye. "I'll talk to you later."

"Yes, I'm sure we will speak again before you leave town."

Evan watched his friend leave and then returned to his meal.

It was late Friday evening before the crowd left and Frank was able to close and lock the front doors. The Grey Horse staff was happy to hear the lock click into place; they were completely worn out from the hordes of people asking questions about what had happened. It was the busiest day in the Inn's history and the most exciting thing that had happened in Clearbrook since King Kenilworth had marched through town thirty-five years earlier to defend Thalacia against invading armies.

Fatigued but feeling better, Evan trudged up the stairs to his room and went to bed. The night passed uneventfully and he awoke feeling refreshed. Listening for the sound of a crowd, Evan heard nothing. No noise from downstairs wafted up to him. Evan got out of bed, washed, and dressed. He was about to leave his room when the sound of many voices all talking at once reached him. When he went downstairs, the foyer was filled once more with people. He sighed with disappointment.

He pushed through the crowd and made his way to the common room only to find most of the tables taken. Evan scanned the room, spied an unoccupied spot, and sat down.

Frank whizzed by carrying a stack of dirty plates. Concern showed on the innkeeper's face; he did not know how he was going to serve all these hungry people. Although Iriel had returned to her job as a serving girl, it had taken both of them to keep up with the demand yesterday afternoon. He was in no mood to repeat yesterday's experience. Then he remembered that there was one person he could ask for help.

"I was planning to interrogate the elf we captured," said Evan. "I'm afraid my priestly duties must come first."

"I understand," said Frank, as his face grew longer.

"Besides," Evan continued, "I've never been good at waiting tables. I'm all thumbs."

"I know, but Iriel and I can barely keep up. Since I've got the chambermaids watching the registration counter, there's no one else to ask." Frank gave Evan a plaintive look.

Evan shook his head. He felt his resolve crumble. The Michaeline priest could not in good conscience abandon a friend. "All right," Evan agreed, "if I finish the questioning early, I may be able to help before the dinner service."

Frank smiled. Evan shot up a hand. "But no promises."

"No, absolutely not," replied the innkeeper. He slapped Evan appreciatively on his back.

James did not fare much better than Frank. He told and retold the story of the theft until he was nearly hoarse. By noon, James was tired and wanted to leave the great hall to rest; however, too many people had jammed into the hall around him, making it impossible to leave. He wished the hole in the wall had not been fixed so quickly; it would have given him an escape route.

Resigned to his fate, James tried to push through the crowd but relented after a few minutes when he saw how hard it was to move about. Sighing, James sat down next to Daniel, who was meditating and talking to Aure.

Daniel, I must thank you for rescuing me.

The honor is mine, Aure.

Thank your friends, too.

I will.

CHAPTER 46
ST. SEBASTIAN'S WEEK ENDS

After he finished his meal, Evan went up to his room and grabbed his first-aid kit. Then he went back downstairs and stood in the doorway of the great hall. He peered into the room as he looked for James and Daniel. Evan saw the hall was full of people standing around waiting to catch a glimpse of the *Aglari*. He scratched his head.

How am I ever going to find them in that throng?

He sighed, pushed into the room, and excused himself as he slipped among people. Evan headed toward the corner of the room where Daniel usually sat to meditate. With luck, the lad would be there and would know where to find James.

A few minutes later, Evan stepped in front of Daniel, surprised to see James sitting next to the teen.

"Why are you sitting on the floor, James?" Evan asked.

"My voice is nearly gone," James said, hoarsely. He coughed. "So I'm trying to rest it."

"Well, roll up your sleeve. I want to examine the burns from the lava."

"Oh, right," said the bard. "I'd mostly forgotten about them. They don't hurt any more."

"Nevertheless, I need to make sure the burns are healing properly."

James rolled up his shirtsleeve and Evan undid the bandage from the day before. To his surprise, the skin under the bandage was new and pink; most traces of the wounds were gone. "Iriel's salve works well. I don't think you need another bandage."

The bard looked at his arm and grinned. "Amazing. I'll have to ask her how the salve is made. It might come in handy later."

"Daniel?" said Evan. "Can you hear me?"

The lad's eyes popped open. "Yes."

"Give me your injured hand. I want to examine the burns on it."

Daniel extended his hand and Evan removed the bandage from it. Several small burns pocked the back of the lad's palm. "Have Iriel apply some salve to these burns. If it works as well on you as it did on James, these should be healed in a day or less. In the meantime, I'll put a fresh bandage on your hand to cover the burns and keep them clean."

Evan stood after he completed his work. Daniel closed his eyes again.

"Where are you off to now?" James asked.

"To the stables to check on Alsvinn."

"Okay. See you later then."

"See you later," repeated Evan.

The priest pushed his way through the crowd again and reached the lobby several minutes later. He went back up to his room, put away his first-aid kit, and then came back down before leaving the Grey Horse altogether.

His first stop, as he had told James, was to check on Alsvinn. He hadn't had much time to supervise the grooming or feeding of his horse; now seemed like a good time to correct that oversight.

When Evan walked into his steed's stall, Alsvinn seemed happy to see him.

"Sorry for neglecting you, boy. I've been busy."

The horse brayed and nodded his head.

Over the next few hours, Evan examined the equine, talked to the grooms, and made sure his saddle and riding gear were in good order. The clock tower was striking noon when he left and headed toward the town square. As he crossed to the north end of the quadrangle, Evan saw Eric coming from the other direction. The priest waved to his friend; the guard lieutenant changed direction and approached Evan.

"Where are you headed?" asked Eric.

"To jail; I'm going to interrogate the elf."

"I'll come with you. I want to hear what he has to say."

They reached the prison a few minutes later. The jailhouse was a small brick building with iron bars on all the windows and a heavy portcullis for a door. Guards stood on either side of the entryway and saluted Eric as he approached. Eric returned the salute, pointed to Evan, and said, "He's with me."

"Yes, sir," acknowledged the lead guard, as he opened the gate.

Eric went inside and led the way down a narrow corridor to Ebalin's cell. They moved past several doors on both sides of the hallway before the guard lieutenant stopped and drew out a ring of keys. He inserted one into the lock on the door to his left and opened it. Then he gestured for Evan to enter.

Evan stepped inside and saw Ebalin chained to the wall. Manacles encircled his wrists and ankles and a gag was tied around his mouth. Eric entered the room, closed the door, and locked it. Then he drew his sword and pointed it at the elf.

"I'm going to remove your gag," announced Evan to Ebalin. "If you try anything like casting a spell on me, my friend here will run you through, understand?"

Ebalin nodded his head.

Evan removed the gag. "I have a few questions for you. If you cooperate, I'll talk to the magistrate on your behalf."

Ebalin worked his jaw briefly and finally said, "All right."

"We'll begin with you. Are you an elf or a dukef?"

Ebalin smirked. "Do you know any dukef that would work with a human?"

Evan didn't get the joke. "No, but most elves wouldn't assist dark mages either since necromancy is a perversion of the natural order, which elves love so much."

The elf half shrugged. "But stealing a gem to make a magic item isn't necromancy."

"Not technically, but why would you give aid and comfort to a necromancer?"

"Why not? He pays well."

"I see. Where did you meet Jormundan?"

"Elvenwood, at a tavern."

"Was it a prearranged meeting?"

Ebalin shook his head. "I live in Elvenwood. I had gone to the tavern to relax. He approached me and said he wanted to hire me for a job."

"To steal any Elf-gem you could find?"

"No, just to locate them, initially."

Evan narrowed his eyes. "Why you?"

"I don't know. Maybe because most elves would refuse and report his interest in the *Aglaril* back to King Everron."

"But not you?"

"No, I happen to believe the dukefs are right about humans." He smiled maliciously. "'Better dead and red.'"

Evan grimaced. "I see. But why did he need an elf rather than a human or a dwarf?"

"Because only elves can get into the Vault of Legends."

Evan paused, one eyebrow raised. Tindolen had mentioned the Vault of Legends the other day. If Ebalin had been there too, then he knew as much about the fabled jewels as there was to know. If he passed that information along to the necromancers, they would have inside information on the *Aglaril.* Perhaps that is how they had learned to enchant the jewels so effectively.

"When did theft become part of the plan?"

"A few months later."

"Why the change in plans?"

The elf shrugged again. "I don't know."

"How long have you been looking for the Elf-gems?"

"Several months."

"How many have you found?"

"Before this, none."

"What parts of the kingdom did you search?"

"I've traveled over all of northern Mirrya, including much of Thalacia."

Evan scratched his head and furrowed his brow. *I would have thought after several months of searching, he would've found at least one or two of the other* Aglaril. *Has the prophecy somehow prevented Ebalin from finding any gems? Is it really guiding events, as Tindolen said? And what of Daniel and the others? Will they fare any better?*

Evan had no answers to these questions and, after a moment considering them, moved on.

"What plans did Jormundan have for the other Elf-gems?"

Ebalin snorted. "I have no knowledge of any other plans he may have had."

"I see." Evan looked at Eric. "Any questions for Ebalin?"

The town guard shook his head. "No, I'm all set."

"All right." Evan replaced the gag over Ebalin's mouth.

Eric unlocked and opened the door. Evan went out into the hallway, followed by Eric, who locked the door again.

"We didn't learn much, did we?" asked Eric.

"I rarely do," said Evan. "Necromancers, and their associates, almost never say too much. Ebalin, however, was more talkative than most. So I learned more than I expected."

"Really?" the guard lieutenant inquired with a quizzical look. "Some of what he said seemed of no importance to me."

Evan smirked. "I understand. Remember, I have more of the big picture than you do." He snorted. "Although not much more."

"I don't envy your job. It must be hard getting information from the few wizards you capture."

"It's hard sometimes, but worth it, considering the alternative is to be overrun by demons and to live in anarchy."

Eric nodded his head in understanding.

Evan returned to the Grey Horse as the clock tower chimed two in the afternoon. He went into the common room to have lunch.

A few minutes later, Mayor Bigsbee stepped into the Grey Horse. No one had warned Frank that Bigsbee was coming. When His Honor did waddle through the Inn's double doors, the chambermaid on duty at the registration desk gawked at the sight. Then she collected her wits and ran off to find Frank.

Behind Mayor Bigsbee trailed two of his assistants. The crowd hushed as His Honor stood in the entrance and looked around, a pleased look on his round, red face.

Frank came running out of the common room and pushed through the crowd, with Evan and Iriel right behind him. "Mayor Bigsbee, welcome to the Grey Horse."

"My pleasure." He smiled with satisfaction. "You have a cozy little place here, Jones."

"Thank you, your Honor."

"Now, where is the gem exhibition?" asked Bigsbee, his eyebrows knitted.

"Over here." Frank gestured toward the great hall. The room was still full of visitors; the townsfolk, seeing Bigsbee approach, got out of the way.

Bigsbee entered, squeezing through the doorway, his round face growing redder from the effort. Bigsbee paused a moment to catch his breath and straighten his checkered vest and mottled gray overcoat. That done, the Mayor of Clearbrook stepped up to the display case. The townsfolk filled in behind him as Bigsbee moved. He glanced at the jewel, then Bigsbee turned toward the crowd and raised his arms. He beamed at them, as if proud of something.

"My friends, this has been a historic week for our quaint little town. We have witnessed not only the beginning of our awareness about elves, but also the foiling of evil plots to steal Tindolen's precious gem."

The crowd cheered.

"And for that brave feat of heroism, I now present a hero's medallion to each of the guards who spoiled that evil scheme."

One of Bigsbee's assistants opened a leather case he was carrying to reveal its velvet lining and five engraved bronze medallions with a leather cord attached to each. Bigsbee took the first medal. "Iriel, of the clan Mealidil."

The elf emerged through the press of people. She smiled and a hint of color showed on her face. Bigsbee placed the medallion around her neck. Iriel accepted it and kissed Bigsbee on the cheek. Frank laughed; he didn't think it was possible, but Bigsbee's face went dark red like a fine elven wine.

Flustered, Bigsbee fumbled for the next medallion. "Er … James Claymont."

The bard looked up as he heard his name, his eyes round and full. He stood and stepped forward, with a smile. "Thank you, your Honor," James said. He accepted the medal and shook Bigsbee's hand.

"Daniel Salvatori."

Daniel opened his eyes and sprang to his feet. He approached, bowed, and accepted the medal. He looked at it, his head cocked to one side.

James knew that look. "What's wrong?"

"I don't understand what purpose this medallion serves."

"Later, Daniel. I'll explain later."

Daniel bowed again.

"Brashani Khumesh."

The wizard slowly made his way through the crowd and at last pushed his way to the front, where Bigsbee shook his hand and placed the medallion around his neck.

"Thanks," said Brashani.

"And finally, our own favorite son, Father Evan Pierce."

From the doorway, at the back of the crowd, Evan looked up, surprised, and came forward slowly.

"Your Honor …" Evan began.

Bigsbee put his hand up for silence. "I know we disagreed about how best to protect Tindolen's gem and it seems more precaution would have been prudent. Nevertheless, you have foiled the schemes of both thieves, so please accept this medallion with the thanks of the town and as a personal apology from me."

Evan was speechless. Bigsbee had never apologized before; at least Evan could never remember him asking for forgiveness for anything. Humbled by the moment, Evan inclined his head and accepted the medal.

Bigsbee addressed all five, "You all acted, charging forward into danger to recover the gem. For that one deed alone, you all deserve our praise and hearty thanks."

The crowd applauded.

Bigsbee raised his arms again and smiled.

"And on that cheery note, I proclaim St. Sebastian's week concluded."

CHAPTER 47
BEST LAID PLANS

That night, Brashani sat alone at a table in the Grey Horse Inn thinking about the *Aglari*. Given the events of the past few days, one thought kept running through the wizard's mind.

How safe are these gems to use?

He had to conclude they weren't safe at all unless you were worthy, as judged by the Elf-gems themselves.

Which begs the question: is the boy worthy?

Brashani couldn't answer that question, but he suspected the answer was *no*. That could mean trouble ahead. The image of a crazed *Qua'ril* master flashed through Brashani's mind.

He shuddered as Iriel came to take his order.

"Is there a problem?" asked Iriel.

"No, I was just thinking. Do we know whether Daniel passed the Test of Purity?"

Iriel shook her head. "Actually, I don't. But I do not think he took the Test. Only people who use the gem must submit to that scrutiny."

"Then it is coincidence that Tindolen gave him the gem to carry?"

"I would think so. Or, as Uncle Tindolen said, 'Amelidel's prophecy is guiding events.'"

That seemed like hogwash to Brashani; but given the power and skill of the elven seer Amelidel, he wondered whether the prophecy was more like a magic spell. Brashani had never heard of a spell so big and powerful that it shaped events and he knew little of divination aside from pyromancy. He supposed the principles were the same but the execution of the spell was different.

"But Tindolen doesn't know that the prophecy is guiding events," the wizard said, after a pause. "He only thinks it is."

"He would not say a thing were so if it were not. And I remember Uncle telling me that he has spoken with Amelidel, who knows the prophecy is working."

"But how could one seer and mage cast a spell to affect the entire world?"

"Amelidel has knowledge handed down to the elves from the Makers of the World. Who can say what he can and cannot do?" Iriel replied.

Brashani scratched his head. "Hmmm. All right, I'll concede that. But that does not answer the question of whether Daniel can use the gem. And if he can, think of the power he could accidentally unleash!"

"As a master of the Art, he is obligated to keep his life in balance," stated Iriel with reverence. "I think he knows using the power of an *Aglari* would upset that balance."

Brashani wasn't convinced. As he saw it, something had to be done to safeguard Daniel, the gem, and the rest of the group — not to mention an innocent passerby who might become the victim of the gem's power unleashed in a weak moment.

I might be able to help if I could hold and study the gem we have. The idea resonated in Brashani's mind.

But how? Daniel seems reluctant to part with the one we have. And I don't have the equipment I need to study it. The best I can hope to do is analyze the magic used to enchant the gem and that will tax my power reserves without the support of another mage.

Realizing the scope of the task, Brashani turned his attention to the first step of his goal — finding a way to get hold of the gem so he could study it. If he could even spend a little time with the gem, he would gladly exhaust himself casting spells to unlock whatever secrets he could. And there were other simpler spells he could try first to see what effect they would have.

"What will you drink?" asked Iriel.

Brashani looked up at her. "Hmmm? Oh, sorry. Have any Old Troll Ale?"

Iriel scratched her head. "I don't know, but Mr. Jones did say a new ale arrived today."

"Well, if it's Old Troll, bring three steins. Otherwise, bring me the darkest lager you've got."

"Very good."

Returning to his thoughts, Brashani considered when and where to cast the spells he wanted to try. Ideas began swirling in his mind. They would all need careful thought. With luck, he'd know something before they left Clearbrook.

* * *

James stretched out on his straw mat, thinking about the journey ahead. He hadn't really wanted to give up his job here, but the search for the *Aglaril* would be an experience of a lifetime; he couldn't pass it up. It would be hard and dangerous, and that concerned James a little; he wasn't a fighter, but given his experiences this week he thought he could handle himself.

And when it is over, I can write a firsthand account of the adventure. Maybe I'll compose some poems and ballads about the saga too. Then I can tour the kingdom reciting the tales to large crowds in all the best taverns in the realm. Of course, given what Tindolen was putting up to finance the trip, James suspected he wouldn't need to work for a while once the search was over.

Then again, he thought, *if we find all the Elf-gems and the Crown of Power is remade, war is likely to follow. Who knows what life will be like after that? If we win the war and the royal line is restored, the royal palace, Azahnon, and the old capital, Andropolis, would most likely be rebuilt. If we lose …*

James really didn't want to think about that. He glanced over at Daniel, who was meditating on the straw mat next to him. Daniel's life would likely change the most, assuming they found members of his family. He would probably want to live with them for a while to learn about his past.

And what will happen to Iriel and me?

In a racial war against the dukefs, would they be permitted to marry? Did James even want that? And regardless of who won the war, would racial tensions be any better after the conflict ended? James didn't have answers to any of his questions. Perhaps locating the Elf-gems was not such a good idea after all.

Evan doesn't seem to think it is a bad idea. James trusted the Michaeline priest's judgment. *I just need faith: faith in the future and faith that things will work out for the best.*

He shook his head. *Too bad that's not me. I prefer to take one day at a time and deal with each day as it unfolds. That seems to work just fine for me.*

Iriel entered the room.

"James, it's time to perform."

The bard looked up at her. "Already?"

Iriel nodded her head.

"Okay, I'll be right there."

"Very good," Iriel said and left.

He stood up and stared at the door. He smiled.

Maybe I will marry her, if she'll have me. We'll see. One day at a time.

End of Book 1

Glossary

Aeril (Ay-ril) n. [Elven] The name of Reayl's commander.

Aglari (ah-glar-ree) n: pl **Aglaril** [Elven] A single gem from the elven king's crown. An Elf-gem.

Aglaril (ah-glar-ril) n: [Elven] Plural of Aglari.

Amelidel's prophecy n: A vision from the great elven mage and seer Amelidel (Am-mel-li-del). He foretold the liberation of Andropolis by the heir to the House of Richmond using the Aglaril.

Andropolis (An-drop-polis) n: The capital of Thalacia; once home of King Leonard. The city was captured in 465 by dukefs. King Leonard is believed to have been slain in the invasion along with his young sister Sandra.

Argentos (Are-gent-tos) n: The castle and home of Duke Celaibon MacPherson. His father, Gabriel MacPherson, established Argentos and the nearby town of Ravenhurst, as a center of learning. MacPherson University became Mana University when Marngol was destroyed.

Argol (Ar-gol) n: [Elven] The first elven king. Argol used the magic elven crown, Balodol to defeat demons unleashed by the destruction of Davenar.

Arnax (Are-nax) n: [Elven] A constellation in the night sky. Literally meaning 'the geese', the stars resemble a gaggle of geese flying north.

Asbith (As-bith) n. [Dragon-speech] A constellation in the night sky, which gets its name from the eldest female dragon that ever lived. According to legend King Illium, the first king of Thalacia, killed Asbith.

Aure (Our) n: The topaz Aglari.

Azahnon (As-zah-non) n: The name of the royal palace in Andropolis, home to King Leonard and Princess Sandra.

Balodol (Bal-low-doll) n: [Elven] The name of the elven king's crown. Literally translated, the term means 'Crown of Power'.

Bohbree (bo-bree) n: [unknown] A mythical bird about the size of a turkey with blue and green plumage. According to myth, bohbrees bring bad luck and are harbingers of ill fortune.

Bryford (Bry-ford) n: A city governed by the local mayor, where magic does not work.

Caer Pennarth (Kyre Pen-nath) n. The capital of Pennarth.

Calen (Kal-len) n: The emerald Aglari.

Carne (Karn) n: The ruby Aglari.

Celaibon   MacPherson   (Sell-ay-bon   Mac-fear-son)   n: [Elven/Human] The current duke of Gods' Home, son of Gabriel MacPherson, the first duke of the region.

Chroig (Cr-og) n: [Lizard Man] Brashani's investigative partner in Marngol.

Clearbrook n: A small quiet town at the southern end of Thalacia and the former home of Evan Pierce, one of the main characters in the Aglaril Cycle.

Davenar (Dav-ven-nar) n. The first city of humans settled at the beginning of the world.

Dukef (Due-kef) n: An elf that harbors ill will toward humans and humanity.

Eeril (Ee-ril) n: [Elven] The elf Ahlan kills and Reayl's scouting partner.

Ehzer (Eh-zer) n: One of two moons seen in the night sky. Ehzer is the smaller moon.

Elf-gem n: The human name for an Aglari.

Emeriel (Em-mer-ril) n: [Elven] King Everron's mother, leader of the dukefs.

Erendyl (Err-en-dill) n: One of the three elven clans, specializing in magic and building or inventing new things.

Everron (Ever-ron) n: [Elven] The elven king, ruler of Oldarmare.

Faroth Mane (Far-roth main) n: [Elven] An expression of good luck. Literally, good hunting.

Feadil (Fee-ah-dill) n: One of the three elven clans, specializing in nature and protecting it. Many elven rangers come from this clan.

Fire Mountains n: A range of mountains west of Thalacia, home to many races including dwarves, ogres, goblins, and giants. The mountain range contains the only active volcano in the area, Mt. Surt, home to a family of fire giants.

Freehaven n: A city situated on top of mountain in the middle of the Gods' Home forest. The mountain is man-made and home to Countess Rogath.

garal (gar ral) n: [Elven] A sacred quest performed by Qua'ril masters.

Galieade (Gal-lie-aid) n: The name of a lumber camp located in the southern end of Gods' Home forest.

Gods' Home forest n: The largest forest in Thalacia and part of the MacPherson Duchy. The forest is said to host thieves and travelers are advised to use only well-traversed paths.

House of Richmond n: The royal house of humans. Both King Leonard and Princess Sandra are part of the House of Richmond.

Ibilk (ih-bilk) n. One of two moons seen in the night sky. Ibilk is the larger moon.

Irenrhod (Iron-rod) n: A town in the Duchy of Wrightwood, near Caer Pennarth.

Karsla (Car-sluh) n: A constellation in the night sky, said to resemble the image of a large mythical bird.

Kaudel (Kaw-del) n: The name of a famous wizard and carpenter who specialized in making puzzles, small boxes, and other items of use to his fellow mages.

Kaudel box n: A box for securely holding items of value and made by the wizard Kaudel.

Khuzarreem (Khuh-zar-reem) n: [Dwarven] The citadel of the dwarves nestled in the foothills of the Fire Mountains.

Luin (Loo-in) n: The sapphire Aglari.

Mana n: Magical energy needed to make magic work.

Marngol (Marn-gaul) n: A ruined city and former home of many wizards. It was destroyed in the Marngol Massacre of 465. Orignially built by the elves millenia ago because of the naturally high levels of magic.

Marthesh (Mar-thesh) n: [Elven] An expression roughly equivalent to oh boy.

Martingis (Martin-geaz) n: A small village in the Duchy of Wrightwood, east of Clearbrook.

Mealidil (Meal-li-dill) n: One of the three elven clans, specializing in art, poetry, and music.

Michaeline knights (Mick-kay-lean knights) n: Religious knights that promote and uphold the teachings of St. Michael. The Order of St. Michael fights evil in all forms and especially seeks to stop necromancers and other practitioners of evil who pervert the natural order.

Mirrya (Mere-rye-yuh) n: A large continent in the southern hemisphere of the world.

Montescenia (Mont-tay-seen-nia) n: A city ruled by Duke Phillip Jose Montescenio.

Nethereem (nether-reem) n: [Dwarven] Steel made to be unbreakable.

Oldarmare (Old-dar-mare) n: [Elven] The kingdom of the elves in Mirrya.

Orod (Oh-rod) n: The amethyst Aglari.

Ostrond (Os-strond) n: The elven royal palace.

Pennarth (Pen-nath) n. A barony in the Duchy of Wrightwood.

Pyromancy (pyro-mancy) n: A type of magic divination. Herbs are thrown into a fire and the wizard stares into the resulting smoke to see images of the future.

Qua'ril (Kwuh ril) n: [Elven] A form of martial arts practiced by elves. It forms the basis of elven ranger training. Masters of the Art are highly respected and revered.

Quan' say (Kwan say) n: [Elven] A Qua'ril combat style that emphasizes self-defense, blocking, and deflecting attacks.

Quan' see (Kwan see) n: [Elven] A Qua'ril combat style highlighting how to turn your opponent's energy against him. It is neither a defensive nor an offensive technique, preferring to keep the practitioner in balance at all times.

Quan' sor (Kwan sor) n: [Elven] A Qua'ril combat style that stresses directly attack to immobilize your opponent.

Ravenhurst (Raven-herst) n: The town near Argentos, home to Mana University, where wizards training and study.

Reayl (Re ale) n: [Elven] Iriel's mother.

Rockborough (Rock-boro) A town in the middle of Thalacia, home to James's grandmother and uncle. James spent summer climb the hills of Rockborough and his uncle runs the Claymont Cafe in town.

rokka (roh-ka) n: [Elven] A special type of horse bred by the elves for speed and agility. Rokka are all black chargers.

Sadarxio (Sah-dar-zio) n: The fabled sword used by kings of the royal house of Richmond. Illium used the sword in the wars that untied the kingdom of Thalacia; Kenilworth used the sword to drive back invaders from the south. Only members in direct line can wield the sword so being able to use the blade is proof of one's royal heritage.

Sapilo (Sap-pilo) n: A town in eastern Wrightwood.

Stellingham n: Also known as the clerical city; home to the Supreme Priest and the four orders of the Church. The main campus of the College of Bardic Lore is also here.

Tah-teem (Tah team) n: [Elven] A test of character conducted by the Aglaril to determine if the wielder of the gems is worthy of using them. Only the most worthy are permitted to use the power of the gems. Literally translated, the terms means 'Test of Purity'.

Telep (Tel-lep) n: The diamond Aglari.

Thalacia (Thuh-lay-see-uh) n: A human kingdom along the eastern coast of the continent Mirrya.

Tindolen (Tin-dole-len) n: [Elven] Iriel's uncle and a friend of Evan Pierce. A gem merchant living in Clearbrook who finds an Aglari and gives to Daniel for safekeeping.

udar (you dar) n: [Dwarven slang] A condescending term for people with the ability to wield magic.

Vorn n: The onyx Aglari.

Wrightwood n: A city ruled by Duke Anthony Wrightwood and his daughter Crystal. Duke Wrightwood has been fighting necromancers for the last ten years. He believes this effort is nearly at an end. Only time will time if he is correct or not.

Zehrem River (Zeh-rem River) n: A river that starts in the Fire Mountains, heads east, passing south of Ravenhurst, and empties into the ocean near Marngol.

Zortan (zor tan) n: The name of a demon that many necromancers serve and that King Argol battled, causing the destruction of the Crown of Power.

About the Author

Rich Feitelberg is a poet and novelist. In addition to the books in his popular fantasy series, the Aglaril Cycle, Rich has several collections of short stories and poems, available from this web site and fine booksellers worldwide.

Rich has a Bachelor of Arts in English from Worcester State College. His Master of Arts in Technical Communication was received at Bowling Green State University. Currently, Rich is working on the Aglaril Cycle and writing more poems and short stories.

Also by Rich Feitelberg

Aglaril Cycle
Book 1, Aure the Topaz
Book 2, Vorn the Onyx
Book 3, Telep the Diamond

Short Stories
Magic and Melee
Strange Stories
Space and Speculation

Poetry
Paraphernalia in My Pocket